As I paused on the threshold of the grand room, some sixth sense made me hesitate and glance to the side. A dark figure caught my eye and the hair on the back of my neck stood up.

I was closer to thirty than twenty, a grown woman who was beyond acting like a star-crossed teenager. But even so, my heart sped up at the knowledge that Nicholas Conrad was coming toward me. Dozens of my diary entries between the ages of eight and fourteen were devoted to him. I knew everything about him: his favorite candy from the vending machine in the golf shack, his batting average on Harrison County High School's baseball team, and the type of car soap he had used on his royal blue 1995 Grand Prix. I knew every girlfriend he took to homecoming and why they weren't good enough for him.

And Nick? He didn't even know my real name.

"Hi, Bump," he said.

A Wedding in Truhart

Cynthia Tennent

LYRICAL SHINE
Kensington Publishing Corp.
www.kensingtonbooks.com

LYRICAL SHINE BOOKS are published by

Kensington Publishing Corp.
119 West 40th Street
New York, NY 10018

All Kensington titles, imprints, and distributed lines are available at special quantity discounts for bulk purchases for sales promotion, premiums, fund-raising, educational, or institutional use.

Special book excerpts or customized printings can also be created to fit specific needs. For details, write or phone the office of the Kensington Sales Manager: Kensington Publishing Corp., 119 West 40th Street, New York, NY 10018. Attn. Sales Department. Phone: 1-800-221-2647.

Lyrical Shine and the L logo are trademarks of Kensington Publishing Corp.

First Electronic Edition: September 2015
eISBN-13: 978-1-61650-832-6
eISBN-10: 1-61650-832-9

First Print Edition: September 2015
ISBN-13: 978-1-61650-833-3
ISBN-10: 1-61650-833-7

Printed in the United States of America

For my husband, John, and our daughters. Thank you for your support and a life filled with love.

Where there is love there is life

—Mahatma Gandhi

PART I: ATLANTA

Chapter 1

We were late to the dinner party and I was crushed between my great-aunt and my mother in the backseat of a battered taxi stuck in the slow lane.

"Is my bra twisted, Annie? Something feels like it has a hold on my left bosom and it can't be a man!" The setting sun glared off Aunt Addie's purplish gray hair. I never should have let her dye her own hair last week.

"Let me see what's going on." I shifted my position in the sweltering cab and cringed as I lost a layer of skin on the vinyl seat. Opening the back of my aunt's dress, I took a look at the massive brassiere that was surely more complicated than a seventy-six-year-old woman needed. "You're caught up in the sleeve. Give me a moment to fix this."

"Take your time, my dear. That air is like heaven on my back. Who in their right mind would live in a city that feels like a furnace?"

Our taxi driver convulsively stepped on the brakes and all three of us lurched forward as we crawled through seven lanes of rush-hour traffic on I-75 in Atlanta. I dodged Aunt Addie's head and Mom's shoulder, attempting to fix the bra, and felt a bead of sweat trickle from my armpit to my elbow. The driver leered at me through the rearview mirror.

"Just remember, this weekend is for Charlotte. We can handle a little August heat. Besides, Atlanta will be a lovely place for a wedding next spring," Mom said as I finished with the bra.

"With all your brains and talent I always thought you were going to be the one to live in the big city," said my great-aunt, nudging me with her elbow.

I bit my lip and let Aunt Addie's words roll off me. I'd buried my regrets years ago. The same year we buried Dad.

"I'll remind you about this heat next February when it's ten below and there's three feet of snow on the ground at home," said Mom as she reached behind her back to fasten the top of her own dress. My mother, Virginia Adler, was attractive and calm, even with a layer of perspiration on her face. I had only seen her fall apart once, and a little heat like this wasn't going to rattle her cool composure.

Was it just this morning that we left our inn before dawn and drove three hours to get to the Flint airport? Unfortunately our luckless journey had only begun. Our flight from Flint was behind schedule and the connecting flight in Detroit was delayed too. I guess that's what we should have expected after buying tickets on a website called ElCheapoFare.com. Now, we were getting dressed in the backseat of a steamy cab as we finished the final leg of our journey.

Sometimes I think my family avoids *luck* as if it is a nasty four-letter word. Well, I guess it actually *is* a four-letter word. But so is *love*, and we have plenty of that. I just wished *love* came with air-conditioning and a restroom to change in.

A dinner tonight, wedding-dress shopping tomorrow, and a wedding shower the following night. The long weekend was going to be a whirlwind. I leaned back against the seat and angled my head to catch a breeze coming through the window, marveling at the fact that my baby sister, Charlotte, called this home. It still was hard to imagine anyone from Truhart, population thirteen hundred and dropping, living in a Southern city like Atlanta.

For the past few years, my focus had been on my family and keeping our inn running smoothly. And now I had another goal. I was going to make sure this wedding was everything my little sister dreamed it would be.

At last we pulled up under a large gilded marquee that marked the entrance to the Ambassador Hotel of Atlanta. A man in a dark suit held open the back door of the cab and all three of us awkwardly slid across the sticky seat. By the time my mother disembarked she had to push Aunt Adelaide and me out of the way; we were momentarily frozen in place as we stared through the open glass doors at an opulent room that was nothing like the rustic lobby of our inn back home.

The man cast his eyes over Aunt Addie and her purplish gray hair piled on top of her head, the way she had worn it since the bicentennial of the nation. Then he cast a glance at the three sorry-looking carry-on bags the driver had tossed onto the sidewalk.

"May I help you, ladies?"

My mother stood up straighter. "Yes, you can. My daughter and her fiancé are hosting a special dinner for family and close friends."

"Oh, of course, in the Governor's Room. Will you be staying here tonight?"

"Actually, no," I said. It had been hard enough to scrape together money for the airfare; there was no way we could afford this place.

The man nodded and offered to store our luggage, but Aunt Addie refused to be parted with hers. She insisted that we hold on to them, and my mother and I knew that arguing with her was futile when she had that look in her eye. So we followed suit and shouldered the bags. I cringed to think what Charlotte's guests would think.

Like zombies we shuffled through the main lobby and shivered when the air-conditioning hit us with a cold blast as we walked up a long, winding stairway overlooking the lobby. Standing near a curved bar was a group of elegantly dressed people who stopped talking and stared as we walked past.

I lifted my chin, trying to look as if we weren't totally out of place.

Mom wore a pink cotton dress that she'd worn to our church's fiftieth anniversary last spring. I wore my black go-to skirt with a wilting gauzy white blouse, a silver chain, and hoop earrings.

And then there was Aunt Addie.

Blue cabbage roses shouted out from her floral polyester dress, in stark contrast to the chic black elegance of the room around us. Wearing a dress with an elastic waistband that cinched her large girth, and sensible shoes, she looked like a 1950s throwback. No matter what Aunt Addie did to herself, she resembled a cross between Minnie Pearl and Betty White. Out of habit I double-checked my aunt for handwritten price tags from the church thrift store and safety pins that showed at the hem.

Then I saw Charlotte. She stood in an ornately framed doorway absently listening to an older man as she chewed on her lip and looked at her watch. She looked up and our eyes met.

"Annie!" she squealed, rushing our way.

My worries dissolved as I dropped my bag and closed the space between us. I forgot the imposing room and all the curious faces as we crushed each other in an embrace that brought tears to my eyes.

Almost a full year had passed since Charlotte had left Truhart for Atlanta to become the newest sweetheart correspondent on the nationally televised *Morning Show*. Every time I saw her face on TV, I still wanted to reach out and touch the screen to make sure it was real.

"It's so good to see you," we said at the same time.

"Jinx," we said, then laughed.

We pulled apart and Charlotte was immediately captured in a hug from my mother and then Aunt Addie.

"I am so sorry we're late! The plane out of Detroit was delayed and we did the best we could," Mom explained.

"Oh, that's all right, Mom. I'm just glad you're here." The smile Charlotte flashed us assured me she was the same blue-eyed angel who used to pour glitter in the sand traps at our inn's golf course, to make pixie dust. But she had changed as well. Dressed in a black sleeveless dress with a chiffon overlay, her blond hair pulled back in a sophisticated chignon, she appeared every inch the celebrity she was becoming.

"You look wonderful, honey," said Aunt Adelaide, grabbing Charlotte's left hand. "Good Lord, that engagement ring is bigger than a lump of coal in a Christmas stocking. I'll bet that didn't come from the Sears catalogue like mine did."

"And you should see the new car Henry bought me," Charlotte exclaimed.

"Just in time! Annie is really excited to drive that SUV back up to Michigan. A new car for you and our old car back to us," Mom said.

My car had broken down a month ago, and I had been pricing used cars in Gaylord. Now I could reclaim the Ford Escape my dad had bought ten years ago and take it back to Truhart.

"I still can't believe you are getting married," I said.

"Of course I wish you could have told us before you announced it on *The Morning Show*," Mom added.

"That Marva O'Shea still brags about the fact that she knew about it before I did," complained Aunt Addie.

Charlotte frowned. "Oh, Mom, I hope you didn't mind too much!"

We all protested, of course. No point in making Charlotte feel guilty after the fact.

"This must be your family, darling." The three of us stopped to stare as Charlotte's fiancé joined her.

I was prepared to resent this man who was stealing our Charlotte away from Michigan for good. But something in the way he looked at her before he turned to greet us made me love him on sight. Adoration was written all over his face. It was as transparent as the picture window in the lobby of the Amble Inn after spring cleaning week. His blond hair was cropped short to his thinning hair line, and his broad shoulders made up for the fact that he wasn't overly tall. He wore a sharp black suit with a starched white shirt and blue-and-gray striped tie, the perfect complement to Charlotte's sleek style.

"Henry, this is my mother, Virginia, Aunt Adelaide, and, of course, Annie."

I held out my hand politely, but Henry surprised us by swallowing each of us up in a big hug. His Southern drawl came with a whole hunk of charm, and Aunt Addie was already half in love.

"I am so sorry you didn't get a chance to rest before this party," Henry said.

An older woman stepped in front of Henry and held out her hand. I was overwhelmed by a heavy dose of expensive perfume and bling. Her wrists dripped with gold and matched the lamé trim on her form-fitting dress. Her blond hair was pulled back and for a moment I wondered if the tight hairstyle was the reason no wrinkles showed around her eyes. But when she spoke and her generous upper lip barely moved, I had my answer.

"Why, it is so nice that you made the trip to our little part of the world. I am June, Henry's mother." We took turns reaching out for her limp hand and I winced when Aunt Addie shook it too hard and June Lowell flinched. June put her arm around Charlotte's shoulders in a proprietary manner. "We just love Charlotte, our little Northern bride." It sounded so old-fashioned that I resisted the urge to look around for hoopskirts. "Do y'all want to freshen up or change before the party? I know you probably didn't have time."

Something about the way she said the word *party* made my breath catch in my chest. I stole a glance at Charlotte. "This is just close friends and family, right?"

"Well, the Lowells have a lot of friends." I could have sworn that her smile was painted on because it didn't waver. I was conscious of the music and laughter in the room nearby.

Mom placed her hand over her heart. "Would that happen to be the Governor's Room?"

June Lowell's eyes darted to the pin on Aunt Addie's dress, made of lace and shells. She had bought it at last year's church craft show. "Why, yes. Everyone is so excited to meet you. But as I was saying, you are welcome to change in the ladies' lounge."

"No need to change. We're fine," said Mom with that hint of ice in her eyes that I recognized as stalwart Adler pride. "That is, unless you feel we should. We are late enough as it is . . ."

"Oh, you look lovely just as you are, Mrs. Adler. I can see where Charlotte gets her beauty. We wouldn't want to miss your presence for another minute," inserted Henry, giving his mother an annoyed look that lifted him up another notch in my estimation. "Let me get someone to take your bags so you can have a chance to relax."

Henry signaled to one of the waiters, who put down his tray and held out his hand to take Mom's bag. After I handed over my bag, he turned to Aunt Addie. She clutched hers with both hands and narrowed her eyes suspiciously. The young waiter looked startled when he saw her fierce expression, but Mom and I wrestled the bag from her death grip and looped it around his free arm.

A serious-faced young girl appeared at Henry's elbow. "Virginia, Addie, Anne, I would like you to meet my little sister, Jessica," Henry said. The girl was in her early teens and it was obvious that she wished she was anywhere else at the moment.

June pushed Jessica forward and I heard her whisper sharply, "Shoulders!" as the miserable girl readjusted her slouch. She was painfully thin and wore a purple dress dotted with sequins. It looked like something her mother might have picked for her. She held out her hand and greeted each one of us without actually looking us in the eye. Then she reached up to fiddle with her hair.

"Jessica, how nice to meet you," my mother said warmly. "Are you in school in Atlanta?"

"Actually she boards at the Delaworth Academy in Connecticut."

"Boards?" asked Aunt Addie. "Is that some kind of new sport these kids do?"

"No, she lives at a boarding school," corrected June. "We flew her here for the weekend so she could come to the party."

I tried to navigate the conversation away from any comment Aunt

Addie might make about boarding school. "It must seem pretty strange to think of your big brother getting married, huh?"

Jessica nodded and looked over at Henry, showing emotion for the first time. Hero worship.

Henry reached over and patted her back. "Actually I keep telling her how great it will be for her to finally have a sister!"

Jessica's glance shifted to Charlotte and I noted how Jessica shut down before Henry led us into the Governor's Room.

As I paused on the threshold of the grand room, some sixth sense made me hesitate and glance to the side. A dark figure caught my eye and the hair on the back of my neck stood up.

I was closer to thirty than twenty, a grown woman who was beyond acting like a star-crossed teenager. But even so, my heart sped up at the knowledge that Nicholas Conrad was coming toward me. Dozens of my diary entries between the ages of eight and fourteen were devoted to him. I knew everything about him: his favorite candy from the vending machine in the golf shack, his batting average on Harrison County High School's baseball team, and the type of car soap he had used on his royal blue 1995 Grand Prix. I knew every girlfriend he took to homecoming and why they weren't good enough for him.

And Nick? He didn't even know my real name.

"Hi, Bump," he said.

Chapter 2

My unfortunate nickname was bestowed on me when I was five years old. I was playing with my stuffed animals along the large stone hearth in the cavernous pine lobby of the inn. My Puffalump teddy was being chased by Alf, the ugliest stuffed animal ever created. I'd like to blame it on Alf for being so aggressive, but I lost my footing and fell forehead first into the corner of a coffee table in front of the fireplace. The result was a substantial knot right in the middle of my forehead. The nickname "Bump" stuck.

So, there I was, with a droopy collar, hair sticking out on one side of my head, and a dried layer of sweat on my body, flashing a crooked smile at a man who called me Bump.

He leaned forward to kiss my cheek at the same time I reached out to grab his shoulders for a hug. We ended up colliding in an awkward nose-smashing greeting. I laughed and jumped back. He managed to look as if nothing unusual had happened.

I felt thirteen again.

"Hi, Nick."

"Welcome to Atlanta."

"It's great to finally be here." I smoothed my hair, conscious of the uneven side. And then I added a huge insight to the conversation. "It's hot."

"Consider yourself initiated to summertime in Georgia," he said, narrowing his gaze to the side of my head where I was trying to tame that curl. "Sorry to hear Ian couldn't come."

Why my brother, Ian, and Nick got along so well was completely beyond my understanding. Ian was a long-haired college dropout who spent half his life with a guitar in his hands playing dimly lit bars from Indiana to the Upper Peninsula. Nick was a former high school star pitcher with near perfect standardized test scores, who earned a full ride to Vanderbilt University and joined one of the most successful architectural firms in the South. He was driven to succeed the same way Ian was compelled to loaf. Yet their friendship had lasted all these years.

"You know Ian. He had a gig in Grand Rapids last night and said he would help with the inn this weekend." I didn't add that we only had one guest booked tonight. The summer had been a struggle.

"Nick! It's so good to see you," said my mother, coming up behind us with Aunt Addie.

Aunt Addie squealed, "Nicholas Conrad! Look at you, dressed up in a suit like a fancy businessman."

"Aunt Addie . . ." Nick started, before being swooped up in a sloppy bear hug.

"It's been way too long since you were home, young man," Aunt Addie said. "We can't have you turning all soft and getting Southern on us, can we?"

She said it loud enough that a few people nearby frowned.

Nick cracked a smile. "Don't worry, Aunt Addie. I still know how to fire a muzzle-loader and wrestle a four-wheeler."

"Hmm," she said, examining him closer.

"Darling, are these the people from your hometown you have told me so much about?" said a breathy voice followed by a sinewy bare arm that wrapped itself around Nick's elbow.

Nick nodded to one of the most beautiful women I had ever seen. She had long black hair, perfect bone structure, and blue eyes framed by thick black lashes.

"Brittany, these are the Adlers. Virginia, Adelaide, and—"

"Annie," I said, holding out my hand before he introduced me as Bump.

Brittany batted her eyelids and stared at Aunt Addie's blue cabbage roses as if they were slightly out of focus. After a moment she looked toward me, leaning forward until my view was taken up by her generous cleavage. Her eyes traveled from my fake designer shoes to the top of my frizzy head. She shook my hand, turned to Nick and smiled. "You never told me how cute they are."

Cute? Should we have put our hair in pigtails and painted freckles on our faces?

"How nice to meet you," said my mother, ever aware of her hostess manners, even when she was away from the inn.

Aunt Addie's gaze hadn't moved from Brittany's chest and I had to jab her with my elbow to get her to stop staring. Nick saw me and his mouth turned down at the corner. If I didn't know him better I would think he was suppressing a smile. But Nick didn't smile much, at least not at me.

The last time I'd seen Nick was several years ago, as he had stood beside his father's grave. As long as I lived I would never forget how he had looked that cold April morning. His mother and sisters had clung to him, their breath coming out in billowing clouds of white and their gloved fingers clutching tissues as they failed to hold back tears. He had stood stoically in a gray wool overcoat, practically holding his family upright. His face had been pale, and his lips were compressed to thin lines. As if something had made him too angry to cry. I cried for all of them, and maybe a little bit for myself that day too. My own father's grave was just a few rows away.

I realized that Nick was gazing intently at me. He stood with his head tilted and his hands in his pockets. Did he know what I was thinking about?

"Where's your camera?" he asked. "I'm used to seeing you with a camera around your neck all the time."

"She doesn't do that as often anymore, Nick. Remember how much she loved it?" Aunt Addie interjected.

Explaining how I had given up photography for teaching wasn't something I wanted to discuss. I had just been laid off from the local high school and didn't want to elaborate on my apparent double failure.

Charlotte left Henry's side and looped her arm in mine. "I can't wait to introduce you to all my friends."

Henry hailed a waiter and grabbed several drinks from his tray. "These are a house specialty. Gin, tequila, and a secret ingredient. You have to try them," he said, handing them to us.

Aunt Addie's eyes grew wide. "I love a good drink."

Ian always watered down my mom's and Aunt Addie's drinks back at the inn. I started to caution them, but Charlotte grabbed my arm. "Let me introduce you to some of my friends."

"Wait. You know how Mom and Aunt Addie are with alcohol. Maybe I should warn them—"

"They'll be fine," Charlotte said, dragging me into the Governor's Room.

With every hour, the party grew louder and the night stretched longer. The room was brimming, and I couldn't even fathom how all these people knew Charlotte and Henry. I found myself introduced to dozens of relatives and friends of the Lowells. Names started running together and I was pretty sure we met more people than lived within the city limits of Truhart.

Several of Charlotte's friends commented on her success and I tried not to brag. With help from Nick, she had landed an amazing job as a correspondent on *The Morning Show* last year. But it wasn't easy. She worked long hours and everyone knew she had to deal with a difficult and demanding lead anchor. Scarlett Francis.

"So far, Charlotte has been able to avoid her tantrums. But we have a bet going on how long it will take before she gets her first tongue-lashing," confided one of Charlotte's coworkers.

"Is she really that bad?" someone asked.

A balding man leaned in and said, "Oh yeah."

"We keep telling Charlotte to keep her head down and pretend she has connections on Capitol Hill. God forbid the woman finds out she is from the flyover zone," said a red-faced man who waved down the waitress for another drink.

I couldn't help myself. "Charlotte doesn't need to justify herself. She has worked hard making a name for herself and it shouldn't matter where she is from."

The red-faced man grabbed a glass of champagne from a passing tray and looked beyond me. "Sure she works hard, but let's be honest—she is young, blonde, and pretty . . . all the things that make her GATE material," he said, mentioning the name of the network they all worked for.

"She was a weekend anchor on our local station by the time she was twenty-two, and was doing headline stories in Detroit before moving to Atlanta."

"Dime a dozen," the man said, guzzling half his glass as if it was water.

"She even won an award for her feature on abandoned houses in the city. That one put her right in the thick of some of the most violent neighborhoods in the nation."

"If you say so," he said, looking at the man next to him and winking.

I could feel heat rising to my face. My voice sounded shrill. "I suppose just because Charlotte is young and pretty people think she is only a piece of fluff, but I would like to see half the anchors on TV get out of the newsroom and actually visit the flyover zone . . . even Scarlett Francis."

It took me a horrified moment to realize that everything was quiet and my comment practically echoed off the ceiling. I looked behind me and saw that everyone was holding their drinks in the air. June Lowell tapped on her glass and beckoned everyone to turn their attention to Henry and Charlotte in the center of the room.

I wanted to shrink into the carpet but instead smiled and raised my glass.

"Thank you, everyone, for coming," Henry said. "I never thought I would meet someone who would make me as happy as Charlotte has . . ."

As he continued, any reservations I had about Charlotte making a hasty decision disappeared.

"And one last thank-you to my good friend Nick Conrad, for introducing me to Charlotte and being a constant source of support to both of us. Nick, thanks for everything and I am so glad you agreed to be my best man. With you nearby for moral support, nothing can go wrong."

Nick extended one of his rare smiles to the couple and his gaze traveled the room. Our eyes met for a moment and his turned cold. I could practically hear him say, *"Getting yourself in trouble again, Bump? Just like old times."* And then his gaze rested on a point beyond my shoulder and I turned to see what was there.

I recognized Scarlett Francis immediately. She was shorter in real life, but no less imposing than she seemed on TV. Her cropped red hair glowed in the light of the overhead chandeliers. Her severely cut green dress could have been made of silk, but on her it looked more reptilian. Her vivid green eyes narrowed on me like laser beams. Had she overheard my earlier comment? Judging by the disapproving expression on her face, I had to say the answer was a resounding yes.

I turned back to the center of the room and raised my glass higher as everyone around me finally said, "Here, here" at the end of Henry's toast. Then I drank the entire glass in one gulp.

Behind me someone shouted, "Who is your maid of honor, Charlotte?"

"Why, my sister, of course!" she said without hesitating. "Annie!"

I choked up . . . literally, when the bubbles from the champagne flew up my nose.

While I sputtered and my eyes watered, everyone clapped politely. Then I felt a solid hand pat my back. I looked up at Nick through wet eyes.

"She is really touched, isn't she, Charlotte?" he said loudly. Everyone laughed and went back to their conversations.

Except me and Nick. He stared at me, that unnerving expression plastered on his face. He reached for my glass and put it on the table next to him.

"Can we have some water here?" he asked a passing waiter.

"I'm okay," I assured him.

"Are you?" he said, sounding like he didn't want an answer. Before I could say anything, he put his arm around me and practically pushed me toward an oversized potted plant at the side of the room.

"What's wrong with you?" I asked.

"I'm just saving your hide from getting ripped open, Bump."

"What—"

I looked back to see Scarlett Francis waylaid by an older woman.

"You had better hope she forgets that little comment you made, or else you will be speared and roasted over an open fire."

"Are you suggesting I'm like a pig on a spit?"

Nick frowned, looking me up and down. "No. You definitely don't look like a pig . . ." I could have taken it for a compliment, but I knew better. "Did you even get a chance to eat something?"

"Yes, I did. I had a bite of the fish paste on a miniature piece of bread . . . Oh, I mean the salmon pâté." I bent my wrist daintily for emphasis and grinned.

"You're not that out of place and you know it."

"You're right. But someone forgot to tell a few of *these* people."

"Charlotte seems to enjoy it here, and she's made a lot of friends."

He ruined my fun. I knew I was being childish. "Well, I have to admit, I like Henry a lot. You met him in school?"

"Studying for our statistics final, freshman year."

I imagined Nick diligently working away in the library, surrounded by textbooks and friends. But that was where my imagination stopped. I knew so little about him since he'd left Truhart.

"How are things back home?" Nick asked, changing the subject.

I couldn't help but notice he said *home*, not *Truhart*. It made my heart beat just a little faster. But I had to stop myself. He hadn't said it deliberately. Since his father's death, Nick seemed to avoid Truhart like the plague. Sometimes I wondered if he was ever coming home again.

I couldn't think of anything dramatic to say that would make us more interesting than this fancy hotel and his globe-trotting friends. So instead of trying to compete, I tucked my hair behind my ear and gave him Aunt Addie–style news.

"We are having a beautiful summer. A little dry, but at least the temperature has stayed in the eighties. Echo Lake has been full of boats since Memorial Day weekend. Ian caught a pike last month that came in second in the Truhart Fishing Derby. The Timberfest is starting in a week, and I hear the planning committee is splurging on a giant bouncy slide this year. That might bring in the younger crowd! And . . . oh, we have a new bakery next to Ike's Hardware."

His brown eyes flickered in the dim light from a nearby sconce and he smiled. I loved it when he smiled. It made me proud to know I had caused it.

"Are you coming home anytime soon?" I couldn't help asking.

"I'd love to, but we're in the middle of a big project right now."

"Oh." I looked down at the glass in my hand and tried not to let him see my feelings. "How are Jenny and Melissa?" Nick's sisters were old friends of mine. He smiled for the second time. I was on a roll.

"Once in a while there is a little drama with a boyfriend, but they manage to stay out of trouble these days."

"They never were in much trouble. You made sure of that."

"Not always. I seem to recall a few occasions where they landed in a hornet's nest or two, Bump," he said.

I rolled my eyes, irritated at the mention of an incident I would rather have forgotten. "That was a long time ago. Thanks so much for bringing it up, Nick. And you know very well that I was the only one who landed in the nest."

"That was your punishment for spying."

"We weren't spying."

"Really? You and my sisters were just passing through and you happened to see some of us guys swimming?" Nick crossed his arms and tilted his head again. His dark gaze made me feel like he could read my mind.

"Exactly." Well, I guess we had been curious. The summer before high school, Melissa and I decided that big, hairy seventeen-year-olds were a major point of fascination for us girls. While they swam in the tiny lake behind our golf course, we prowled around them, ducking from tree to tree, trying not to let the boys hear us giggling.

"How was I to know there was a hornet's nest next to the lake?" I asked.

Unfortunately, one wrong step on my part blew our cover and had us screaming like babies as the angry swarm stormed the shore. While most of the boys laughed, Melissa and Jenny ran far from the emerging swarm and joined the boys by the opposite bank. But I couldn't see because I'd closed my eyes in a panic. I heard a deep voice yelling nearby, but my mind didn't register the words. The next thing I knew someone tall and strong hauled me up and ran with me, away from the buzzing mass. My rescuer and I hit the water hard. I came out of my panic in Nick's arms as he unleashed four-letter words I had never heard him say before. After a few terror-stricken moments, while Nick repeatedly dunked my head under the surface, the hornets dispersed. Then he carried me, sniveling and shaking, out of the lake. As soon as my feet touched the grassy shore I began to weep in his arms, feeling the first effects of the stings. Poor Nick, I'm sure he was absolutely horrified to have such a pitiful soggy mess on his hands. He quickly passed me off to Ian, who dragged me, bawling like a baby, all the way home.

Miraculously, like the demigod he was, Nick wasn't stung at all.

Unfortunately, I had not been so lucky.

"Poor Bump. At least you suffered no real harm."

I rolled my eyes. "I started high school three days later," I said, grinning despite myself. "I have never been so mortified in my life."

"No lasting damage," Nick said as he scrutinized my face for bumps.

"Are you kidding? There I was on the first day of high school with three calamine-covered welts right in the middle of my face. I suffered an indignity beyond description. Everyone laughed at me."

"No, they didn't," Nick said.

Well, that was true. Every time I passed one of my brother's friends they pointed at me and made faces. But not Nick. He just frowned. I used to fool myself into believing that Nick cared. And now as he stood in front of me, I almost could believe it was true.

"There you are!" came a familiar cloying drawl. Brittany and her D-cups had arrived. "You are missing all the fun tucked away in this little corner, Nicholas. I have someone I must introduce you to." She paused for a moment, looking at me through her overly long eyelashes. "Oh, and you can come too, if you want, Anne."

"Oh no, thank you. Nick and I were just talking about the new septic tank in our trailer park . . ."

She blinked at me, not sure if I was joking or not.

Nick tilted his head and pressed his lips together. Then he gave me a quick, impersonal peck on the cheek. "It was great seeing you," he said before leading Brittany away.

"Bye, Nick," I said quietly, resisting the urge to cradle my hand over the spot his lips had touched. My cheek throbbed as much as those hornet stings all those years ago.

Later that night Charlotte and I sat on the balcony of her midtown apartment. Aunt Addie and Mom had staggered and giggled the whole way up to Charlotte's floor. Now, Aunt Addie snored happily from the sofa, and Mom slept in Charlotte's bed. We propped our feet up on the railing and enjoyed the view overlooking Piedmont Park. From eight stories up the city at night looked like a string of fireflies and neon sparklers being waved around in midair. The lights were so bright they crowded out the stars that filled the night sky back home. I lifted my camera and took a picture, mourning the fact that I had left my vintage Canon at home.

The great love of my life—besides Nick, of course—was an old 35 mm film camera that my father gave me when I was ten. I took that camera with me everywhere, shooting pictures of an embarrassing number of flowers, dogs, and sunsets on the lake. That first camera started something inside me that grew way beyond those blurry photos from the early years. It led me out of Truhart to New York, where I followed my dream of studying photography. It stayed with me during the difficult times when my father was sick and I drove home almost every weekend. And it made the final trip with me when I left school early and returned home.

The camera I now held was digital. Like Nick, the old film camera didn't have a place in my life anymore.

Charlotte let out a deep breath and I lowered the camera. She said, "Sorry about the party tonight. It really did start small. But before we knew it we had almost a hundred people coming."

"That's all right. Just warn me next time. I'll make sure to take Aunt Annie and Mom to the outlet mall. Maybe I could convince Aunt Addie to purchase shoes that were made in this century next time."

"Oh, Annie, do you think Mom is upset that we're planning an Atlanta wedding?"

I had been secretly relieved when Charlotte had mentioned her plans to hold the wedding in Atlanta. There was so much that needed fixing at the inn that I wasn't sure we could handle a wedding. The last big event we had hosted was Harriet Knopf's ninetieth birthday party. "We completely understand why you want to get married here. Before tonight Aunt Addie was upset . . . but since she is the new belle of Atlanta, she may be coming around. How much do you think she drank?"

"Who knows? Oh my God, did you see her try to give the Lowells' financial adviser a lesson in ice fishing?"

"That wasn't nearly as bad as when she hoisted her leg up on the chair and readjusted her garters in front of Mrs. Lowell."

Charlotte drew her knees up and rested her chin in her hands. "That's classic Aunt Addie! Where does she even buy garters these days?"

"Believe me, I don't even want to ask."

"Thank goodness I warned Henry. Now maybe he'll believe all the stories I tell."

I looked over at Charlotte and put my hand on her arm. We had long since changed out of our dresses into T-shirts and loose shorts. "I am so glad you found someone who loves you as much as Henry seems to."

"Me too! Oh, Annie, he is so wonderful. And you know how worried I was about how his mother would handle Aunt Addie? He was twice as worried about how all of you would like his mother!"

"Really?"

"Well, come on. You had to have noticed. Don't be polite. She *is* a bit uptight."

"Well, I don't know . . ."

"Annie! June Lowell is—well, she's not Mom. Henry says his father was the grounded one in the family."

My antenna went up. Charlotte's distress was more than just a fleeting concern.

"How does she feel about you marrying her little boy?"

"Henry won't tell me what she says to him. I think it's still taking time for her to adjust to the fact that her only son is marrying not only a Yankee but a small-town country girl. He says not to worry. I like his little sister, Jessica. Too bad she won't talk to me. But his mother? She never seems happy. Henry says she is always like that. He says she would complain that her ice cream was too cold."

"Well, you can charm anyone, Charlotte." I leaned back to take her picture and just before I released the shutter she stuck her tongue out.

She grinned and put her hand out. "Annie! Stop it."

It was a common scenario, her making faces at me. Then she continued. "I guess I am being too critical. June can be nice. And I think we are growing a little closer. But she has already given me an initial guest list. It's longer than the IRS tax code."

"Just how big is this wedding going to be?" I asked tentatively.

"Henry and I insist it has to be below three hundred. But June has bigger ideas. Evidently her country club holds more than five hundred and she wants to fill every corner so she can break the record."

"Wow. It sounds, well, really fancy," I said, wondering how our family would ever pay for such an extravagant celebration.

"Don't worry, Annie. Henry and I insist on paying for a lot of it. That is why we refuse to give in to June's pressure."

"They say mothers-in-law are some of the biggest problems in marriages. It's not going to get much better, Charlotte. Do you think you can handle her?"

She shrugged. "I don't know. If I thought Henry wanted me to change, I would have been out of this relationship so fast . . ." She took a deep breath and sat back. "But Henry tells me every single day that he loves who I am. He isn't disappointed in a single thing about me."

"Why should he ever be disappointed? You are the best. Besides, you're an Adler. 'Our ancestors cleared virgin forests with their bare hands, rid our county of wolves, and—' "

" '—brewed beer for the town during harsh winters,' " we finished in unison. God knows we'd heard Aunt Addie say it often enough over the years.

"We may be politically incorrect, but a little snobbery isn't going to bring us down now," I added.

She giggled. I couldn't see her face very well in the shadows, but I hoped she was feeling better.

"So, is something going on with you and Nick Conrad?" Charlotte asked.

"What? No. Nothing." I heard her chuckle. "Oh, come on! Don't laugh at me that way. I was something like ten years old when I had a crush on Nick. It isn't even worth talking about."

"I don't know, he certainly kept watching you tonight."

"Yeah. He was probably making sure I didn't break the crystal."

"Annie, sometimes you are so blind! You are a beautiful woman who men find attractive."

"Don't worry, I am going to be your maid of honor no matter what. You don't have to compliment me."

Charlotte slapped me lightly on the shoulder. "Annie! You are one of those women people are drawn to. It's not just that you are attractive, which you are, by the way. It's that you are so, I don't know, so easy to talk to, and I know Nick—"

"Hey, you know how you said Henry loves everything about you and would never want you to change? Well, when Nick Conrad thinks of me, which isn't very often, I might add, all he probably wishes is that I stay far away from him. Like *another continent* type of far away. He sees me as a walking booby trap."

"I think you're exaggerating."

"Only the part about him actually thinking of me."

Charlotte paused for a moment. In the silence she drew a circle on her knee. "I don't know . . ." she said.

A siren blared in the distance and I tensed involuntarily. Sirens in cities always reminded me of a time in my life I wanted to forget about.

Charlotte interrupted my thoughts with another giggle. "Well, it will be fun to see you dance with Nick. You know the maid of honor always dances with the best man," she said in a light, singsong voice.

I had forgotten about that. Good Lord! I was probably going to break his toes. Or worse, force him into a potted cactus!

"Thanks a lot, Sis!" I said sarcastically, trying not to let myself get excited about the prospect of Nick holding me in his arms.

"Are you going to be all right driving back to Michigan alone?"

"Of course I will. Mom will take Aunt Addie on the plane and I will have a nice, relaxing ride home. Besides, you are saving my checkbook by letting me have the truck."

"It's the least I can do for my maid of honor."

I stared out at the Atlanta skyline and wondered what Charlotte would say if she knew how much her giving me the car helped, and how tough things were back in Truhart. We hadn't wanted to bother her with bad news. At least not yet.

In the old days the inn was full of people playing euchre in the lobby. Self-described hackers lined our nine-hole golf course, despite the fact that the greens were indistinguishable from the fairways. And tipsy octogenarians sang camp songs by the piano in the dining room at midnight.

But times had changed. Charlotte didn't need to hear the depressing details of the inn's slow demise.

"I am really excited about your wedding, honey. This is going to be a wonderful time in your life." I sounded as artificial as that jolly weatherman with the big hair on Charlotte's TV show. Well, everyone on *The Morning Show* sounded like that, so maybe she wouldn't notice my lack of sincerity.

She didn't.

Instead, I heard all about her wedding plans. As Charlotte talked about Atlanta and the future, I looked at the twinkling lights of the city, thinking about how everything was changing, and felt a stab of pain in my gut.

For a moment, I wished I could reverse the clock and return to the good old days. The bucolic summers when we swam in the spring-fed lakes of Truhart, rode our bicycles through ruts in the dirt, and caught fireflies at dusk with leftover jelly jars.

But things were going to be fine. Our inn was surviving somehow. Seven years after my father's death, Mom was finally happy again. Even the town was managing to survive. I had no regrets about my life.

I let the sounds of the traffic and the distant sirens engulf me.

Cities never slept. They were always changing, always frantically buzzing with activity. Even after midnight. The lights and noises swirled around me in a restless haze.

For a moment it seemed like I was the only person on earth who was standing still.

Chapter 3

If anyone ever thought gin, tequila, and women over age sixty were a good combination, I would tell them to take a good, hard look at my mother and my aunt the morning after the dinner party.

The moans and the sounds of retching had started at 5:00 a.m. Of course Charlotte had slept through all of it. I, on the other hand, ran back and forth holding heads and trying to offer ice chips whenever possible. By the time Charlotte woke up, I was so tired I wanted nothing more than to stay in my sweatpants and camp out on her couch for the rest of the afternoon. But we had things to do.

Charlotte paced the small hallway of her apartment. "Have you seen them? There is no way they are going to make the bridal boutique today."

I peeked through the crack in the door to the bedroom where both women slept in Charlotte's bed now. Unfortunately she was right. "Do you want to cancel?"

She shook her head. "It will take at least a month to get another appointment."

"Go without us. Don't sacrifice for us," Mom croaked from the bedroom.

"I'll take a picture," I promised.

Charlotte bit her lip and started to say something. But the phone rang and she turned away. I quickly showered and dried my hair, only applying a little mascara and lipstick before changing into a black pair of cropped pants and a gray tunic.

"Are you excited?" I asked, running my hand along my sister's shoulder. Something about the tenseness in her posture made me wonder if there was another reason she was uptight.

"Well—" A buzzer interrupted her before she could finish. We moved into her living room. She pressed the intercom on the wall. "Yes?"

"Mrs. Lowell is waiting for you in the lobby, miss."

I raised an eyebrow. "Mrs. Lowell?"

"I kind of invited her at the last minute while you were in the shower. She said I needed a mother's helping hand in this."

Evidently a sister's help wasn't enough. I grabbed my camera bag and tried not to let the fact that June was coming bother me. It made perfect sense to have her help. After making sure Aunt Addie and Mom were comfortable, Charlotte and I took the elevator down to the first floor.

"Actually we have more than just the two of us at the bridal salon," she said avoiding my eyes.

"Oh, don't worry. Jessica is coming, right?" I linked my arm with hers.

"No. There are more—" The elevator door opened and June, Jessica, and Scarlett Francis stood in the lobby. Great! No wonder Charlotte had looked like she'd just swallowed a spider.

"Anne. I hope you slept well," said June with a Southern charm that was a little too sweet for me.

"Like a baby," I lied in matching cadence.

I shook Jessica's reluctant hand and received no smile for my efforts.

"Annie, have you met Scarlett Francis?"

Only if glares were the same as handshakes. I held out my hand and looked Scarlett Francis straight in the eye. "Not technically, but I have heard all about you, Ms. Francis."

I felt her hand squeeze mine in a challenge before I let go. Perfect. This weekend was starting to rank right up there with getting braces and studying for final exams.

We walked toward a driver who waited at the curb next to a shiny black limousine. I looked around for the movie star and realized the car was for us. At senior prom I had ridden in a ten-year-old limousine that my date's uncle owned. But it had been nothing like this. I looked over at Charlotte before she ducked inside, and I mouthed "wow" and winked. She barely smiled.

The conversation in the limousine was civil and small talk remained small. So small that I had time to study Charlotte. She still avoided looking at me.

I wanted this wedding to be perfect for Charlotte. It was my responsibility to help her enjoy the day.

After what seemed like an interminable car ride, we arrived at the Bellasposa Bridal Salon. Classical music and the faint smell of lilacs greeted us as we entered an ornate door underneath a swag-style awning. Two women I had been introduced to last night, Bebe and Patty, approached us.

"It's so good to see y'all again!" exclaimed Bebe. Charlotte's tall, blond friend was wearing pink leggings and an orange tunic. I wished I could make color like that work for me.

In addition to me—the maid of honor—Charlotte had recently chosen Jessica, Bebe, and Patty to be bridesmaids. Bebe and Patty would be fun. But I tried to imagine Jessica walking down the aisle with any sort of smile on her face and just couldn't picture it.

A severe-looking woman wearing all black greeted us with a clipboard.

"It is such a pleasure, Ms. Adler," she said to Charlotte as she looked at June and Scarlett. "And may I just say that I love *The Morning Show* and the GATE Network. Mrs. Francis, your guest appearances on the evening news recently have just kept me riveted to my seat." Scarlett merely nodded and I wondered if the woman was serious. Scarlett delivered the evening news like a preacher giving a eulogy.

We were led to a small room with a loveseat and two chairs. Bebe, Patty, and I took the cramped loveseat while Scarlett and June sat in the comfortable-looking armchairs. Jessica sat on the armrest of her mother's chair and crossed her arms.

"Honey, don't do that with your arms, it makes you slouch," June said, touching Jessica's back. Jessica rolled her eyes. "Jessica is so excited to be included, aren't you, dear?" Jessica regressed to a bored blank stare and it occurred to me that perhaps she could give Scarlett a run for her money as an anchor on the evening news.

I pasted on a smile and glanced at Charlotte. She blinked rapidly as two men entered the room. One carried a professional photographer's light, and another carried a large video camera.

"Oh, here you are, Greg," said Scarlett.

"Sorry," the man carrying the camera said as he held out a light meter and walked around the room. "We got lost on the way from the studio."

"That is what MapQuest is for, Greg. No excuses," Scarlett said.

I looked over at Charlotte, who was chewing on her lower lip as she studied the clipboard with wedding dress pictures. Seriously? I couldn't believe what was happening. It had never been her style to blur the boundaries between her private life and her career.

"Isn't this fun, Annie? It's going to be like that TV show. We all get to help Charlotte find the perfect dress and be in the feature story," said Bebe, elbowing me.

"Charlotte wasn't sure at first," said Patty, "but Scarlett convinced her that it would be perfect for *The Morning Show*. Every woman goes through the uncertainty of finding the right dress."

"And our viewers will be thrilled to be included," finished Scarlett Francis.

What was Charlotte thinking? My gaze rested on Charlotte and I detected the slightest wince as she finally met my eyes.

"And since your mother couldn't come, it will be so nice for her to see the dress we . . . Charlotte chooses," added June.

I said nothing, but ran my fingers through my hair.

Charlotte's lips compressed for a moment. "It will be nice for Mom and Aunt Addie to see."

"And Henry and everyone in Truhart, and of course your entire viewing audience," I said, meeting her eyes. I was amazed that Charlotte hadn't warned me about this. Then again, she knew I would hate the idea of making her dress-shopping experience a spectacle. We always joked about those people on reality shows who lived their lives in front of the camera. I pressed my tongue to the roof of my mouth to block the words I wanted to say, forcing myself to relax.

"Oh, come on, Annie, it will be fun," Charlotte said in a quivering voice.

The only person in the room who noticed the interchange was Jessica. She leaned forward in her chair, looking back and forth between us, for the first time interested in what was happening.

"If it's what you want, why not?" I said, sitting back and crossing my legs. I smiled at everyone around the room. "No problem." My foot bobbed up and down and I kicked my camera bag under the couch. No need to take pictures for my mother now. The whole world would know what wedding dress Charlotte was wearing. The thought of the snarky comments from couches across America made me cringe.

The camera crew set up around us while Charlotte changed into her first dress. Within moments her head popped out of the dressing room. "Are you ready, Greg?"

He gave the thumbs-up, adjusted the video camera on his shoulder, and out walked Charlotte.

I lost it.

It sounds cliché, but I didn't expect to feel so overwhelmed the first time my baby sister put on a wedding gown. The cameras and the people in the room fell away from me. Charlotte could have been walking down the aisle right then and I wouldn't have felt any more emotional. She had grown up right in front of my eyes, from a little fat-kneed baby to an awkward, metal-mouthed teen. And now she stood beautiful and elegant in a simple strapless A-line gown that was gathered ever so slightly at the waist on one side. My throat tightened and my eyes grew alarmingly wet. I don't know whether it was Bebe or Patty, but one of them handed me a tissue.

And then everything turned bright. It took me a moment to realize that the camera was trained right on me. Wonderful! I had just rounded out the perfect wedding segment: emotional family member crying over her baby sister's wedding dress.

"Are you all right, Annie?" asked Charlotte. She sounded amused and breathless.

I gulped, trying to dig up some dignity. "It's just that, you look so . . . beautiful."

Charlotte stepped up on the small platform in front of a three-way mirror. Her head tilted to the side as she looked at herself. A big smile spread over her face.

"Oh, it's just what I was looking for . . ." She turned to all of us and searched our faces.

"You look great," Patty said, while Bebe gave the thumbs-up sign.

We all turned to Scarlett and June. They stared fixedly at the dress.

After a long pause, June said, "I don't know . . ."

What didn't she know? It was perfect for Charlotte.

Scarlett just stared, her eyes narrowed into tiny slits as she squinted. "Of course, everyone loves the first dress they try on, my dear." Now the camera focused on Scarlett. She smiled and waved her hand toward the open door of the dressing room with a flourish.

"But look at all those beautiful dresses. June and I have chosen some others for you to try on as well. You never know, you might find something you like better." The other ladies bobbed their heads enthusiastically toward the dressing room. They didn't want the show to end.

The next dress Charlotte tried on was similar to the first, but not quite as perfect for her. From the less than enthusiastic smile on Charlotte's face, I suspected she felt the same way.

Then she put on Scarlett's choice. It was monstrous. Not only did the transparent corset cinch Charlotte like a character in *Gone with the Wind*, but the dress had more spangles than a circus performer. Jessica, who wasn't so bored anymore, broke out in laughter the moment she saw it. June kicked her.

"What?" she said, looking back at her mother. "It's really awful."

Scarlett ignored Jessica and stood up to get a better look. "It's a Nina Formosa. Her styles are all the rage this year." Circling Charlotte, she came to a halt in front of the camera and posed in a flattering stance.

Poor Charlotte. She looked back at herself in the mirror and forced a fake smile, no doubt trying to figure out how to tell Scarlett that it was the most god-awful creation ever conceived.

"If you like this, I will make sure to get you a personal introduction and fitting with the designer. She is a close family friend," Scarlett purred.

"Let me think about it," Charlotte said, and I wasn't the only one who breathed a sigh of relief.

The last dress Charlotte tried was June's pick. We waited patiently as Charlotte took longer than normal to come out of the dressing room. During that time, Scarlett left a long voice mail that sounded like someone was about to be fired, and Bebe and Patty talked endlessly about what kind of bridesmaids' dress would go with each gown. The camera crew leaned against the wall, trying hard not to look bored and failing miserably. I could only imagine what men thought of this whole process.

Finally, the door to the dressing room opened. We held our breath as Chantilly lace and organza spilled out like an overflowing froth of whipped cream. Then Charlotte appeared, gently guiding each successive layer of fabric through the dressing room doorway with her hands. Once through, a longer swath of frilly material followed her. As she moved, the sales attendant poofed and fluffed each layer with as much fuss and fanfare as a lady-in-waiting.

The dress was absolutely stunning . . . and completely wrong for Charlotte.

An asymmetrical neckline was fringed with silk rosette flowers that draped over one shoulder and crisscrossed a ruched bodice adorned in crystal flowers. Even more dramatic, the back of the gown dipped impossibly low and was swathed in a trail of silk petals that gathered every few inches to form a train worthy of a Disney princess.

Everyone in the room exclaimed at once.

"Oh my God!" Bebe was the loudest. "You have got to get it!"

"Truly special," came the self-satisfied response from June.

"This dress is something of an original," explained the sales attendant. She helped Charlotte stand on the platform in front of the mirrors as the camera crew circled her.

I watched Charlotte carefully. She looked at herself from head to foot and turned to see the back of the dress. "It's gorgeous. But . . ."

"What?" asked June. "You will make such an impression coming down the grand stairway at the club. Honestly, Charlotte, they'll be talking about it for years to come."

"Yes, but it's really out of my price range." She told us the price and I was the only one who looked shocked.

"Oh, honey," said the sales attendant. "Believe me, everyone thinks they can't afford the dress. But remember, you only get married once . . . Well, I got married four times, but who's counting?" She laughed at her own joke and looked nervously at the camera.

"You know, honey, we all want this wedding to be perfect for you. I am sure your family and I can work something out to make this happen." June looked at me for support. She got no response on my end. I didn't have the financial authority to make this decision. The dress cost more than the total budget my mother had already figured out for the whole wedding.

"No. I told you, June, Henry and I are both working. We want to handle a lot of the costs ourselves."

Scarlett laughed. "Oh, you kids! You're so practical these days." She looked at the camera and leaned forward. "In my day we knew how to enjoy each moment. God, I would have never bought anything or taken a risk if I thought I had to *afford* it first."

June and Scarlett nodded to each other. Everyone started talking at once. Except me and Charlotte. She caught my eye in the mirror. Was she pleased? I couldn't tell.

Charlotte had never been a fussy dresser. Maybe it was our Midwestern roots, but we had always shared a similar taste for simple styles. A little black dress that looked nice on most people was divine on Charlotte. She would do nothing more than twist her hair in a graceful chignon and add a pair of chic earrings and heads would turn. It was her trademark. For all the glitz and glamour of this magnificent dress, the first dress was simply Charlotte. Sadly, I was the only one in the room who felt that way.

It took me a moment to realize that the camera had cut away and was focused on me.

"Well, Annie? What do you think?" Charlotte asked.

Why did I have to be featured in this decision? I didn't want the responsibility. I felt like a jury foreman who had been told to make the life-or-death decision on the fate of the favorite local son.

The room grew quiet and I saw the camera cut away to Charlotte and back to me.

"It is very beautiful . . . and so is the first dress . . . it was so simple and elegant." I could feel my face turning warmer under the glare of the other women. "Of course this dress is so detailed and umm . . . well, fancy . . . I can't imagine the number of hours that were put into making it." I was blabbering like an idiot. I looked at everyone as they leaned forward in their chairs and at Charlotte, who seemed so unsure. Was she just looking for my approval?

I curved my lips into a smile and hoped my nose didn't grow longer. "But, if this is the one you like the best, you should get it."

The other ladies exhaled an audible group sigh. Charlotte glanced back in the mirror and smiled tentatively.

"Well, I know Henry is going to love it! You will be everything a man dreams of in a bride," said June with a confidence that put me to shame.

Charlotte's eyes lit up and I knew the moment she made the decision. Her tongue touched her top lip just like it used to when she was a little girl deciding on her favorite ice cream flavor at the Dairy Cow.

"Yes, I think I'll take it."

Chapter 4

"Why don't you just drop us off at the Fifth?" Charlotte asked June when we climbed back in the limousine.

I had no idea what *the Fifth* was. And it was the last thing I cared about right now. We had stayed at Bellasposa for an hour, waiting for Charlotte to work out fitting details for her dress and to wrap up a few shots with the camera crew. After calling to make sure my mother and Aunt Addie were on the mend, I spent the time trying to reconcile the Charlotte I knew and this stranger she had become. She seemed dependent on everyone else's opinion, especially June Lowell's.

"The Fifth is Nick's apartment building. Henry is over at Nick's watching baseball," Charlotte explained. "He invited us to come over after we finished this afternoon. Is it okay with you? I know Nick would love to see you." The mention of Nick made my heart miss a beat.

Oh, this was just perfect. After the scene at the bridal salon, I would probably do my usual foot-in-mouth routine and make an idiot of myself when I was around him. Hopefully there would be no breakable crystal or hornet's nests.

"Can I come too?" asked Jessica. She perked up at the mention of her older brother.

"No, Jessica. You don't need to pester everyone," June said.

"It's not a problem, June. Really. Jessica can hang out with us girls while the guys watch their baseball." Charlotte put a hand on Jessica's shoulder and was immediately rejected as the girl squirmed away.

"I like baseball!" insisted Jessica.

"Well, all right. But have Henry make sure Jessica is home before eight. We have guests coming for dinner tonight and, Jessica, you promised to play piano for us."

Jessica rolled her eyes and dropped her head back against the seat. "I don't want to play the stupid piano for your friends."

"I told the Frasers that you would play for them, dear. We wouldn't want to disappoint them, would we?"

"Mom, I hate it when you do that." Jessica rolled her eyes and stared at the ceiling of the limousine.

I couldn't decide if I should feel sorry for Jessica or not. Sensing my gaze upon her, Jessica turned her head and our eyes met. For a split second I could see the pain of a teenager reflected in her gaze, then she made a huffing sound in her throat and looked out the window, ignoring the conversation in the car the rest of the way.

The limousine dropped us off on the sidewalk in front of a towering high-rise made of glass and steel. This was where Nick lived? As Charlotte and June arranged a ride home for Jessica, I craned my neck to see the top of the building. The neighboring high-rises cast strange shadows across the façade, and I had to shade my eyes from the glare of the sun against the glass.

When we entered the gaping lobby a man behind the desk recognized Charlotte and waved. We walked past endless walls of gray granite toward a bank of stainless steel elevator doors. I tried to shake off my mood. A dull ache had started behind my eyes. I was just tired, I kept telling myself.

The three of us were quiet as we waited for elevator doors to open. When they finally did, we entered and I retreated to the corner with my back against the wall and drew in a deep breath.

"So . . . you okay, Annie?" Charlotte asked.

I paused for a moment. Then I answered very slowly, "I'm okay, Charlotte . . . and you?" It was a simple question, and I wasn't sure she understood all the meaning I had put into it.

"I'm great," she said, turning her eyes to the numbers above the elevator door.

Finally we stopped on the twenty-sixth floor. I walked off the elevator first and paused in the long, dark hallway.

"Why don't you go on in; we'll be there in a moment," I said, turning to Jessica. Jessica looked at us with sudden interest. After a moment, she reluctantly slouched away and I made sure she was out of earshot before I turned to Charlotte.

"Charlotte, I had no idea there were going to be cameras. I am surprised you made today a TV show," I blurted out.

"It was only a last-minute idea. And it's not like the wedding is actually going to be a TV show, Annie. Just a segment on *The Morning Show*. Our ratings were slipping a little and Scarlett thought this might get us some viewer interest. It's harmless really," she added. "She thought it would make a great story about the trials and tribulations of getting ready for a wedding. And according to the surveys, our female audience relates to me."

I wanted to say that most women weren't going to relate to someone who bought a dress that cost as much as a small car. But I took a breath and pointed out, "You have always said you planned on preserving your privacy if you made it big. I never thought you would take your once-in-a-lifetime chance to shop for a wedding dress and let America in."

"Oh, come on, Annie. It's no big deal."

"What comes next, TV cameras at the wedding?"

Her eyes widened and she backed up until her shoulders hit the wall.

"Oh, Charlotte! Tell me you aren't going to make your wedding the story featured in the eight o'clock segment!"

"No. I wouldn't do that."

I had said too much. I could see tears forming in her eyes and a tremble in her lips. Charlotte looked like I had run her over with a tractor instead of a few words.

"You don't understand. It has been really hard . . ."

I hadn't seen her tears in years. Not since Dad died. I took a deep breath. Suddenly I felt ashamed of myself. It was obvious this wedding was stressing her out. And here I was, adding to it. I put my hand on her arm. "Listen, honey, I didn't mean to upset you . . . I am so sorry. I was just worried."

"Why are you worried? I'm marrying the man of my dreams. Don't you like Henry?"

"Henry's great!" I didn't need to lie about that.

She started to say something, then stopped and took a deep breath. "You know . . . it's just hard to plan a wedding."

I placed my hands on her shoulders and looked into her soggy eyes. We never argued and I didn't want to start now. I pulled her close and hugged her.

"I'm not having the wedding on TV," she mumbled against my shoulder.

"I'm sorry. I didn't sleep all that well last night and I wasn't expecting to be videotaped this afternoon."

"You don't like the dress, do you?"

I looked over her head at the wall behind her, trying to keep my voice calm. "I love your dress . . ."

"No you don't," she said, pulling out of my arms so she could see my face.

I put my hand under her chin. "Listen to me, honey, I am telling you the truth. That is one of the most beautiful dresses I have ever seen."

Her lips formed a tentative smile. "Really?"

"Yes." I didn't add that it swallowed her up like a marshmallow. If she loved it, well then, that was all that mattered.

With our arms around each other we walked to the door of Nick's apartment. Jessica had left it cracked open and we could hear the baseball game on TV. Stepping inside, we moved slowly down a long foyer with bleached wood floors and bare gray walls that made me feel like we were in an empty exhibit at the New York Museum of Modern Art. I followed Charlotte as she turned the corner into a huge open space and for a moment I just stared.

Henry, Jessica, and several men sat on a white leather sectional that took up the middle of the room. I didn't see Nick.

Henry spotted us and jumped up. He walked over to hug both of us.

"I hope you had a great time shopping for a dress. Of course, you would look great in a potato sack," he said, putting his arm around Charlotte. He rubbed his hand along the back of her neck and I saw her relax.

"Hello! I'm Richard," said a shorter, dark-skinned man who rose from the couch to greet me. He wore a smile that lit up his face, and he tried to block a taller blond man who introduced himself as Kevin.

"Ignore these two clowns, Annie. They may be my groomsmen, but they aren't good enough for you and they don't know a thing about baseball," Henry said.

I laughed and found myself relaxing around Richard and Kevin. They reminded me of Ian's friends back home, never serious and highly competitive about their sports. After a moment, Henry murmured something to Charlotte and the two of them wandered off toward the windows.

Richard handed me a beer and we all moved to the couch for an exciting third-inning rally. As they were engrossed in the game, I had a chance to get a better look around. Steel-framed windows made up the outside wall. The other three walls were white and blank and rose up at least fifteen feet to the ceiling. Other than the sectional, the only piece of furniture in the space was a glass table in front of the couch. In fact, the only sign of human habitation in the entire room was the gargantuan flat-screen TV mounted on the wall and several beer bottles on the glass table.

Jessica brooded from the corner of the couch. I tried to talk to her while Kevin and Richard yelled at the umpire for a bad call.

"How is school going?" I asked her.

"Fine."

"What are your favorite subjects?"

"I don't have any."

I asked her a few more questions, but she looked at me like I had two heads. I remembered my own mother's personal mantra during the teenage years: Don't take it personally. I'd repeated it often to myself when I'd taught high school, and this was a perfect occasion to use it again.

I restlessly grabbed my camera out of my purse and wandered over to the window. I was an avid baseball fan. But I had to admit, if it wasn't a Detroit game, I usually lost interest. The sun was setting lower over the Atlanta skyline and I wanted to get a shot of the orange and violet ribbons peeking out between the buildings.

"What do you think?"

I turned to see Nick standing behind me. My heart did its usual cartwheel and I wanted to slap it down.

He stood with his hands in the pockets of a worn-looking pair of jeans. An untucked blue-striped button-down hung lazily over his pants. That, plus the fact that he must have forgone a shave in the morning, made him pure *GQ* material.

He stared at me like he was waiting for something and I realized that I had forgotten his question.

"Do you like it, Bump?" he repeated.

I blinked, on the verge of making an inappropriate comment about his appearance. Then I realized he meant the room.

Did I like it? It was a masterpiece of modern architecture and design. It could have been on the front cover of one of those expensive magazines that most people never actually bought. The view of the Atlanta skyline was magnificent. I suspected he had a lot to do with this building's design and architecture. And looking at him now, as he watched me for my reaction, I knew he was proud of it.

But it was like Charlotte's dress.

It wasn't Nick. At least not the Nick I remembered.

Nick was raised in a house with antiques, scuffed wood floors, and dogs in every room. I wouldn't call the Conrads' house in Truhart cluttered, but it was homey. Walls were lined with hand-painted pictures and family photos. Furniture that his father and grandfather had made graced every room. I knew for a fact that his dad Russell had taught Nick how to make his own furniture. The two had spent many hours together, hammering away in the barn. I had a vivid memory of the day Nick had shown us the first piece of furniture he made. I remember how he ran his hands along the finely sanded arms of the rocking chair and his eyes lit up.

Where had all those little pieces of Nick gone?

The pounding behind my eyes returned. Would it be cruel if I told him that all the place needed were some inscriptions on the walls and a few urns? "It is really . . . clean. And so . . . white," I said instead.

Nick's mouth looked pinched and I thought he was going to smile, which would have been crazy, given the intensity in his eyes. He shook his head with a grimace and hugged me, planting a kiss on my cheek that made me feel branded. "Never mind," he said in my ear. "I can always tell how you feel about things, even when you don't say a word."

I started to protest but was too overcome by his nearness. I breathed in the faint musk he was wearing, resisting the urge to lick his neck. When we broke apart I felt heat seeping across my face. I needed to find a corner to hide in before I made a fool of myself.

"How was dress shopping?" he asked.

"Great. Charlotte found a beautiful dress that everyone liked a lot."

Nick tilted his head and I hoped he wasn't reading my mind again. Instead he looked across the room. "Well, it's Charlotte. What could look bad on her?"

"Of course."

I, on the other hand, would have looked like a white goose in

Charlotte's dress. Charlotte was the only one who had inherited my mother's petite beauty. I was just awkward and tall.

"I didn't get a chance to tell you last night, I saw your mom last week. She said you've been busy," I said.

"We've been getting a lot of corporate business lately. It's been crazy. I was just on the phone in the back room, dealing with a new client."

I nodded and looked out the window, wondering at how successful he seemed to have become.

Nick came to stand beside me. "That's Peachtree Center over there."

"Oh." I aimed my camera in the general direction and released the shutter.

"And that other building is the Sun Trust building."

I lowered my camera and nodded. He was standing close enough that I could smell that musk again.

"And if you look farther, you can see Centennial Park, built for the 1996 Olympics." He leaned closer and I prayed he couldn't hear the racing of my pulse. It rivaled the speed of any Olympic runner. I turned toward the room, clutching my camera between us like a shield.

"So are all your buildings modern like this?"

Even though I was tall, the top of my head still only came to his chin and he had to tilt his head to look down at me. He was so close I could practically count his eyelashes.

"You don't like it at all, do you?"

Unfortunately, we were back to my views on his apartment. "I didn't say that . . . This place is actually quite striking."

His mouth tipped up in the corner and I clutched my camera tighter, trying to think of the words to use.

"It's really different from what you grew up with, though. You were raised in a house that was so full of—color." I wanted to say *life* but the mortuary image needed to be put to rest . . . so to speak.

He stepped away and his face shuttered. "That is the point of modern architecture. It is all about focusing on a single object, like the view out this window. No distractions by the debris that occupies most spaces."

"Well, antiques and family pictures are hardly trash."

"I didn't call them trash. But they clutter up a lot of things. People don't realize how little they need until they eliminate it. It's liberating."

"I guess I never thought of it that way." My racing heart stopped cold somewhere in the middle of this conversation. "So, did you design this building?"

"My firm did. I usually work with corporate spaces and there are offices on the other floors of this building. Our residential and corporate groups do a lot together in the city."

"Where is your office?" I asked.

"Not far from here. But I don't spend much time there. I'm usually on project sites and meeting with clients. I hate sitting behind a desk."

So, he designed corporate spaces but didn't like sitting in the office much? Interesting. If his office was anything like his apartment, I wouldn't want to spend time there either. I wondered if he saw the irony.

I smiled sweetly. "It looks like you love your work."

His nostrils flared and he returned my smile, only it didn't reach his eyes. "Speaking of work, how have things been going for you in that department?"

I blinked. Beneath his smooth veneer I must have gotten to him. My lack of enthusiasm had hit a sore spot. Unfortunately for him, I was pretty thick-skinned about being jobless.

"You know art—it's the first thing to get cut in the budget crunch in schools these days," I said with a laugh, referring to the layoffs in the high school arts programs.

"Actually, I was surprised you went into teaching. Wasn't photography your dream?" he said, touching the top of my camera.

Touché. I subtly pulled back from his reach. He noticed, and dropped his hand.

"It's okay. I am happy to be back home in Truhart . . . helping my family." I put the emphasis on the words *home* and *family*.

He barely nodded and rubbed the back of his neck.

"Your mom mentioned you probably weren't coming home anytime soon," I blurted.

"I don't think so. It's just too tough to get away."

"She misses you." It was such a pathetic way to guilt him into coming home.

"We talk several times a week, Bump. And she says she is busier than ever with the dogs and the church."

"I know that's what she says." If he had no idea that his mom missed him, I wasn't going to explain.

"She visited Atlanta last spring. And I told her to bring Melissa and Jenny in December. They love the city at Christmas. The weather is great, there is so much to do here, and it isn't so—" He opened his mouth to say something else, then seemed to think better of it.

Wasn't so *what*?

We were interrupted by a shout in the room behind us.

"Hey, you're missing it, the Braves have loaded the bases," called Henry.

Kevin and Richard waved me over to a spot they had created between them. I smiled and walked away from Nick. For the next hour, my ego enjoyed having Richard's and Kevin's attention. Nick sat mutely across from us. He kept his eyes on the screen the entire time, looking like a gloomy fan as his team suffered four strikeouts in a row and the injury of a key player.

The game ended and Richard stood up. "Who's up for a night out? Let's go drown our sorrows in good food and better drink."

Two hours later I found myself in the middle of a chic midtown martini bar. Blue lights lit the room's borders and cool jazz energized the under-forty crowd. From the moment we pulled into valet parking, I'd felt out of my league. Once inside the Double Olive, we found ourselves in the crush of an upscale crowd dressed to the nines in designer clothes and lots of bling. I was conscious of my simple clothes and the scuff marks on my discount shoes.

Our group had grown larger since we'd left Nick's apartment. Two other couples, friends of Charlotte's and Henry's, had joined us. And wonder of wonders, my favorite D-cups made an appearance. Brittany wore a sheer white top over a low-cut matching camisole, a black miniskirt, and high-heel boots that made her legs go on forever, or at least up to her armpits. She sat to Nick's right and leaned into him sickeningly as she curled her perfectly manicured hand around her martini glass. I secretly hoped she would spill the chocolate martini she wielded so gracefully down the front of her Ds.

As I clutched my glass, Kevin described a sand trap he had played on the seventeenth hole overlooking the bluffs of the Australian coast. Both he and Richard had moved closer as more people joined our table, and Kevin's hand rested on the back of my chair while he talked.

"I know we are probably boring you with all this golf talk, Annie, but the game is addictive. Have you ever played?"

I pressed my lips together, trying not to grin. "Just a bit."

Richard leaned in and gestured toward Kevin. "Anytime you do play, Annie, don't let this guy give you pointers. You'll never get out of the rough."

Kevin laughed. "Spoken like someone who spends a lot of time in the rough. You should know all about sand traps, Rich."

"Say, Annie," said Richard, "we're playing in a really laid-back tournament at the club tomorrow and there's room in our group. How about you let us give you some pointers. You never know, you might get hooked once you know a little bit more about how to play."

Across the table Nick froze, his glass of scotch raised halfway to his lips. He looked over the rim at me and our eyes met. Nick knew all about my golf game.

I had grown up with a golf course in my backyard.

"I don't know, I guess it could be fun," I said, lifting my shoulders.

Charlotte laughed nervously from farther down the table. Although she had never been very interested in golf, she was a decent player and had witnessed my hustling firsthand when she worked the golf shack snack bar.

"Charlotte could loan you the new clubs she bought last summer, Annie," Henry said. "But are you sure you want to play? You don't have to make these buffoons happy." Judging by the twinkle in Henry's eye, I guessed he had already heard about my golf game.

Nick sent me a warning look. But I wasn't paying attention, or at least I pretended I wasn't.

"Well, it sounds like it would be fun to give it a try. You men just tell me what time to be ready and I'll be there." I frowned down at my shoes. "Is it okay if I wear these?"

"God no!" said Richard. "You have to wear golf shoes. Charlotte, you played with Henry a few times. Do you have shoes Annie could wear?"

"My feet are a little smaller, but she could probably squeeze into them if she wears thin socks," she said with a hint of wariness in her voice. I flashed her a grin, hoping I could loosen her up a little.

I raised my hands and looked around the table. "Special shoes? I thought I could just wear an old pair of sneakers. I had no idea I needed special shoes." Henry slapped the table and laughed. I caught him winking at me. It was nice to know I had found a kindred soul.

Nick rolled his eyes and sent me a withering look. Okay, perhaps I was lathering it on a little thick. But I was having fun for the first time since arriving in Atlanta, and the part about the sneakers was actually true. I wasn't a stickler for golf formalities.

"Do you want another drink, Annie?" Kevin asked.

I looked down and realized that my glass was empty. I nodded my head. I hadn't eaten since lunch and a warm, mellow feeling relaxed me. I was only too happy to keep the feeling going.

Nick leaned forward and said in a low voice, "Be careful, Bump. A martini is a lot stronger than a bottle of beer."

"Thanks for warning me, Nick. After watching Aunt Addie and Mom last night, I would never have figured that out," I said, aiming a dagger of sarcasm his way.

Brittany readjusted her blouse, which further exposed her breasts, and raised her voice. "I can't imagine you get too many martinis up in Michigan, Annie."

"What?! You haven't lived until you've tried the Truhart Twister." I made that up, of course.

Nick closed his eyes and shook his head as if he had just undergone surgery without anesthesia. I couldn't help it. I really liked Henry and the boys, but Brittany was a snob through and through.

"You'll have to make it for us sometime," said Kevin. "So, another one?"

"Yup," I said, smothering a hiccup as Nick focused on his glass.

"So, tell us what it was like growing up in Truhart," Henry said.

"Yeah," added Richard. "I'll bet you have some great stories about Nick."

"And Charlotte," added Henry from farther down the table.

I breathed a sigh of relief. Now I was in my element. Telling childhood stories about my two favorite people in the world was almost as good as finding the perfect photo opportunity at sunset.

I began with my story about Charlotte as Mary in our church nativity play. That was the year Charlotte had been on a Disney kick and had to be coerced out of her Little Mermaid dress to wear a robe for the part of Mary.

After I had warmed up on Charlotte, everyone begged for stories about Nick. I took great pleasure in telling them about his rather colorful adventures with my brother, the summer they discovered WWF wrestling on TV. Of course they had only been twelve, but their pitiful attempts to mimic the great Hulk Hogan had kept our mothers in a state of continuous anxiety.

Even Brittany laughed at the image of Nick shirtless in a cape. After I finished and the conversation moved on, Nick tapped the table, staring absently at his fingers. I had a feeling he was remembering more than just my stories. I hoped he was remembering good things about growing up in Truhart. Something more than whatever was keeping him away.

Then he raised his eyes and met mine. I tilted my head and grinned, but his expression remained stony.

A moment later Brittany put her hand on Nick's arm and he turned away. "You are still playing with Daddy and the Vanderbeeks in the tournament tomorrow, right, Nick?"

"Of course," he said. Then he flashed her a heart-stopping smile.

Brittany had just performed her own hustle. I had been waiting all evening for that smile—but Nick had given it to her instead.

Chapter 5

It had been a while since I'd played a round of golf and I was eager to see if I still had my game. I whistled my favorite *Caddyshack* tune as I opened the refrigerator door in Charlotte's kitchenette and grabbed milk for my cereal. Charlotte lay on the couch, in the pink Pokémon pajamas I bought her for Christmas last year, and sipped coffee while she watched her *Morning Show* on TV, doing its customary jump from perky topic to headline news.

"So, Annie . . . you aren't really going to do anything crazy today, are you?" she asked casually when a commercial came on.

I stopped whistling and put my cereal bowl in the sink. "Crazy? Who, me?" I said, winking at her.

"No. Really. You are just going to have a little fun, right? You aren't going to cheat Richard and Kevin out of any money or anything like that, are you?"

"Nah," I said. "Don't worry. They'll still be able to buy you and Henry a great wedding gift when this is over."

Her mouth compressed and she smoothed her messy hair back. Once again I sensed something bothering her and I promised myself that we would have another talk soon. She seemed perfectly happy when she was around Henry, but when she was with me she acted edgy. Aunt Addie would say she was as nervous as a long-tailed cat in a roomful of rocking chairs.

The phone rang, and the doorman announced Kevin's arrival.

"Oh jeez, I'm late," I said, grabbing Charlotte's clubs. She had left them for me by the door.

"As soon as they are up and ready to go, I am going to take Mom and Aunt Addie to Bellasposa to see the dress. But I can pick you up if you need me to, Annie," Charlotte said, trailing after me. "We should be getting ready for the shower no later than five o'clock. Bring your phone in case you need me to get you early. Okay?"

I nodded as I stuffed my phone into a zippered compartment in the golf bag and arranged the strap over my shoulder. I was more excited to play golf than to attend the bridal shower, but I would never let her know that.

When I hopped in Kevin's car I was surprised by the sight of Richard sitting in the backseat with his hand wrapped in a bag of ice.

"What happened?"

"*Someone* closed my hand in the door of the car," he said.

"Only an idiot would put his hand on the door frame when I was about to close it," Kevin retorted.

"I was trying to open the back door so I could move the clubs you stupidly put in the front seat. And you're the idiot for not looking to see who might be standing there when you pushed the damn door closed."

Fortunately, from the way he moved his fingers it looked like Richard's hand wasn't broken. But it was turning an alarming shade of purple.

"Are you sure you're going to be okay?" I asked.

He nodded. "At the very least I'll drive the cart. Besides, I wouldn't want to leave you alone with this amateur. You would never learn a thing from this duffer."

For some reason I felt right at home with Kevin and Richard's bickering. They reminded me of my brother Ian. By the time we arrived at the Thorn Hill Golf Club in the heart of Atlanta, the conversation had deteriorated to a discussion of who had broken the most bones over the years. I shook my head at the way men loved to brag about injury and pain and flexed my fingers inconspicuously, anticipating the feel of my first drive off the tee.

After we had unloaded our clubs and put on our shoes, we lined up at the registration table. Thankfully, it was windy and eighty degrees, cool for Atlanta in August. The weather report predicted rain from the first tropical storm of the season, but it hadn't reached us yet.

"They might make us combine teams since Richard here can't play, Annie. But don't let that make you nervous. Like I said, this is a pretty laid-back tournament. Not that we don't occasionally have an older member who thinks he's at the Masters. But for the most part, this is just a friendly Saturday game."

I ran my hand through my hair and tried not to look like a fraud. I felt a twinge of guilt, but it wouldn't hurt a thing if I went along with Kevin for a short time. They would be laughing along with me by the end of the round.

"Don't worry, Annie. I got your back on this," Richard added. "I may not be able to play, but I'll help you as we go." He popped another ibuprofen in his mouth and I double-checked his hand. It hadn't swelled much more, but it looked painful.

The lady at the registration table shook her blond ponytail and leaned over to whisper to an older woman next to her. The older woman placed her elbows on the table and said to Kevin, "I hope you don't mind, young man, but we might need to put you into a foursome. We have another team with two players who canceled this morning . . . if that is okay with you?"

Richard leaned on his bag. "We don't mind much, but we have a beginner with us and she might feel awkward." He nodded my way.

"I don't mind if no one else does," I said.

"Well, let me call the other team over and you can talk before you decide," the woman said.

I looked around for a group of two. Amid the sea of navy and white polo tops I didn't see anyone who looked like they were missing players. Until I spotted two familiar faces.

Nick and Brittany leaned against a golf cart talking to a white-haired man. That must be "Daddy." The gentleman bore the angles of privilege: a long patrician nose, square jaw, a good head of white hair, and height. Every pore screamed money, and I could see a faint resemblance to his daughter.

Then I noticed our registration lady approaching them and nodding her head in our direction. Nick's brown eyes turned black as he looked our way. I could see a muscle twitch in his neck, even from where I stood. The older man smiled and started walking our way, followed by a reluctant-looking Brittany and a moody-looking Nick.

"Well, well, boys. It looks like you are as stranded as we are."

"Hello, Mr. Hartwick, sir." Kevin and Richard's immediate deferral to the older gentleman and the way they stood up straighter as they shook his hand caught my attention. This man was important.

Mr. Hartwick looked down at Richard's injured left hand. "Hope you didn't do any permanent harm, boy," he said.

"The only permanent harm done is to a good friendship, sir."

Kevin rolled his eyes but said nothing.

Richard stepped aside slightly. "Mr. Hartwick, in case you didn't meet her at the dinner party, may I introduce Annie Adler. She is Charlotte Adler's sister, soon to be Henry's sister-in-law. We thought we would introduce her to the game of golf. Annie, this is Travis Hartwick, Brittany's father and owner of the GATE Network where Charlotte works."

I raised my eyebrows and tried to pick my jaw up from where I dropped it on the ground. Really? Brittany's father was the owner of the GATE Network?

"My wife has told me all about you, but she didn't mention how pretty you are," he said, smoothly gripping my hand and holding it in his.

"Your wife?" I looked over at Brittany, sinking further into confusion. But before I repressed a shudder, he replied.

"Scarlett, of course."

My smile froze on my face. I looked from Brittany to Nick and then back again at Travis Hartwick. I must have been the densest person in the world not to make the connection between Scarlett and Brittany. In my defense, their hair and uh . . . bra sizes were nothing alike. And Scarlett must have been using her maiden name in her profession rather than her married name. But if I looked past the makeup, I could see a faint resemblance in the shade of their eyes and the tilt of their brows.

"The Hartwick and Lowell families have been close friends for thirty years now. Henry's father and I went to Ole Miss together and started out in business years ago before going our separate ways. Henry is like a son to me. In fact, there was a time when I thought he would be my son—that is, until your Yankee sibling came along."

I was beginning to understand why Charlotte was nervous about this wedding. Still, Brittany seemed far more interested in Nick than Henry.

As if reading my mind, she said, "Oh, Daddy. Henry is like a brother to me. I always tell you that. Dating him would have been like dating a member of my own family." She smiled and for the first time I saw warmth inside her ice princess exterior as she looked up at her father. The moment was shattered as he reached over and touched Nick's shoulder.

"Well, I guess we will have to settle for some other fine young gentleman who'll make my little girl happy, right, Nick? Glad I could introduce her to someone as smart as this guy. You know Nick Conrad, right? He is a rising star in one of the country's top architectural firms . . . that I just happen to own as well." He was so smug it grated my nerves.

Nick's attention was elsewhere and his face was partially hidden from me as he turned to Richard and examined his hand while Travis was talking.

"Actually, I met Nick a long time ago. I think I was about two," I said, smiling brightly.

The older man raised his eyebrow and looked questioningly at Nick.

"Annie and I were neighbors growing up. Her brother was my best friend," Nick said with a simple nod my way. His eyes brushed over me and I could tell he was irritated at the way the day was unfolding.

"Well, then it sounds like we have ourselves a golf game. You two know each other . . . from Ohio, was it?"

"Michigan," Nick and I said in unison.

But Travis kept talking. "If you two know each other from your little Northern town, and I know everyone else, we should get along brilliantly, my dear. As for your golf game, little lady, I am sure I can give you some great pointers on the sport. Down here in the South we pride ourselves on our mastery of the links. Not everyone appreciates the game." He nodded toward Brittany. "All it takes is one great shot and you're hooked. And I have the fortunate habit of making great shots so often I am downright addicted!" He laughed at his own joke and we all chuckled.

Why did every man I met this weekend have such a driving need to teach the "little ladies" in their lives all about the game of golf? I rubbed my hand along the side of my bag and relished the moment when I could let myself enjoy the game.

Once the ladies at the registration table were assured that there would be no problem with our new foursome, Brittany kissed her daddy good-bye and we walked to the first hole and waited for our start time.

While the others were busy with their equipment, Richard took me aside and whispered, "Whatever you do, don't bet with Travis."

"Why not?" I whispered back.

"He's a rotten cheat. He'll do anything to win. It's probably why the Vanderbeeks canceled on him."

I raised my eyebrows. Well, well, Brittany's daddy was a cheat and a snob. This was going to be very interesting. A piece of the old hustler in me was rising to the surface and I could feel my pulse throb in excitement.

The others gathered near the first tee and Kevin approached, taking his job as my mentor very seriously. "So, we all tee off by these markers, but because you are a girl your tee is farther up, a little closer to the hole way over there. Can you remember that?"

"Oh yeah. That's really nice of the people who make the rules," I said innocently.

"Well, golf is a gentleman's sport, Annie," he assured me. Kevin and Richard reminded me of all the basic rules of golf and I nodded my head as they explained all about bogies, birdies, and pars.

"Just take it one shot at a time, Annie. No pressure. Okay?" Richard said.

While Richard and Kevin wandered over to talk with Travis and Brittany about the scoring and rules of this particular scramble, Nick came over and stood beside me.

"Pretending you can't play golf with just Kevin or Richard is one thing. But now that you're in the middle of a real tournament, playing with a whole group of people, things are much more complicated. Do you ever consider that maybe you should think before you act, Bump?"

I did feel a little regretful, to be sure. But it wasn't going to get messy. "It's not going to be a big deal, Nick. I'll start slow and get a little better as we play. Once the guys realize I can actually play, we are all going to relax and enjoy ourselves."

He studied my face. "I hope you're right. But I know you and you're not going to be able to resist winning this game. Everyone around here knows Travis Hartwick likes to win. You have no idea what you are getting yourself into. Every time you assume something is simple it ends up being complicated. You step into trouble the way some people step into shoes, Bump."

I put my hands on my hips and looked up at him. "I had no idea we would be playing with anyone else, so don't blame this on me. And what do you mean, I'm always in trouble? Everything that isn't business is trouble in your book. Do you even know the meaning of fun? I'm surprised you don't have a tie on."

Nick started to say something, but Kevin interrupted. "Hey, Nick and Annie, it's tee time."

I stormed away from Nick and joined the others. Richard drove his golf cart with his good hand and we decided to take turns walking. He pulled up alongside the tee while Kevin and Travis Hartwick selected their drivers.

"Let us men start, little lady. We'll show you the right way to swing the club. Then we'll let you try," said Travis. He held up the tee and placed it in the grass before balancing his ball on it. "Now this here is the Vardon Grip, it's the right way to hold your club. You want to stand like so," he said as he showed me the basic golf stance. Unfortunately, he was leaning all wrong from the hips up. "Make sure to balance your feet and keep your head from bobbing as you swing."

Travis went into great detail. He explained how his shoes were the same ones Phil Mickelson wore and revealed how much they cost. If he thought that would help his stance he was an idiot. I tried desperately to look attentive as he continued. I held the club all wrong and Kevin corrected my grip and smiled at me when I did it right. Nick just leaned against the cart and glared. Fortunately, I was the only one who knew he was glaring. To everyone else he looked like he was sending me an encouraging smile. I barely heard Travis Hartwick as he continued with his tutorial. I kept thinking about Nick's words. Why did he take everything so seriously?

We waited patiently as Travis practiced a minimum of ten times before actually taking his shot. The shot faded slightly, which I could have predicted by the way he was standing. He marched back to the cart and said nothing.

Kevin and Nick went next. They hit their balls in a nice arc and landed a good distance down the fairway. While Kevin demonstrated his swing, Nick did not acknowledge me in any way, but as he lined up to swing I couldn't help peeking. His wide shoulders and trim backside made my mouth go dry. Even as annoyed as I was, Nick made me feel like a schoolgirl watching the quarterback from the bleachers. When he swung I was reminded of what a good athlete he had always been. Whether it was golf, football, or baseball, he was a natural.

I swallowed and moved toward the ladies' tee. I feigned worry as I looked back at the group behind me. "Am I going to be okay? What if I hit someone?"

"Don't worry, Annie, the group ahead of us is almost at the next hole. You'll be fine. We'll give you a few practice swings," said Kevin.

He walked over to me and stood behind me with his arms around my shoulders as he moved me through a swing. Richard made a comment about Kevin's enthusiasm and I laughed nervously, glancing back at the carts. Nick was seemingly fascinated with his clubs and never glanced my way.

Stepping back, Kevin encouraged me to try on my own. I slowly moved the club, getting the feel of the grip in my hands and adjusting to its length. Then I stepped back in place, gauged the ball with my driver, then readjusted for a miss, and swung.

Afterward I looked down at the ball. It was still on the tee. "Oh no!"

"Don't worry, it happens to everyone, although you Northerners have a habit of over swinging and topping the ball, I must say," said Travis. "Try again."

I tried two more times before I finally hit the ball. I wasn't going for power at this point, just a nice easy swing. I struck the ball fairly well, I had to admit. It sailed forward and landed about ten yards behind Kevin's ball, right in the middle of the fairway. I was pleased.

A silence fell over the group behind me.

"Wow. That was pretty good, Annie."

"Well, I had great teachers," I said, smiling.

As we played the first few holes, I tried to keep it low-key and shot just to the right of the green. I found myself enjoying the challenge of purposely missing my target.

My brother used to say that for people who sing well, it is really hard to deliberately sing off-key. But for golf, I found I could challenge myself to hit the ball at a different target, say ten yards to the right or left. It was kind of fun. For a little extra entertainment I found myself aiming for Nick's ball. If we were playing croquet I could have knocked him right out of range into the lake near the third hole. For now I had to settle for a little amusement by getting in his way and messing up as much of his game as I could. He remained unruffled and it only fueled me more.

I kept thinking of his comment about me stepping into trouble. "Trouble, my—"

"What was that, Annie?" asked Richard when he heard me muttering under my breath.

"I'm having trouble with my grip, that's all."

"Here, let me show you again," said Kevin eagerly.

"You're holding us up, Annie. Practice it when you aren't ready to putt," said Nick.

The testiness in his tone made my blood sing. Finally, I had managed to annoy him as much as he annoyed me.

"Now, Nick. Don't hurry the little lady," Travis said magnanimously. "Everyone can just wait. We aren't in any kind of rush. Annie is from a small town in Ohio and they don't know this game like we do in the big league. You should know that."

It turned out I wasn't the one holding us up. Travis Hartwick took more practice strokes than anyone I had ever seen. Even though his form was off, he commented to me about every swing as if he was a golf pro and I was his student. At one point, we stood on a putting green at the eighth hole. Nick was getting ready to sink a long putt. Just as he started his back swing, a shrill ring went off. He missed the hole by yards and his ball ended up going downhill toward the lake on the side of the green.

Travis pulled a phone out of his pocket.

"What's up, Hal!" he said so loudly that the players on the adjacent hole looked our way.

I stared at him and wondered if he had lost his mind. Even on our laid-back golf course back home we turned off cell phone ringers. I watched in astonishment as Travis Hartwick told Hal all about how he would call him back after he finished playing with his young friends from Ohio. I sent Nick an exasperated look and he just crossed one foot over the other with casual unconcern. We ended up letting the group behind us play through.

"Whoops. Let me get back to you, Hal. It looks like everyone's getting impatient," Travis finally said. Turning to the rest of us, he made things worse. "Now, where were we? Oh yeah." He picked up his marker, which sat at least six feet from the hole. "Sorry about that call. This one's a gimme, I believe," he said, marking it in his score sheet.

I started to say something, but Nick put his hand on my shoulder, turned me around, and squeezed hard. "Don't worry about it," he said.

We continued to play, but I could sense everyone's lack of enthusiasm.

Travis Hartwick was a cheat.

If he went into a bunker he dropped the ball practically in the middle of the fairway before playing it again. He called his own "short" putts gimmes. He flirted shamelessly with the girl on the beer cart, trying to squeeze her behind when she handed him his third beer. And I couldn't even think about his scoring. By the second half of the round I was ready to smash a club over his head.

By the thirteenth hole I made up my mind it was time to revive my hustling ways.

I shanked the next tee off on purpose, aiming for the lowest branch of a nearby oak tree. I brushed a leaf on a hanging branch and had to mask my satisfaction at the shot. "Aww. Just when I thought I was getting it."

"It's okay, little lady. That happens. Now this hole is a dogleg. You want to use an iron on that next shot and stay left of the water." I watched as he squared up to the tee and took practice swing after practice swing. We had just waved another group through on the last hole.

"Now in Ohio I know you probably play on some pretty small-time courses . . ." He began another endless golf lecture. I nodded my head and forced a smile.

Now, if you ever asked anyone from Michigan if they thought the day would come when they would defend a person from Ohio, they would say "no way." But I was getting defensive about the derogatory comments.

When we started the final hole, I said, "You gentlemen have been absolutely wonderful to teach me today. I feel like I am finally getting the hang of this game." I sighed. "Why, if I were a betting woman I would bet a whole dollar on this hole, but of course I'm not." I giggled and pulled the wrong club out of my bag.

Travis Hartwick whistled softly. "Why, honey, there's nothing I like more than a little green in my golf, and I don't mean the grass." He chuckled at his own joke.

"What's that?" I said, pretending to miss his meaning as I practiced teeing off with an iron.

Travis walked over and laughed. He pulled a driving wood out of my bag and handed it to me. "Well now, how about we each stake a hundred dollars on the last hole."

"One hundred dollars!" I put my hand on my chest in shock. I could feel my blood racing in my veins. This was the challenge I had been waiting for.

"Sure. It'll keep this last hole from getting too tedious, you know?"

Kevin reluctantly agreed and Nick said nothing. He had become strangely quiet over the last few holes and I knew he was probably thinking all about me and trouble again. Well, I was tired of worrying about trouble. Travis Hartwick was a bully and an old snob, just like his wife.

Besides, there was the whole state of Ohio to defend!

I lined up at the tee and let it rip on the sweet spot, packing more power than even I thought was possible. A hushed silence fell over the group. I smiled absently and just said, "Wow."

Nick and Kevin hit well, but landed behind me on the fairway. Travis Hartwick shot low, failing to get the height he needed, landing short of the rest of our shots.

My next shot was clean and straight and landed right on the green. If I stayed focused I was sure I could birdie. Travis Hartwick landed in a bunker on his third shot. I watched incredulously as he dropped his ball close to the middle of the fairway, a move any self-respecting golfer could never get away with.

"That's kind of taking liberties, Mr. Hartwick," I said.

He acted like he hadn't heard me.

I looked to the other gentlemen for some support. They said nothing.

Fine. I could win this without their help. Travis Hartwick would probably shank the next ball.

The only trouble was that by sheer luck he made a good chip to join us on the green. Before I knew it, he and I were the only ones left to win the round. Nick and Kevin had overshot the green and Travis and I hung back, letting them finish since they were out of the running with a double bogey each. Nick sank his putt and stood nearby with his hand in his pocket, watching Kevin's final shot sink in the hole.

When the ball dropped, I leaned against my putter and watched in trepidation as Travis Hartwick picked up his marker and turned to the men. "Too bad, gentlemen. You may need to practice more than you think. Let's see how I do . . ." He took two sly steps closer to the hole and placed his ball on the green, farther from his marker and closer to the hole.

I opened my mouth to say something. "You—"

"—should make sure to clean that ball, Travis," interrupted Nick.

"But—" I started.

"—of course it is up to you," he said, butting in again.

I was livid. I turned to Nick to say something, but he just shook his head fiercely at me. I couldn't believe he was being such a wimp. I looked at Kevin and Richard near the cart, waiting for someone to say something. But they stayed silent.

Travis turned toward the hole and went through the irritating routine of practice strokes that we were nauseatingly used to by now.

Then he lined up and gently pulled his club backward . . . just as his phone went off in a shrill ring.

The ball stopped four feet short of the hole.

A flurry of four-letter words escaped his mouth as he stomped around the green, pulling the phone out of his pocket. "Well, shit! No one is even there! I don't even recognize the goddamn number," he said, staring at the phone. "That's a mulligan!"

He lined up again and repeated the previous routine, practicing his putting form over and over until I wanted to clobber him with his clubs. Finally he was ready. Just as he pulled back, the phone rang again and the ball went off the other end of the green into the water.

I laughed.

He threw his clubs down and let loose a string of obscenities. Picking up the phone, he turned it off and threw it in the cart, continuing to swear up a storm. By the time he took the shot again he was too frazzled. Even without the phone ringing it took him several attempts to sink it and he ended up shooting three over par.

"Your turn, Annie," said Kevin as Nick shifted nearby, his hands still in his pockets as if he hadn't a care in the world. I stepped up to my ball and measured the shot with my eye. I was about thirty feet from the hole and no one expected me to make it in one shot. But putting was a particular specialty of mine. It reminded me of looking through the lens of a camera. I measured the distance and angle like a photographer. I often wondered if Jack Nicklaus or Greg Norman were good photographers, because it took a certain eye to understand a putt. Anyway, it would have been an interesting study. I smoothly rotated my shoulders backward and tapped my ball with the putter.

It was a thing of beauty.

All eyes watched as my putt rolled across the length of the green and made an incredibly satisfying plunk into the hole. Behind me Richard gave a whoop and Kevin clapped. Travis looked like he had swallowed a ball. Nick just sighed.

"That was a lucky shot!" I said. "I didn't know I had it in me."

I looked back at Nick's impassive face and felt like sticking my tongue out.

My victory was sweet. Kevin and Richard were elated and we exchanged high fives all around. If they were embarrassed by my new-found giftedness they said nothing. They both drove off to return the cart and promised to say good-bye later.

Once recovered from his initial shock, Travis Hartwick finally pulled himself together enough to mutter his congratulations. I couldn't help the satisfaction that rolled through me as he shoved his clubs in his bag so hard he might have bent them. He sulked the entire way to the clubhouse, insisting that golf had changed since cell phones were invented and he would never bring his phone to the golf course again.

We stopped at the side of the clubhouse near the parking lot and Travis Hartwick looked around to make sure no one was watching. Then he pulled his wallet out of his pocket and fished out two fifty-dollar bills.

"Maybe we can have a rematch sometime?" he said with a shade of bitterness in his tone.

I smiled brightly. "Sure."

Then he walked into the clubhouse, leaving me alone with Nick behind me. I turned around and realized he was closer than I thought. Looking up, I waited for his reaction to my victory. Although I knew I was probably going to get my usual reprimand from him, I searched his face for a sliver of approval.

Nick remained poker-faced, neither congratulating me nor scolding me. I should have been used to his nonresponses, but I was disappointed that he hadn't stood up to Travis Hartwick.

The sun was sinking lower in the sky and I knew I should touch base with Charlotte and make sure I wasn't late for the bridal shower.

As my hand grazed the bottom of the golf bag, fishing for my phone, Nick held his hand out.

"You dropped your phone, Bump."

"Thanks," I said, reaching for it. "I could swear I zipped the pocket."

He tilted his head, studying me. A breeze blew a wisp of hair over my face. He reached out and gently curled the stray strand behind my ear, leaving his hand near my chin. For a brief moment I thought he might say something. I leaned closer, hoping to encourage him as his eyes moved over me like a caress.

I heard Kevin calling me from the path near the clubhouse.

Nick let his hand drop and stepped back. "See you later, Bump," he said as he turned around and picked up his clubs.

I watched him walk away and felt a familiar pain in my chest. I had almost lost my head over a simple touch. How pitiful was that? He hadn't even wished me a good trip back to Truhart. Instead, it was just a casual "see ya later." As if I were the bagger at a grocery store. No. One of the ladies at our local Family Fare would have gotten a better good-bye than that. It was time to take my heart off my sleeve. Nicholas Conrad was an unfeeling, wimpy, cold-blooded man. Crushes were for teenagers.

I took a deep breath and looked at his retreating figure. *Good-bye, Nick.*

Chapter 6

"Are you going to wear *that*?" asked Charlotte. She stood in the doorway of the bathroom in her apartment, watching me as I applied mascara to my eyelashes.

I looked down at myself and wondered what the problem was. I wore a camel-colored silk shirt with a simple matching scarf, black cropped pants, and my favorite low-heeled sling-back shoes.

"What's wrong with this?"

"Nothing, it's just that you are all sort of . . . casual. That's all."

I popped the mascara wand back in its dispenser and stepped out of the bathroom to get a better view of what she had on. Charlotte wore a sleeveless black lace dress with a shimmering gold sheath underneath. The dress hugged her body like a glove and I was momentarily struck by her splendor before it hit me that it was a little dressy for a shower, even if she was the bride.

"Wow. You look great."

She hugged her arms around herself and nodded her thanks, shifting from foot to foot.

"Uh, Charlotte, this is a wedding shower, right?"

"Well, yes. But they kind of do it up in the Lowell family. It's just that the club is pretty fancy. We are in a small room, not the big hall where the wedding is being held. But they tend to overdress here."

"I had no idea." A cold feeling passed over me as I realized that I was missing something significant about my sister. Something just beyond my reach that I needed to understand.

"Oh, Annie. Don't say anything to Mom and Aunt Addie. I didn't mean to make you feel bad. You look absolutely wonderful. Really. I should have warned all of you. But it's not a big deal at all, really." She exhaled with a feeble laugh.

"Something tells me it is a big deal. As a matter of fact, Charlotte, something tells me this whole thing is a big deal—more than just a wedding, actually. Is there something going on that I'm missing?"

"Oh, don't be silly."

Mom and Aunt Addie were watching the end of an old movie in the living room. I backed up into the bedroom and dragged Charlotte in with me. "At first I just thought you were a nervous bride, but now I know there is something else going on."

"What? There's nothing—"

"Sit." I pointed to the bed.

Charlotte blinked and put her hand to her throat, as if she were trying to say something.

"Sit!" I said more firmly. The Adler alpha-woman in me was rising to the surface. Aunt Addie would have been proud.

"Okay, okay . . . But really, there is nothing to—"

"Yes, there is. Is there a problem between you and Henry?"

"No," she said emphatically, and I believed her.

"Well, then there is something else going on." I crouched down in front of her and a worry popped into my head. "Char, honey, are you pregnant?"

A startled look passed over her face, and she smiled. "No, Annie. Oh my God, no!"

I sank back on my heels with relief. A baby would have been wonderful under any circumstances, of course, but better to be wonderful *after* the wedding.

"Well, at least we don't have that little complication to deal with."

"Oh my God, I can't imagine having to explain that one to June and Scarlett," she said, rubbing her hand across her temple.

"But we have other things to explain to them? Is that what you mean?"

She scrunched up her face as if she was deciding what to say. It bothered me that she had to consider what to tell me and not to tell me. I always used to be her confidant. But now I just felt helpless and out of touch. I stayed quiet, gazing steadily into her face, willing her to talk like the old days.

Finally she tilted her head and said, "It's just that I think the Lowells, well, actually . . . I think June, Scarlett, and their friends, kind of think I am . . . well, they think that our family is . . ."

"Yes?" I prompted.

"They think we are . . . not really worthy."

"Worthy?" I tilted my head sideways, trying to understand. Worthy? It sounded archaic. Like a term that belonged in King Arthur's court.

"I know it sounds strange, but they think we are beneath them."

"Because we live in a small town?"

"Yeah, and well . . . you know how Aunt Addie was at dinner the other night?"

I was beginning to get the gist of what she was saying and it made my blood turn cold. "But a whole lot of people at that dinner were really nice to Aunt Addie. In fact, remember how we laughed about it? She was the hit of the party." Of course, deep down I understood. I wasn't oblivious to how our small-town ways must look to others. Was I embarrassing too? I clenched my fist. This wasn't about me. I needed to remember that. Taking a deep breath and loosening my fists, I urged her on.

"Don't get me wrong. It's not everyone who notices. It's just June and Scarlett mostly. And maybe a few friends of the family. You see, Henry's family always assumed he would marry into another family just like his. And when he chose me, at first they thought that's what I was. With my college background and my manners, even if I wasn't from around here, they thought our family was some sort of Northern version of the Lowells. Until the other night. Aunt Addie kept clutching her old suitcase and she wore that awful dress. And even Mama was a little dowdy looking and unsophisticated."

"And me . . ." It wasn't a question. I let my voice trail off as I remembered how I had behaved on the golf course.

"No, Annie, you were fine. It really was no big deal. I am probably imagining all their comments . . . And besides, at the dinner party they knew you were really tired from all that travel."

I wasn't about to mention my own loud comment about Scarlett before the toast. I had almost made things worse than Aunt Addie ever could have.

"So that's why you're trying so hard with this wedding. The dress, the reception here in Atlanta. And it worked just fine . . . until we came into the picture."

"Oh, Annie, that sounds so melodramatic. I just want to be careful it doesn't look like I am marrying Henry for his money. And anyway, this is so stupid. I am too old to care about all this."

"And does Henry care?"

"No," she said quickly. "Henry thinks your funny stories are charming. He keeps asking all about growing up in Truhart. In fact, he wants to come for a visit as soon as possible."

Well, thank God for that. I didn't think I could bear it if Charlotte was keeping Henry from the truth.

"I don't know why I am letting it get to me, Annie. It just seems like every time something about the wedding comes up, I look at things through their eyes. I don't want them thinking I'm a gold digger."

"It really matters what they think?" I asked quietly.

"It doesn't. It shouldn't." She shook her head. "It's so stupid, isn't it? I appear on national TV in front of thousands every week and here I am, super nervous about this wedding."

She stopped and looked at my face, then placed her hand on mine.

"See? This is why I didn't want to tell you. I knew you would be upset with me. I'm being way too sensitive. I'm just a bundle of stupid nerves."

For once I kept my mouth shut. A sense of disappointment washed over me. But if I was honest with myself, I understood all about being the odd man out. When I lived in New York I suffered my share of insecurities and embarrassments. It was bad enough that they insisted I had a Midwestern accent—which I still say I didn't. But people in the art community were always making fun of my lack of sophistication. How would they understand what it was like to live in a small town, where garage sales were big events and everyone knew one another's names?

But I didn't feel like sympathizing with her right now. Between my mental divorce with Nick this afternoon and Charlotte's apparent desire to defect from her small-town roots, I wanted nothing more than my own lumpy bed in the back annex of our inn, and a box of tissues.

"Forget I said anything, Annie. This is silly."

I shook my head and stood up.

"This is nothing. Really. I am just imagining everything."

I opened the bedroom door and walked back to the bathroom, trying to swallow the lump in my throat and erase the heaviness behind my eyes.

Charlotte appeared at the door of the bathroom. She put her hand on my arm.

"Please forgive me, Annie."

I forced a smile, but a quick glance in the mirror told me it looked more like a grimace.

"I love all of you! And I would never, ever want any other family." Charlotte put her arms around my shoulders and hugged me. When she was little and couldn't swim well, Charlotte used to cling to me in the lake just like this. Sometimes I felt like she was dragging me underwater.

After a pause, I returned her hug. "It's okay, Char."

I wasn't going to let her drown. We might be uncouth, but we were Adlers. We watched out for each other. It was my job to keep Charlotte happy and this wedding on track. I could handle bruised pride.

I pulled away and gripped her upper arms reassuringly. "Let's go to this fancy shower."

She chewed on her lip and I lightened the mood with a glance down at my shoes. "My big feet are already sore from squeezing into your golf shoes. But I think I could be persuaded to wear those cute designer shoes you were wearing at the dinner party if you think that would dress me up."

Her eyes widened. "Oh my gosh! No way, Annie! You'll stretch those out with your big feet. Your shoes work fine!"

That was the same argument she always used when I wanted to borrow shoes. I laughed and ruffled her hair. Nice to know in all this wedding craziness some things hadn't changed.

Charlotte insisted that all four of us squeeze into her sporty red compact car for the drive to the Lakeland Hills Country Club. An early-season hurricane that was downgrading to a tropical storm was knocking out power from Jacksonville to Charleston. Georgia was supposed to be hit with the remnants later that night and I wasn't relishing the drive in the muddy aftermath of the rain that threatened. Even now, the clouds were building as we drove down a long drive tucked into a low-lying area of Buckhead.

Charlotte paused at a guard house and gave her name to a man who raised a gate for us. As we wound our way around a small river and the private drive that led to the clubhouse, I made Charlotte stop for a moment so I could grab my digital camera and take a few pictures. Aunt Addie and Mom climbed out and insisted that I take a picture of them with the impressive view in the background.

Aunt Addie giggled. "Oh, wait till I show these pictures to the ladies back home. Marva O'Shea is going to be at a loss for words."

"That would be a first," Mom added.

A shiny Mercedes passed us as I framed a shot of a large magnolia tree with the club's white pillared portico in the background. A woman in the passenger seat stared at me as the car passed. Even if I couldn't hear what she was telling the driver, there was no mistaking her raised eyebrow. *Who let these people in?*

I nodded to her and helped Aunt Addie back into the car, ignoring Charlotte's nervous sigh. "You aren't going to take that inside, are you, Annie?"

I clutched the camera to my chest, then put it on the seat. I guess I would have to keep my camera in the car for the evening.

When we approached the club I pointed out several open parking places, only to realize when a red-vested man ran to open my door that the parking was valet only. Charlotte stopped the car and handed her keys to the valet. Mom and I grabbed the stack of presents from the trunk.

Our arms were overflowing and Charlotte tried to help, but I waved her off. "Nope, you can't carry any. You might guess what they are," I said with a grin.

Well, in all fairness, I didn't really know what they were either. Besides the fine linen my mother and I had ordered from a catalogue, we had brought presents from the ladies at the Family Fare, Nick's mom, Mary Conrad, and Aunt Addie. Judging by the way Aunt Addie had smiled when she packed hers, she had put a lot of thought into her gift.

A sense of déjà vu hit me when we entered through the heavy oak-paneled front doors of the club. I wondered if the person who designed the room had also designed the Ambassador Hotel. Or perhaps it was just the overly formal sophistication that I recognized. Two matching crystal chandeliers and a baby grand piano graced the elegant, deep-brown paneled lobby. A set of stairs to our left led down to a room that looked a little like last night's chic nightclub. But it was the grand-looking room ahead of us that captured my attention.

Up several steps and through a wide corridor I could hear the sonorous hum of a large crowd. In the background I could make out the sounds of a string quartet. Just as I walked over to investigate, a short woman carrying a black leather notebook stepped in front of me. She asked in a low, hushed voice if we were wedding guests.

"We are here for a shower. This is Charlotte Adler," I said, nodding to my sister behind me.

"Of course. It is nice to see you again, Miss Adler," the woman said, staring at the presents in our hands covered in rainbow-colored toucans, silver confetti wrapping paper, and peel-and-stick bows.

"We have been waiting for you. Your party is in the Peach Blossom Room. Follow me."

"Is there a wedding going on in the main ballroom?" Charlotte asked.

"Oh yes. As you know, we are busy with weddings and other special events almost every weekend night of the year," said the woman. "You were so lucky we had a cancellation in the spring for your reception. It would have been a whole year and a half until we could have fit you in."

We turned to the right down another corridor lined with windows. I could hear the sounds of "My Melancholy Baby" coming from a piano down the hallway.

"So, that room back there is where your reception is going to be held?" Mom asked Charlotte.

The woman looked back at us. "Yes. And I must say that it will look so wonderful with the springtime blossoms out the windows."

"Oh, can we just peek for a minute?" Aunt Addie asked. "I would love to see what it looks like. Maybe we can get a few ideas, Charlotte. Marva's daughter had a great balloon archway at her wedding."

The woman sent her a startled look. "I'm sorry," she said with a crisp voice. "We pride ourselves on assuring all our guests' privacy. It just wouldn't do to have everyone who comes to our club peeking. I'm sure you understand."

"Of course," said Charlotte quickly as we continued to follow the woman down the hall. I narrowed my eyes and scowled at the lady's rigid back as our feet clicked on the shiny polished marble floor. Charlotte sent me a pleading look. I'm sure she was worried I might say something rude. How little she trusted me. I usually only *thought* rude things.

As we entered another room I could see pastel-colored couches arranged in small groupings and a man in a white tuxedo playing a baby grand piano on our left. To the right were a half dozen linen-covered tables set with rose-colored glasses and hurricane lanterns, surrounded by small arrangements of pink and white roses.

I blinked at the women around the room. Charlotte had been justified when she worried about our clothes. From the sparkling jewelry dangling from their ears and necks to the spiked heels on their feet, these women were dressed for the kind of event that could grace the pages of a high society magazine.

"Charlotte," a familiar voice called from the other side of the room.

Charlotte waved to June, who stood with several well-coiffed older women. She wore a silk suit that shimmered with a subtle hint of silver. Jessica stood beside her, looking bored to tears, in a pink chiffon dress with a brown bow at the waist.

I sighed. Now I knew just how underdressed we were. Even the teenager's clothes looked nicer than Mom's cotton pants and gauzy blouse and Aunt Addie's blue polyester dress.

"What's wrong?" asked Charlotte.

"I should have stolen your shoes anyway. And maybe that cute little black purse with the sparkles."

"No way, that was a Michael Kors. I would never have let you borrow that one." Charlotte gave a nervous laugh and put her shoulders back before walking across the room to greet June. I shifted my weight, trying to balance the gifts in my hands. Maybe we should have left them in the car.

"Can I take that from you?" asked a young woman in black pants and a vest from behind me.

"Oh, if you just tell me where to put these, we can manage."

She pointed us toward a table that looked like it had been designed especially for the room. Then I realized it was actually mounds of shower gifts that made it look so gorgeous. Dried-flower bows and elaborate ribbons adorned the beautifully wrapped gifts. The wrapping paper alone probably cost more than what Mom and I had paid for Charlotte's present. After Mom put her armful down and wandered off with Aunt Addie, I tried to find an unobtrusive spot near the back for our gifts. Would anyone notice if I hid them under the table?

"Excuse me," said a blonde wearing a white suit with a fur collar, as she skirted by me to put her gift on the table. It was wrapped in yellow and white toile wrapping paper with real calla lilies tucked in the bow.

"Wow. Nice," I said under my breath. I wasn't just talking about the gift. The lady looked like she belonged at Buckingham Palace.

"I know," confided the waitress. She helped me make room on the table.

"Do they even own jeans?" I didn't realize I said it aloud.

"I doubt it," the waitress said under her breath.

"Well, there is always a chance they're wearing granny underwear from the dollar store. At least that's what I'm going to tell myself all night."

She started to laugh and caught herself. "I'll get you a big drink—how's that?"

"Perfect."

I turned back to the room and found myself face-to-face with a willowy woman in a peach-colored lace dress. "You're Charlotte's sister," she said, holding out a limp hand.

"I'm Annie." I tried not to squeeze her tender hand to death with my firm grip. Several other women joined us.

"How nice you could come down here for the shower. I hope the weather holds, but I hear it's going to pour tomorrow. When do you have to fly back?"

"Oh, I am driving. I'm planning on going back tomorrow."

"Driving? Oh my. Is that a long way to drive? I am trying to remember where Charlotte is from . . . Ohio?"

What was it with Ohio around here?

"No, just a little farther north. Michigan."

"Michigan? Near Detroit?" She looked a little shocked.

I had several friends from Detroit and I wished I could have said yes. I almost pulled out my hand to show where Truhart was on the mitten. Using our hands as a map was a little inside trick we did in Michigan, but that might have been beyond this woman.

"Oh." I could see her trying to figure out what to say after that. We stood smiling at each other for a moment and I was just about to ask her about herself when she blurted out, "I drove to our condo in Hilton Head last year and that was over four hours away. The traffic was really bad at one point and I almost gave up and turned around. How long is your drive?"

"About sixteen hours with stops."

Her eyes grew large. I could see the wheels turning in her head. A lady nearby laughed, thinking I was making a joke. I looked back at her with a straight face and she realized I was telling the truth.

"But I will make a lot of stops to break it up."

"Of course . . ." she said as her voice trailed off.

"What do you do in Michigan, Anne?" asked another woman.

"I teach art. But I'm unemployed right now."

They looked at me in embarrassed sympathy, not sure what to say.

"Well, this economy is just so terrible right now, isn't it?"

I nodded and faded into the background as they changed the subject. Growing up in an inn, I had learned how to converse with people easily. Everyone in our family was fairly good at the art of small talk. Aunt Addie would have chased us with a wooden spoon if we had ever shown a drop of rudeness. But even with that background, tonight I was having trouble.

I tried to talk to Jessica, but she had zero interest in talking to me. Within a half hour after we arrived she was on the couch playing a game on her phone. I almost wished I could join her. Mom and Aunt Addie stayed close to Charlotte, and I tried not to look at the way she bit her lip whenever Aunt Addie said anything around her friends.

At one point I stood by the piano player, just needing a break before my smile cracked. I patted the piano in time to a Michael Bublé song. In between sets the piano player let me look through his list for a song I might like. He suggested a Barry Manilow tune and I shook my head. "That's my little sister's least favorite artist."

"Really?" he asked. I nodded. "That's kind of un-American," he commented.

Nobody could disagree.

"We have an old upright piano at our inn back home. Sing-along nights happened all the time growing up. But God forbid if a Barry Manilow tune was requested by one of our guests. Charlotte would run to her room with her hands over her ears by the end of the first verse."

The piano player laughed and started playing a Nat King Cole song. Charlotte caught my eye from the other side of the room. I figured it was time to mix with the crowd again. I broke away from the piano and walked around the room, pausing every once in a while to join conversations, but feeling mostly invisible.

I stopped by the ladies' lounge in the hallway outside the Peach

Blossom Room. When I pushed open the door I almost laughed. It figured. Even the bathroom was nicer than my bedroom back home. Pink wallpaper, gold-plated fixtures, and a plush velvet chaise made me want to recline in the room for the rest of the evening. Maybe no one would miss me.

Several minutes later, as I turned the knob to exit the spacious room-sized stall, I heard a voice in the main lounge. "It is going to be a beautiful wedding, June. I know you had your reservations about it, but Charlotte seems like a lovely girl."

Now I really felt guilty.

"Yes. She does seem that way," June replied mildly.

"You sound worried."

"Well, you know what they say. Family is everything. We don't really know her family. and between you and me, things may be a little . . . well, shall we say uncomfortable?"

"Oh, now that you mention it, that aunt is a character, isn't she?"

"Well . . . we can't always choose who our children marry, can we? Fortunately, Scarlett has been a godsend. She assures me that she will tutor Charlotte on everything she will need to know as she joins the family."

I raised a shaking hand to my throat and tried to swallow my anger. I was going to tell June just what I thought of her. But I caught myself. That would have proven her point.

Taking a deep breath, I straightened my shoulders and opened the stall door. I stepped into the main lounge and turned to June. It was a pleasure to watch her smooth, wrinkle-free face turn mottled and blotchy from embarrassment. The other woman sputtered something unintelligible.

"Excuse me, ladies," I said with a smile. I moved in front of June and washed my hands, forcing myself to remain calm. When I finished I reached across her for a towel and then I paused. I looked her directly in the eye.

"This has been a beautiful shower, June. My mother and the rest of my family are so appreciative of all your graciousness in accepting Charlotte into your family. I just wanted you to know that. My mother taught me quite a bit about good manners."

With that I walked away.

It was almost the end of the evening. I just needed to get through the rest of the night and then I could leave this nauseatingly elegant place. I clenched and unclenched my fists as I walked the rest of the corridor. A pressure was growing in my chest, and the throbbing behind my eyes wouldn't go away.

When I joined the shower again I looked around, disoriented and wondering if I was in the wrong place. More than a dozen men lingered by the couches.

"Either those are strippers or I am in the wrong room," I mumbled to the waitress as she walked up to me with a tray of champagne glasses.

She raised her eyebrows and shook her head. "Oh God, I hope not."

As I looked more carefully it dawned on me that she was right. I caught sight of Travis Hartwick. Ugh. Just the thought made me take a hearty swig from the glass she handed me.

Charlotte walked over, seeing my look of confusion. "Henry and the guys ate downstairs in the men's grill. They're going to join us for the gift opening. June thought it would be a nice touch since Henry and I registered together."

My heart dropped and I felt a new panic. Great. I knew what that meant. And true to my fears, I spied Nick at the back of the room. He caught me looking at him and looked away, taking a deep gulp of his drink. Did I make him uncomfortable? It dawned on me that Nick must feel that same way Charlotte did. I suppose now I knew why he never came home to Michigan.

"Annie, are you all right?" asked Charlotte.

"No," I said after a moment. "My stomach is just a little upset, honey. But I'll be fine."

From behind me, June entered the room.

Avoiding my eyes, she clapped her hands. "Are you ready for gift opening, Charlotte?" Maybe she couldn't wait for this evening to end either.

We formed a half circle. I was offered a seat next to Charlotte and Henry. The waitress handed me a pen and paper.

"You need a paper plate so you can put the bows on it, like we do back home," Aunt Addie shouted from her chair. "Every bow she breaks means a baby."

"She has to pull the ribbon off without untying the bow," Mom explained to a confused woman on her right. "It's a tradition. We put all the bows onto a paper plate, and Charlotte can use it to hold as a bouquet for her wedding rehearsal,"

I bit my tongue as a waitress brought my mother a paper plate. We had just given June more reasons to ridicule us.

Nick stood behind the seated circle of onlookers. I turned away and straightened my scarf. I wasn't going to think about Nick anymore. I reminded myself of my mental divorce from him. The documents were signed and sealed in my mind.

Charlotte and Henry took turns opening gifts of fine china, crystal vases, a nineteenth century silver-rimmed decanter, and a full set of hand-painted sushi plates and chopsticks. I struggled to keep up with recording each gift while not letting my jaw drag on the ground. If these were shower gifts, what would the wedding gifts be like?

Everyone oohed and aahed over the gifts, and Henry joked about all the dinner parties he would have to give to put these fine items to use. Aunt Addie reminded him that with all the broken bows, a dinner party was out of the question. Too many children to watch.

I had just finished recording a set of Wedgwood serving pieces, when I sensed a nervous rustle from the crowd. Charlotte held up a box decorated in familiar silver confetti wrapping paper. I wanted to rip it out of her hands before anyone saw what was inside. She read the Hallmark card my mother and I picked out last week and peeled off the wrapping paper. Part of me refused to feel intimidated. Lifting the lid of the box, she pulled out four sets of white cotton towels. I couldn't bear to see the disappointment in her face, so I kept my head down as she pulled out the towels and thanked us with a hug. The crowd clapped politely. But I sensed their flat response to the gift. With alarm, I could feel my eyes growing moist and I struggled to hold back stupid tears. Fortunately, Mom smiled, oblivious to the direction my thoughts were taking.

Next, Charlotte was handed a gift with colorful toucans dancing across the wrapping paper. Charlotte explained that the gift was from several ladies back home and I cringed as she lifted out a commemorative plate from the shopping channel, bearing the likeness of the president of the United States.

Aunt Addie beamed from her chair. "Everyone should collect something. The ladies thought this would be a great way to start!" Several women in back laughed and I scanned the room quickly, smiling through gritted teeth before fixing my eyes back on the pad of paper in front of me.

I stared down at the words that wavered in my vision and tried to collect myself as Henry opened a small gift next.

"Who is this from, I wonder?" he said.

I looked up as he wagged his eyebrows at the guests around the room. Everyone turned their heads, looking for someone to claim the gift. Tilting his head, he joked about the mystery gift and then he ripped open an envelope and pulled out the embossed card.

Reading it out loud, he said, "'A trip for two to Italy for your honeymoon. Enjoy your time together. Love, June and Jessica.'"

The room exploded in applause at the unprecedented generosity. Henry and Charlotte jumped up and hugged June. Scarlett loudly offered to give Charlotte time off for a honeymoon next year, and everyone laughed.

If the gift had come from anyone else, if it had been opened at any other time, I would have been happy for Charlotte. But now I wanted to burn the card in the hurricane lantern on the table until it turned into tiny pieces of ash.

After everyone stopped gushing over June's gift, we were back to the next present: Mary Conrad's gift. I stole a look at Nick as Charlotte read his mother's card. Was he feeling this? He didn't seem the least bit affected.

After pulling off the wrapping paper, Charlotte lifted the lid of a box and pulled out a beautiful log cabin quilt that must have taken Mary weeks to make. I saw the lady who couldn't handle a four-hour drive to Hilton Head whisper something to Scarlett. Charlotte was polite enough to exclaim over the beauty of the quilt and I wondered vaguely how it would have looked in Nick's barren apartment. Of course he wouldn't have used it.

Heat rose to my face and I felt like the room was closing in around me.

From the perimeter of the crowd I caught a glimpse of Nick edging toward me. What did I do now? Wasn't I smiling properly? I swallowed past the thickness in my throat and clutched the pen so hard my knuckles were turning white. Henry said something about blankets and bedding that made people laugh, but I wasn't listening anymore.

My deepest prayer was answered when the last gift was eventually handed to Charlotte. This couldn't end soon enough! But my heart dropped when I recognized the silver wrapping paper. Aunt Addie had walked around with a smug smile after shopping in Gaylord two weeks ago. She wouldn't tell anyone what she had bought Charlotte, and I hadn't given it much thought.

Until now.

It was Henry's turn to open the gift and with every tear of the paper I felt a piece of my composure shred.

Henry lifted the lid of the box and held up Aunt Addie's gift in wonder.

A burst of laughter and exclamations erupted around the room. Aunt Addie's was the loudest. The men in the back jeered and pointed. Henry grinned as he held up the gift. A transparent black negligee with feather fringe and lace thong underwear.

I thought I would die.

Tears rushed to my eyes and thankfully no one noticed as they continued to exclaim over the tawdry gift. Gift opening was finished. Everyone left their seats and made their way toward a dessert table, I jumped out of my chair and ran through the doorway. I headed toward a set of doors that led outside and barely made it before a sob escaped my throat.

It had been a very long time since I'd cried. It wasn't that I never felt sad, I just never felt tears ever did any good. But as I braced my arms against the stone wall, I sobbed. For my father who wasn't here, my sister who was never coming home again, and for myself—because I felt so helpless. I had no idea how long I stood there, but after a while I became aware of a steady rain falling and a dark form standing nearby. Nick leaned over me, shielding me from the rain. Somehow I wasn't surprised. Nick always seemed to be around for my most embarrassing moments.

As he stood with me under the dark overhang, I thought about how good it would have been to cry into Nick's wide shoulder. But I couldn't. Even in the middle of my emotional breakdown, I was too proud to cry on Nick's shoulders.

He was the enemy.

He lived in a cold and desolate apartment.

He was friends with all these people.

He never came home.

And I had divorced him . . . figuratively, at least.

He handed me something. I looked down at a handkerchief. I didn't know men still used those, but I took it gratefully and blew my nose indelicately.

With clear sinuses I became aware of the smell of wet cement and pine needles, carried by the stiff breeze. They helped the fuzziness in my head recede as I wiped the last of my tears away. When I was ready to face Nick, I turned around.

The first thing I noticed was the way the breeze lifted damp tendrils of Nick's hair and how much I liked it that way. The second thing I noticed was the shadowed expression on his face.

"Are you all right, Bump?"

I nodded and an unexpected hiccup escaped my mouth.

"What happened in there?"

What could I say? He had been there. He'd witnessed the whole thing. Extravagant and elegant gifts from Henry's friends. Tacky and cheap gifts from the Michigan friends and family. I waited for some acknowledgment from him. But he just stood there, staring like I had grown horns.

"God, Nick! Didn't you notice?"

"Notice what?"

"*What?* Are you kidding me? Are you that unaffected by the snobbery of these people?" I stomped on the cobblestone walkway, wishing his foot were beneath my shoe.

"I don't get it . . . what?" he said.

How could he be so dense? I was so frustrated that I pushed the heels of my hands against his chest. "You don't get it? I can't believe it. *You don't get it?*"

"Hey, Bump, calm down," he said, grabbing my shoulders. "All I know is that with every present Charlotte and Henry opened you looked like you were falling apart a little more. I thought you might break out in tears right there in front of everybody."

My hands were buried under his sports jacket and I had no memory of how they got there. I clutched my fingers around his lapels and felt the solidness of his muscles beneath my knuckles. How many times in the past had I wanted to be in this position? Unfortunately, I never thought it would be in the rain with mascara smeared on my face.

I tilted my head up and tried to control my voice. "Nick . . . the Lowells, Scarlett Francis, their friends, almost everybody . . . they are snobs. Every time Charlotte unwrapped a gift from home, they were looking down on us with complete . . . I don't know . . . condescension. Like we were hillbillies."

Nick put his hands on each side of my face.

"Annie . . ."

I tried to pull away and he held me, bringing his face closer to my own.

"Annie . . ." he said again. I felt his hot breath against my cheek. He smelled like scotch and something more masculine. The traitor in me wanted to lean in farther and capture his mouth. But then he continued. "You need to understand. No one was half as affected by this as you. Your mom and Aunt Addie didn't care. Even Charlotte was taking it all in stride."

"No. You don't get it! Charlotte is going to get eaten alive by them. She is going to turn into an upper-crust professional snob who cares more about the label on her purse than the people around her. She is going to live in some cold house with marble floors and granite tables with no warmth, and she'll never return, Nick. She'll stop wanting to come home because we're shabby and common and worthless to her."

He let go of my face and took a step back.

"Is that what you think of me, Annie?"

I shook my head feebly, missing his nearness. "No . . ."

"Is that how you think everyone is? All the people you've met and talked with . . . and laughed with? Kevin and Richard and Henry?"

"No. I don't think they're like that . . ."

"Well, that's what it sounds like you're saying."

I felt abandoned and leaned backward against the cold wall.

"We should go back," he said after a minute, running his fingers through his damp hair. The rain had spattered his shoulders, forming sparkling droplets that glistened in the dim light. I focused on those droplets now, trying hard to compose myself.

"Are you driving back tomorrow?" he asked after a moment.

"Yes."

"You should wait a day. You've got to be tired." I should feel flattered for his concern. But it was hard to feel flattered when I knew he just wanted to be done with me.

"I'll be fine," I said as we took a step toward the doorway. I pulled my hair behind my ear and stopped. "Look, Nick. You would understand what I'm trying to say if you had heard some of the things June Lowell was saying—"

"I've heard a lot of things, Annie! And if you ask me, the only person who has been acting like a fool is standing right in front of me."

I turned back to him and stopped. "Are you calling me . . . did you just blame all this on me?"

"Maybe I am just pointing out that you're taking every negative little thing about the Lowells and their friends and turning it into something overblown and exaggerated."

"I'm not imagining things. Even Charlotte tells me she feels nervous about Henry's family."

"I'm sure every bride feels the same way. Charlotte is going through a lot of changes right now. Atlanta is a big city, and she's just gone nationwide with her career. Of course she feels overwhelmed. But she doesn't need her big sister egging her on!"

For the first time I understood what the expression "seeing red" meant because my vision was flashing crimson and I was losing control.

"Oh, now I see it! Well, I'm not surprised. I'm the bad guy in this. No one else is at fault, are they? You are going to make excuses for everyone else because it's easier than looking inside yourself."

Nick looked at me as if I'd grown two heads. "Me? Are we back to me? Go ahead, Annie. Spit it out! What is it you really want to say?"

I lifted my finger and pointed it at him. "You really want to know?"

"Yeah! I really want to know," he said, raising his voice for the first time.

I shifted and took a deep breath, winding up to strike.

"You have turned into a stuck-up, coldhearted snob." I could see a muscle ticking at the side of his cheek as I continued. "Something happened to you when you left Truhart. You barely smile. You live in a mausoleum. You rub elbows with people who cheat at golf . . . and I might add . . . you let them cheat as long as they are rich and they are your boss!"

I was just getting going and I couldn't stop myself. "You never visit your mother or home. And why is that? Are we too common for you?"

He stepped back and crammed his hands in his pockets.

"And last but not least, you have horrible taste in women! Brittany is a stuck-up daddy's girl with a bra size bigger than her IQ!"

"Are you finished now?" he asked curtly.

"Yes. I am," I said after a moment.

"That was low, even for you, Annie," he said hoarsely.

He reached around me and swung open the door. Without looking back, he walked inside and left me standing alone in the rain.

His words rang in my head. *"That was low, even for you."* Nothing he could have said would have made me feel worse.

Chapter 7

The wind howled through the parking garage as I loaded my suitcase in the backseat of my SUV the next morning. Power had already been knocked out in one Atlanta suburb and forecasters were predicting several inches of rain by late afternoon.

Last night as the hurricane crept inland and broke apart in Georgia, rattling the windows of Charlotte's apartment, I had tossed and turned on Charlotte's couch. What little sleep I did achieve was haunted by garbled images of crystal chandeliers swinging from knobby trees and a desperate search for a wedding I couldn't find.

Despite a headache from lack of sleep, I was anxious to hit the road. Mom and Aunt Addie were hoping their flight would not be delayed by weather. As for me, if I could get to Kentucky by early afternoon, I could avoid the worst of the storm. The prospect of my own bed and familiar surroundings fueled my need to get an early start. Rude guests and clogged toilets sounded relaxing compared to worrying about the Lowell family.

"Well, I think that's everything," I said as I readjusted my suitcase on the backseat. I turned to Charlotte and willed myself to smile through a fog of sleeplessness.

Charlotte wrapped her arms around her small frame. Her pink Pokémon pajamas peeked out below her jacket and, judging by the dark circles under her eyes, she looked like she needed more sleep, too.

Last night when I returned to the wedding shower after my meltdown, Charlotte and I didn't have a chance to speak. The crowd milled around the doorway saying their good-byes and no one noticed my damp hair and red-rimmed eyes. I helped Charlotte and Henry load the shower gifts into June's car, where they would be stored at the Lowells' house until after the wedding. Nick was nowhere to be seen. He must have left right after my tirade.

Charlotte and Mom recapped the evening as I sat in the backseat, numbly watching the city lights flicker off the damp pavement, while Aunt Addie snored. When we arrived home, Henry picked Charlotte up for a nightcap, and I sensed that they wanted time alone. Ever polite, Henry asked me if I wanted to join them. But I had no interest in doing anything other than lying on Charlotte's couch and wallowing in my shame. In the early morning hours when Charlotte returned to her apartment and paused by the couch, I pretended to be asleep. For the first time in years, I wasn't up for late-night girl talk.

Where had it all gone wrong? Somewhere between the dress shopping and my reckless outburst, the weekend had turned into a nightmare. How could I accuse Charlotte of being ashamed of our family, and then dump all that fury and jealousy on Nick? It was like I had started the weekend as the perfect maid of honor, and ended it as the wicked witch.

"That was low, even for you, Annie." Nick's parting comment washed over me like a bucket of ice water. Now all I wanted to do was to click my heels together three times and go home.

And, oh my God! Did I really mention Brittany and her bra size?

I closed the back door of the car and turned to Charlotte. A gust of wind sent a blond ringlet across her eyes and I reached out to clear it from her face. I kept my hand on the side of her face and she leaned into it.

"It was great to be here this weekend," I said.

"Oh, Annie. It was so nice of you to come all this way for me. I hope I haven't been too much of an emotional wreck this weekend." She grabbed the hand that cupped her face and gave it a squeeze. "What would I do without you for support? Thank you so much for keeping me grounded."

"Not at all," I said, stepping closer and wrapping her in a sisterly hug. I hoped she would never find out about my own meltdown.

"Give everyone back home a hug from me."

"Well, think about coming for a visit and doing it yourself," I said into the top of her messy blond head. Stepping back, I clutched my keys. "I know you are busy, but maybe between Christmas and New Year—"

I was interrupted by the sound of tires screeching around the corner of the parking garage. A wet, black BMW, its wipers still thrashing against the windshield and tossing out streams of water, pulled into the empty spot next to us. I was just getting ready to comment on the rudeness of the driver when he jerked open the door and bounded out.

"Nick?" said Charlotte. "Is everything all right?"

He ignored her as he pushed a button on his key fob and opened the trunk of his car. For a moment I thought I was hallucinating. Had my guilt conjured up the one person whose voice had echoed in my mind all night? I dumbly watched the rivulets of water fall from his car onto the cement floor of the parking garage, and said nothing as he pulled out a small suitcase and shut his trunk.

Turning back toward us, he said, "I need a ride."

I blinked.

"Why?" Charlotte asked, looking confused.

"I'm supposed to fly to Detroit for an important meeting. But my flight was canceled. Since you are passing through Detroit, Annie, I thought I could go with you."

Now I knew this was truly the weekend from hell. Not only had I pissed off the man I had loved for twenty-odd years, but I was going to be confined to a five-by-five-foot space with him for the next ten hours. Just yesterday I would have jumped at the chance to spend time in the car alone with Nick. Now being with a man who thought so little of me seemed like torture.

Besides, I had been looking forward to a good cry, man-bashing Taylor Swift songs on the radio, and stopping at the greasiest fast-food restaurant I could find to gorge myself on french fries and pity. But if Nick came along, I was going to have to either grovel to him until I lost my appetite, or face the silent treatment with nothing but sports radio playing in the background.

I opened my mouth and started to protest. "I don't think—"

"Thanks!" he said without giving me a chance to talk. He opened the back door of my car and threw his bag in next to mine. Taking the keys from my hand, he nudged me out of the way. "I'll drive first."

I couldn't believe it. "But I didn't say yes. This is like being abducted!"

"I'll pay for the gas and buy lunch."

"Are you trying to bribe me?"

He folded himself behind the wheel and moved the seat back to accommodate his long frame. "See you later, Charlotte."

"But what if I'm not going through Detroit?" I protested, grabbing the driver door before he could close it on me.

Nick placed his hand on the steering wheel and glared, daring me to argue with him. "Get in the car, Bump."

I looked back at Charlotte, who was staring. She must have decided I wasn't being kidnapped because she said, "I think you should give him a ride, Annie. It must be an important client or something if he is acting like this."

"Whose side are you on?"

"No one's. I just think it would be good to have someone to take turns driving. This weather is pretty bad," she added.

Nick put the key in the ignition, started the car, and revved the engine impatiently.

I stomped over to the passenger side and yanked open the door. "Fine! But I get to play my music, do you hear me? No sports radio!"

As we backed out and turned to leave the garage, I rolled down the window and shouted my good-bye to Charlotte. She waved back and I noted that the corners of her mouth were turned upward in an amused smile.

When the car pulled out of the garage, the full brunt of the storm pummeled us. Rain whipped across the pavement in blanketing gusts and I rolled up my window and gazed toward Nick. His lips were pressed together and his jaw was clamped shut while he concentrated on the road. His hair was mussed, as if he had used his fingers instead of a comb this morning. He wore an old black jacket I remembered from years ago, and it was awkwardly off-kilter. One side of his collar was out and the other tucked in, as if he had been in a rush and forgotten to check the mirror this morning. The faint stubble on his chin and the redness in his eyes made me wonder if he had slept as poorly as I had.

As we made our way toward I-75 North, and the car was buffeted back and forth in the wind, I had to admit to a sense of relief that he was behind the wheel. The weather really was horrible.

I crossed my arms and made a little humph with my breath. I did it again, just to let him know I was not okay with his Attila the Hun impersonation.

He ignored me and turned the radio on to the news and weather station. The newscaster listed traffic accidents and road closures. Nick was probably telling the truth about his canceled flight. Still, a part of me wondered if he was just trying to find a way to torture me for everything I'd said the night before.

I kept my mouth shut. I didn't trust myself to say anything that made sense around Nick anymore.

The local news ended and I leaned forward to see if I could find more traffic and weather. Unlike Nick and his Atlanta friends, this truck had no fancy radio that received news by satellite from every time zone around the globe. I gave up and tried my older model smartphone. Unsurprisingly, the signal was too weak to pick up a website.

After a few minutes of frustrated browsing, I asked, "Do you want me to search your phone for any additional traffic or weather problems?"

He didn't look as annoyed as he had earlier. "I can get us out of Atlanta, Annie. I checked the closures on I-75 before I left. We should be out of this by the time we get closer to Knoxville."

"I can drive then, if you want me to."

He sighed. "Just go to sleep. You look tired."

"Thanks so much, just what a girl wants to hear."

"Are you going to keep this up? If you want to continue arguing, it's going to be a long ride to Michigan."

I didn't want to dredge up anything about the previous night, so I let my shoulders sink back in the seat. As I tapped my foot on the floor to the beat of the windshield wipers, my mind started wandering. I thought of all the reasons I should have drooled after John Szymanski in high school, instead of wasting my crush on Nick. Sure, John now had very little hair left, and his gut had grown two waist sizes, but he was a nice guy . . . and he still visited his mother!

I was on reason number five when Nick reached over and put his hand on my bobbing knee. "Just go to sleep, Annie." He said it more softly this time. The warmth of his hand on my knee stopped my breath. Strangely, I grew calm. I didn't want to move for fear he would take it away. I closed my eyes and my exhaustion caught up with me. Eventually, my mind drifted. My last thought was that the sun must have come out because I felt warm all over.

* * *

I knew I was awake, but I didn't want to open my eyes. The steady drone of the engine comforted me like a baby in a rocker. For several minutes I relaxed in a haze that floated somewhere between sleep and waking. I became aware of a softness under my head that hadn't been there before and the way it smelled like . . . like . . . Nick?

Opening my eyes, I lifted my head from where it slumped against the window. Something fell in my lap and I picked it up to get a better look. It was the jacket Nick had been wearing earlier, turned inside out so that the thin flannel of the lining was against my cheek. Years of wear had made it soft to the touch and I brought it up to my nose, breathing in the smell of him.

I was caressing my cheek with the lining when the skin on the back of my neck prickled and I became aware that the owner of the jacket was looking at me oddly out of the corner of his eye. Abruptly, I put down the coat and pretended interest in the scenery outside my window.

We passed a sign that read "Knoxville 21 Miles." The rain had stopped, and the cars around us still had their lights on even though it was getting close to noon. Low-lying clouds chased each other in the sky, but it was obvious that we were out of the worst of the storm.

"Are you hungry?" Nick asked.

"Are you?" I was famished but didn't want to admit it.

"Yeah, I wouldn't mind stopping."

The radio was off and we sat in silence as the miles stretched out in front of us. Ten minutes later an exit sign with the symbol of the golden arches lured us off the highway. We pulled into a parking space and I handed Nick his jacket after he turned off the engine.

He grinned and brought it up to his nose. "It doesn't smell," he said.

I rolled my eyes and jumped out of the car before he could say anything else. A few minutes later we met in line after using the restrooms and I contemplated the menu above the counter.

Even though I was sure the food had been delicious at the shower last night, it had tasted like sawdust and I hadn't eaten much. And this morning I had taken only a couple bites of toast before chucking it in Charlotte's trash can. My food-withholding limit had just expired. I was starving.

Nick was probably going to order some sort of healthy option that the restaurant chain put on the menu to appease health food advocates. The unmistakable smells of burgers and fries made my stomach grumble. My earlier dreams of greasy food had reincarnated themselves into an all-out monster craving. When we reached the front of the line I didn't hesitate. I ordered two double bacon cheeseburgers, biggie fries, and a chocolate milkshake. Nick's eyebrows climbed as I recited the list to the cashier and, by the way his face took on a lopsided tilt, he was trying hard not comment.

"You said you were paying," I said as nonchalantly as possible, waving him to place his order.

He ordered a single, teeny-tiny burger and a coffee. The louse!

"I thought you were hungry," I said.

"I am."

"That wasn't enough to satisfy an old lady."

"Are you questioning my manhood?"

"Just your hunger," I shot back as he pulled out his wallet.

"I figure I'll eat what you can't finish," he said, handing a twenty to the cashier.

"What?! There is no way I am going to share my fries with you!"

Fifteen minutes later I surrendered my second double bacon burger to Nick, who grinned eagerly as he folded back the wrapper and took a bite. My milkshake rested in the cup holder in front of me, only half finished. He had already claimed several sips. I followed Nick's gaze to the french fries and covered the top of the box with my hand. "Not the fries, I'm only resting."

He knocked my hand out of the way and his hands plundered the carton. Well, at least he had kept his Midwest appetite, I told myself. It would have been a big turnoff if he had ordered something wimpy with lettuce.

We sat in the McDonald's parking lot overlooking a ridge while we finished our food. It had been crowded in the restaurant and no tables were available. I was actually glad. Nick and I had settled into a peaceful truce and I was feeling more relaxed as I took in the beautiful view in front of us. Who would have known that the front seat of a car in a McDonald's parking lot could feel as good as a window seat at a fancy five-star restaurant?

When Nick finished the last of my burger and fries he grabbed our bags filled with trash. "I'll be right back," he said, jumping out of the car and heading toward the trash cans near the front of the restaurant.

Impulsively, I reached into the backseat and pulled out my camera. The clouds at the edge of the storm pattern hovered over the ridge in front of me and the contrast between the yellow strands of sunshine that clawed their way out of the low mist and the shadows across the valley were hauntingly beautiful. Farther down the ridge, a church steeple and a scattering of houses gave the picture context. I wanted to capture the moment, but after several shots I couldn't quite get the frame right. I was readjusting a manual setting on my camera when I realized that Nick was standing beside me.

"Oops, sorry. Have you been waiting long?"

"Not at all," he said. He gestured toward the ridge. "Go ahead. I don't mind waiting . . . but only if you let me see the finished product."

I snapped one last picture and put the lens back on. "If you really want it, I'll send it to you. But sometimes what I think is going to be perfect ends up looking canned. It's all the pictures I take that I don't really think about that are my best shots."

He put his hands in his pockets and looked up at a low-flying bird that coasted in the wind. "Really? I've heard that happens. Too much planning and thinking can make a work of art artificial."

"Yeah. You have to lead from the gut and just hope the art follows. I guess it doesn't happen that way in architecture, does it?"

Nick turned to me and the wind blew an unruly piece of hair straight up on his head, making me want to reach out and tame it. "Actually, you would be surprised. You can spend forever planning and working out a fantastic design only to lose the integrity of the project in the details. The easiest solutions are the simple ones that are no-brainers. I always try to remember that when my design gets too complex."

For a moment we just stared at each other and then our attention was caught by the bird again. It was circling lower, looking for something to prey upon. But it wasn't having much luck.

"I can drive now," I said finally.

He handed me the keys with no argument and we walked back to the car.

I adjusted my mirror when we merged back onto I-75. Nick had moved his seat back and looked ready for a nap, which was why I was surprised to see his eyes still open several minutes later.

"Do you want any music?"

"Nope," he said.

The silence continued. Every unspoken moment built into an uncomfortable stillness. I couldn't figure out why. We had been so easy around each other during lunch. But now, fingernails on a chalkboard would have sounded more pleasant than the quiet that had settled in the car.

I finally said what I should have said first thing that morning. "Look, Nick, I don't know what got into me last night. I was tired, and Charlotte mentioned some things about the wedding and our family that got me all worked up . . ."

He grunted and shifted his dark gaze toward the side of the road.

"I took everything out on you last night at the shower, and I know you didn't deserve it. It's just that all this wedding stuff is so, so . . . kind of over the top, if you know what I mean."

"Hmm," was all he said. Damn! He wasn't going to make it easier on me.

"So what I mean to say is . . . I'm sorry."

There. I said it. As soon as the words left my mouth I felt an enormous relief.

But Nick still sat there, his stony expression fixed on the side window as if he hadn't heard me. Why was he so quiet? I had shared my milkshake with him, for God's sake!

"So . . . are we good now?" I asked.

A long pause stretched out between us. The tires ate up the road while the silence continued.

It was several miles before he spoke. "You said a lot of things, Bump."

"I know. I'm really sorry."

"Are you sorry you called my apartment a mausoleum? Or the comment about me being an unfeeling jerk? What about the part about being a snob who doesn't visit his mother? I want to make sure I know where we stand."

I swallowed. I deserved this. "I'm sorry about all of it, actually. I was way out of line." He had turned his head now and I could feel the heat of his stare. "OK, I'm not just sorry I said it. I was wrong to even imagine all those things. I don't think you live in a tomb or that you're a jerk or a bad son. I blew everything out of proportion. And there are no good excuses for my behavior."

"And the part about letting Travis Hartwick cheat at golf? I don't grovel to anyone on the golf course, even my boss. If you can't figure out yesterday afternoon, I'm not going to explain it."

"I know, I know. You're right." I didn't quite know what he meant, but at this point I was willing to agree to anything he said. Something in the back of my mind felt like I was missing an important detail. But I ignored it.

We were both silent while I passed an eighteen-wheeler that was having trouble going uphill. My phone rang and I reached into the backseat for my purse, but Nick was there already and handed it to me.

It was Aunt Addie. For once I was grateful for her call.

She and mom were delayed at the airport and she wanted to talk about how wonderful the weekend had been. I agreed, ignoring Nick's grunt. When she wondered if I had a dog in the car, I explained that I was driving to Detroit with Nick. She immediately asked to talk to him. I tried to keep a straight face as Aunt Addie told Nick how much she loved Atlanta. I was impressed at how patient he was with her, explaining that he would love for her to return anytime. This of course led to the next conversation, which was near and dear to my heart.

When was Nick going to come home?

But he wasn't committing. "I don't have any plans to visit Truhart right now, Aunt Addie."

It was the equivalent of a cold shower for me. I reached out and grabbed the phone before my bubble burst.

"Hey, Aunt Addie, here I am. What's up?"

For the next few minutes I listened to Aunt Addie ramble on about a last-minute event at the inn. Then my mother got on the phone and gave me the full scoop. The Preservation Society, which usually held their annual dinner at the Rose Terrace Hall in Harrisburg, was in a panic. The hall was unexpectedly foreclosed on, and they wanted to hold the dinner at the inn Thursday. My mind calculated the options. A hundred and fifty people. We hadn't hosted a banquet in a while.

When I hung up, I paused with the phone still in my hand. For some reason I kept thinking about Nick and our conversation earlier. I glanced down at the numbers on my recent call list while I tossed things around in my mind. As I looked back and forth between the road and my phone I noticed two unfamiliar outgoing calls from yesterday. They were made in the afternoon, less than a minute apart, to the same Atlanta area code.

A prickly feeling rose up the back of my neck. I glanced at Nick, who was watching me with hooded eyes.

"Problems?" he said.

"Nothing that can't be worked out. It looks like we're going to have a hundred and fifty for dinner Thursday night."

"Sounds like the old days . . ."

"Yeah," I said, not really interested in talking about the Preservation Society dinner. Instead I held up the phone and selected the unfamiliar number.

Nick watched me closely. Then he said, "Uh, you might not want to—"

"Travis Hartwick, here," said a loud and memorable voice.

Speechless, I just stared at the phone. Nick reached out to steady the wheel. Then he grabbed the phone from me with his other hand and turned it off.

"You!" I barely recognized my high-pitched exclamation. The phone call that Travis Hartwick had received just as he was getting ready to putt was from my phone. *That* was the phone call that had sent Travis Hartwick over the edge. A picture of Nick handing me my phone long after I took my winning shot on the golf course rose in my memory.

I looked over at Nick, who still held the wheel. He focused on the road, waiting for me to calm down before letting go. Then he sat back in his seat and cleared his throat. "I take my golf seriously. I don't grovel to anyone, even my boss."

I concentrated on the road again and let the new knowledge sink in. Closing my gaping mouth, I tried to find words. But Nick wasn't finished shocking me.

"And just for the record, Bump, I am not dating Brittany." He leaned back as if punctuating the sentence.

I almost slammed on the brakes. "What?"

"We aren't dating. Although I know it may have seemed that way to you, it isn't the case. We have been together at the same social functions and shared lunch a few times. But we aren't dating."

Well . . . I had no idea. I wanted to do the happy dance but managed to control my enthusiasm.

"Do you think I should still apologize for comparing her IQ to her bra size, then?" I asked, trying to keep the glee out of my voice.

He laughed. "Only if it makes you feel better."

"Well, actually, I don't think it would. So I might not apologize for that one if you don't mind."

For the first time all day I broke out into a true smile. The heavy weight in my chest lifted and I felt as buoyant as the drifting clouds overhead. Now that I knew Brittany's claim on Nick was bogus, this wedding might be a little more bearable. I hadn't wanted to think about it, but the picture of Brittany and Nick making goo-goo eyes at each other during the ceremony—or even worse, making out on the dance floor—had bothered me. Still, the backup warning system in my mind cautioned me to temper my excitement. Nick hadn't exactly claimed that he never intended to date Brittany. Just that they weren't dating now.

My hands flexed on the wheel and I exhaled as relief washed over me. I didn't even complain a few minutes later when Nick turned the dial to a sports radio station.

The Cincinnati skyline was way behind us when Nick and I fought over control of the volume as a Taylor Swift song played on the radio. For the past few hours the sports talk show commentators had debated which teams in the NFL were Super Bowl contenders, and Nick and I had argued over the possibility of the Lions ever making the grade. College football talk followed. We listened in acute agitation as a local commentator speculated on an early victory for Ohio in this year's Michigan-Ohio football game. I wanted to call the guy and tell him what an ass he was, but Nick swore that I would get arrested for that behavior in Ohio. When the possibility of the Red Wings losing our favorite Russian to the L.A. Kings because of player problems came up, Nick thought it would be better for my driving to turn to the pop radio station.

There was a reason I didn't listen to sports radio, and it wasn't because I didn't like sports. Sports talk made me crazy! I could handle football and baseball talk . . . even golf. But I didn't like anyone trash-talking my hockey team.

Unfortunately, pop radio turned out to be a bad move for Nick. He leaned forward in excruciating pain as girl-power vibes emanated from my speakers.

"I need Led Zeppelin," he moaned.

"Don't you touch that dial, Nick."

I was having a great time.

With his messy hair and stubbly chin, there was no denying it, Nick was downright sexy. As he adjusted the radio dial I wanted to run my hand along the back of his neck and feel the coarse hair between my fingers. The outline of his broad shoulders along the back of his cotton shirt sparked a desire in me that was more worthy of Beyoncé than Taylor Swift, and I took a deep breath to cool the heat rising inside of me.

I still wore the black T-shirt I had slept in and an old pair of faded jeans I had stuffed in my suitcase at the last minute. When Nick wasn't looking I performed the stealth move known to men and women worldwide. I tucked my head and raised my arm. I thanked God and Taylor Swift that I didn't smell bad. Still, I wished desperately that I had taken time to put on makeup instead of simply washing my face and sticking my hair in a ponytail this morning. I could feel the loose ends hanging against my neck and I suspected I looked a bit like a zombie at the wheel.

Nick found a station that played classic rock and I racked my brain for the name of the band, but I was always bad at telling the difference between Led Zeppelin and Pink Floyd. Ian was mortified that I was so uneducated about rock. He made such a big deal of it that I purposely sang the wrong words to songs just to annoy him.

Nick pulled out his phone and checked a few messages while the lead guitar played a riff that rose and fell over and over. The low sun was shining through the side window now, and I lowered my side visor to avoid the glare.

"Are you ready to switch drivers?" he asked, turning off his phone and putting it in the front pocket of his shirt.

I was getting tired, I had to admit. We were only about three or four hours from Detroit and I still had to drive several hours on my own from there.

Nick pointed to an exit. "There's a decent rest area up ahead. I used to exit there when I drove back home. Let's stop."

I pulled into the right lane and tried to picture a younger Nick driving back to Michigan. For some reason I had trouble with the image. I couldn't remember a time when Nick had come home on a regular basis. But then again, I had been in school in New York for some of those years. And we had both been busy dealing with the death of our fathers. I suppose I blocked out that time period.

Ten minutes later I stared at myself in the restroom mirror. I had combed down my bed head and fixed my ponytail and looked less like the walking dead. But the harsh overhead lighting made me feel washed out and pale. An older woman walked up next to me and lifted a little girl with spiky lashes and pudgy pink cheeks up to the sink to run her hands under the water. I dug my makeup out of my purse and the little girl stared at me as I attempted to apply mascara to my eyelashes. I tilted my head from side to side, making sure I hadn't left clumps of black on my lower lids.

"What is that lady doin' to her eyes, Gamma?"

"She's making them pretty," said the lady, smiling at me.

"But why? Aren't they already pretty?" the little girl asked.

"Why yes, honey. I believe they are."

The little girl kept her eyes glued to me as her grandma walked her over to the hand drier. I sent a tiny wave and she laughed.

"The pretty lady waved at me, Gamma!"

Like a fairy godmother and her little sprite, the two fellow travelers were a balm for my insecurities. I kept telling myself that it didn't matter how I looked. Nick had seen me from crooked teeth to braces and all the awkward stages in between. He had spent the night at the inn dozens of times and I had a vivid memory of him in sweatpants and a T-shirt, hunched over the breakfast table next to Ian. They would eat Frosted Flakes and roll Matchbox cars across the table while I sat in my pajamas watching *Scooby-Doo* on the couch. I hadn't given a thought to my looks back then. But that was before I had made a connection between personal hygiene and attracting boys. By the time I was a preteen I would shower and dress before coming to the breakfast table when Nick stayed over. Not that he ever noticed . . .

Deciding there was nothing else I could really fix, I followed the little girl and her grandmother outside and watched them absently as the older woman settled her granddaughter into a car seat in the back of the late-model sedan. I looked around for Nick, but he wasn't near the car.

I strode along a path from the rest area's main building to a picnic area out of sight of the highway. It felt good to stretch my legs after the long car ride and I spent several minutes walking farther down the paved path, past empty picnic tables, abandoned for the season. The scent of leaves and dried grasses lingered in the air. At the edge of the clearing I spotted a trailhead. A clump of tall grasses, their long blades faded to yellow, waved in the wind, and I tucked my hands in my pockets as a brisk breeze pulled at my jacket. The wind was the only thing that hinted of a storm farther south. If we hadn't come from that direction, I'd have thought this was typical August weather, not the remnants of a hurricane.

"There you are."

I turned to see Nick strolling down the paved path from the parking lot. My heart did its usual somersault when I spotted him, and I realized all was business-as-usual in my body's reactions. Nick carried my camera case and I raised an eyebrow as he approached.

He nodded toward the trail. "There is a path over there that leads down to a little pond. I thought you might want this," he said with a grin, holding up my camera.

I hesitated. "We'll see."

He lifted his shoulders and turned toward the path. I followed him as we walked along a bed of pine straw that cushioned our steps. We took several turns and passed a row of dogwood and crooked cedar trees before coming to a clearing. The sun flickered off ripples in a small lake in front of us. An old swim raft rested on the far shore and a family of geese basked in the evening light on the graying lake surface. On the far shore maple trees shimmered in the wind and the light reminded me of the trees I had photographed near Nick's mother's house just a few weeks ago. Those trees back home were getting ready to change color, but these were still as green as they had been in June, as the lowering sun made streamers through their branches.

Nick turned and looked at me like a little boy who hoped he had pleased me.

"Here," he said, holding out my case.

I sighed and handed him my purse so I could pull out my camera from the bag. A beautiful view, my trusty camera, and Nick. What else could a girl want?

"What happened to that old film camera you used to use?" Nick asked with surprise.

"I still have it. My dad gave it to me when I was ten. My favorite pictures have always come from that one. It's at home." When I finished switching lenses I looped the strap around my neck, handed him the bag, and turned back to the pond. It was like an empty palette, waiting for my brush to begin.

For the next few minutes I walked around the shoreline, trying to capture the beauty from as many angles as my imagination would allow. At one point, I followed one of the last dragonflies of the season to a cattail, and photographed its silky wings glimmering in the sunset.

When I had captured my fill I turned to look for Nick. He leaned against an old picnic table behind me. Nick had no idea how gorgeous he looked. I wanted to take a picture of him with his arms resting behind him and his legs stretched out. But I didn't. It might have changed the way he was looking at me. And the way he was looking at me made me feel warm all over.

I walked slowly toward him until I stood just a few feet away.

"Why didn't you stay in New York? You had that great scholarship to NYU. I always wondered what made you give up your photography and return to Truhart."

I went stone cold.

He didn't say it rudely. In fact, he said it so gently a person might have thought he was talking to a child. But still it was jarring. I didn't like talking about those days. I looked down at my camera and tried to think of a reason to avoid answering him. But something in the sound the wind made through the trees and the way he waited so patiently for my response gave me courage to start talking.

"It wasn't really one big thing . . . well, it was, actually. But I guess . . . well, I guess you could say I couldn't handle New York." I looked up at him and pressed my lips together before continuing. "I don't know, maybe I'm just not cut out for cities. You saw how I reacted to Atlanta. And that isn't even half as crowded as New York."

He nodded but said nothing.

He lifted my camera bag from the seat of the picnic table and I tucked the camera inside. Then I moved to sit next to him, putting one foot on the bench and propping myself up on the table. It was easier to look out at the pond instead of at him.

"From the very beginning I felt out of place. Everyone in the art program was really talented. They were so worldly and hip, and I was just—just so countrified. They weren't mean about it or anything, but I was this token Midwesterner and they teased me for my accent and . . . well, I didn't wear the right clothes. I didn't know the latest trends. They actually made fun of me out of fondness, I'm sure. But that wasn't a big deal.

"My second year at school, a bunch of us lived in tiny apartments near the East Village. It wasn't the cool area most people know about. It was the kind of place where the convenience stores run twenty-four hours and the hookers come out at night. When they weren't in class, my roommates liked to party. They were into raves and Ecstasy, partying in a way that I couldn't relate to. They weren't that bad the first year, so I didn't think anything about it when we decided to room together. But the second year was tough. That was the year my father got sick, remember?"

Nick nodded and I felt his hand on my back, gently stroking. I clasped my fingers together and took a deep breath. I don't know if I ever really told anyone the full story. Pieces. But never the whole thing.

"I started staying in our apartment when they went out, telling them I had to study, or I wasn't feeling well . . . I made up any excuse I could. Somehow it just seemed so stupid. I mean, every time I went home I watched my dad wither away under the chemo and the radiation. The doctors were doing everything to poison away the cancer that was invading his body. And then there were my friends in New York, partying with other kinds of poison and thinking it was the coolest thing in the world. They told me I was no fun. And then my photos started to suffer. Nothing was interesting. Everything my professors were enthusiastic about seemed stupid and contrived to me.

"After about six months, right around the time the doctors stopped my dad's treatment and sent him home to hospice, I returned from a pretty bad weekend home. He had lost so much weight and was in and out of consciousness. I'm not even sure he knew I was home that weekend.

"My roommates had planned a party on the roof of our apartment building. They convinced me that I should go . . . told me it would be good for me. Since it was right there in our building, I couldn't find an excuse to say no. But I wish I had. It was wild. The drugs were everywhere, the music was insane. I drank but declined whatever drugs they were passing around."

I took a ragged breath. I hadn't talked about it in years, but that didn't mean I had forgotten. I thought about it almost every day of my life. Not consciously, just in short flashes that I banished to the back of my mind. But now, the images burst across my memory as strong as photographs.

"Sometime in the night . . . or maybe the early morning, I'm not sure which . . . a young woman, I didn't know her very well . . . she was a third-year student, super smart, really talented. She stood up on the ledge of the rooftop. She was dancing . . ."

Nick's hand stilled on my back.

"I was the only one who saw . . . everyone else was laughing and lost in their own high. But I watched her standing on that ledge and I knew what was coming. It was like watching something in slow motion. I was just a few yards from her and I reached out to grab her . . . but her hand slipped away. Her eyes met mine and I saw her expression change when she realized what she had done. It was like she couldn't believe it. And neither could I. We stared at each other for a split second. And she just went over.

"The police and the fire trucks were there in minutes. I was the main witness. I stood out on the curb with them for the next hour while the other students walked around, trying to shake off their highs.

"I heard later that her parents were completely broken when they came to pick up her body from the morgue and take it back home . . ."

I exhaled a couple of times, trying to release the tension. My hands were still in my lap, but my knuckles were white.

"My father died the next week. Then Mom . . ." I didn't want to share how Mom fell apart. Not even with Nick. "No one even asked why I dropped out. They just thought I wanted to be closer to home."

Nick rose and moved to stand in front of me. I looked up, but the setting sun's rays were behind him. I couldn't see his face. He raised his hand and caught a tear that was running down my cheek. I hadn't even realized I was crying.

"I sound like a wimp, don't I?"

"No. You sound like someone who needed to come home to people you loved."

"Yeah, but I gave up . . . I couldn't handle New York after that. I mean, I know in my mind it's not a bad city. But I couldn't get past that. I tried once, and I swear I had a panic attack just riding in the cab from the airport."

"Maybe it was just the wrong place for your dream."

I looked up at him and laughed a little. "Maybe." Forgiving my-self for giving up my dream had taken a while. But I was fine with it now. Well, mostly.

Nick placed his hands on my shoulders, rubbing them gently as they traveled down my back. He pulled me closer into the circle of his arms and for several minutes we stayed like that. I could feel his heart beating and his breath along my neck.

I said in a muffled voice against his chest. "Don't tell my family . . ."

"I won't."

He leaned back to get a look at my face. "So, what do you do with all these beautiful pictures you take?"

"Oh, they aren't that good—"

He placed the tip of his finger against my mouth. "Stop putting yourself down."

"Is this a therapy session?" I joked.

"You're trying to be funny. I know that tactic." I could see him better now that he leaned away from the sun. His eyebrows were fur-rowed as he scrutinized my face.

"I haven't done anything with them." I thought about the folders and files of all my pictures and what I really wanted to do with them. But I couldn't say it out loud. So I told him about how I eventually went back to a school near home for my teaching certificate. And then about my short-lived teaching career.

"Actually, I really like working with students. Art is such an im-portant part of growing up and learning to express yourself. Unfortu-nately, art teachers are the first to go when budgets get cut."

"I'll bet you were a great art teacher," Nick said, leaning toward me. "In fact, if I'd had a teacher like you all those years ago, I might have become the next Picasso."

I could feel Nick's breath against my cheek. He was close now and it thrilled and terrified me at the same time.

"Thanks," I said. I barely had enough breath for that one word.

He leaned in closer until we were almost touching. His lips were a hairsbreadth from mine and hovered. I had this strange feeling of bal-ancing on a needle. As if the next moment might change everything.

Then his lips touched mine.

The kiss was light, like a feather. But it was the sweetest I ever felt. He touched me so lightly, it was as if he was afraid I might break if he pressed more firmly. He kissed me again. This time his lips felt more solid. Then the contact stopped as we both inhaled, drawing something other than breath from each other.

Our eyes met and Nick pulled back.

"It's okay, you don't have to feel sorry for me . . ." I said.

What an idiot! How could I blurt something out like that? I had just experienced one of the most beautiful kisses of my life and I ruined it!

But Nick just looked down at me, a funny little lopsided tilt to his mouth. "If you think that is a pity kiss, then obviously I've done something wrong!"

"No, oh my gosh, Nick. I'm a moron. It was so—"

"Bump . . ."

"What?"

"Shut up." He seized my mouth in a passionate, gut-stirring, heart-wrenching kiss that left no doubt about how he felt. He tasted of heat and fire and I smoldered under his touch.

All these years of chasing after Nick, of dreaming about this moment that I never thought would come . . . and now that it was happening I realized how little my dreams had to do with reality. When I had secretly dreamed of kisses, I hadn't been able to feel the heat or taste the desire. Those visions were a weak shadow compared to the way I felt now.

I ran my hands through Nick's hair and along the back of his neck. My legs parted and he fit perfectly between them, lifting me up to him until we were on the same level and every inch of our bodies molded against each other. My heart raced, keeping pace with his. His lips ran down my neck and his hands moved up to cup my breasts. I lifted his shirt and explored him, trying to memorize the feel of him.

For this moment, he was mine.

He leaned me backward until I was stretched out on the picnic table and he was on top of me. Our bodies flexed against each other in rhythm. I could feel his excitement aching against me and took advantage of my new power by pressing my hips closer.

I was beyond rationality, ready for anything . . . when the sound of a phone ringing broke through my frenzy. We both opened our eyes and stared at each other. It took me a moment to place myself back on earth. Back on a hard wooden picnic table with my shirt half up and Nick's hand inside my bra.

I looked around for my purse and saw it lying on the ground nearby.

"It's probably a telemarketer," I said feebly. It finished ringing. I wanted him back on top of me with his hand moving in circles like they were a moment ago.

"Probably," he said, making a trail up toward my face with his fingers. He cupped my cheek gently. "Oh, Annie. What are we going to do?"

"You can still call me Bump."

"I could . . ." he said, moving his hand back to my breast and giving it a playful kiss, "but I don't think it will have quite the same meaning for me anymore."

His lips parted in a Cheshire-cat smile and I felt deliciously evil. I laughed. I was delirious.

He kissed me again. This time with more control. But I wasn't satisfied. I wanted our crazy, plundering kisses back. I wanted the wilder Nick who had almost made love to me. I wiggled beneath Nick in a way that I knew would stir him.

He started to lose that control again when I felt him pulsate against me. I was either imagining something very erotic or another very poorly timed call was vibrating in his pocket.

"Damn!' he said, and the irritation in his face was unmistakable. He pulled his phone out of his pocket. "Who the hell . . ." He looked at the screen and moaned. "Someone from Truhart."

He took the call and I saw his expression change.

"Aunt Addie?" We were close enough that I could hear Aunt Addie's voice. "Yeah, we stopped at a rest area." I was having trouble hearing what she was saying as a breeze whipped at us and tugged on my shirt.

"Yes, Aunt Addie," Nick said, still circling his hand around my breast. He absently looked down at my breast and suddenly jerked his hand away as if he'd been caught with his hand in the cookie jar.

"No. I mean NO! You aren't interrupting anything. Annie is just coming out of the restroom."

Nick's eyes widened and his mouth dropped open. He hopped off the table. I understood his problem. Aunt Addie was the enforcer. And if she had any idea what Nick was doing . . . well, the consequences could be mind-boggling.

"No, no . . . nothing's up," he said too quickly.

I shifted on my elbows and my eyes went wide at the bulge in his pants. Nick caught me. He walked stiffly around in a small circle with a menacing look, challenging me to point out the obvious.

"Hey, Nick. Do you want any coffee from the vending machine?" I yelled, cupping my hands over my mouth.

Nick's scowl was unfair. I was only attempting to corroborate his alibi, after all.

"Sure, she's coming. Let me put her on the phone," he said, trying to finish his conversation before one of us laughed.

I scooted off the table, pulled my shirt down, zipped up my jacket, and took the phone. I expected to hear all about serving dishes and tablecloths.

Instead I heard the panicked voice on the other end. I forgot about foreplay and tried to figure out what was going on. Aunt Addie was rambling and I asked her to pass the phone over to my mother.

"Annie, have you spoken to Charlotte?" my mother said.

"No."

"Well, something horrible has happened."

If June Lowell had done something to upset my sister I was going to turn the car around and go tell her exactly what I thought of her.

But my mother explained the problem. "Rain has been falling all day. Parts of the city are flooded. The GATE Network is asking Charlotte to do a special story about it for the network today. She just called to say that the club where her reception is being held is halfway underwater."

"Oh no!" I pictured that beautiful room with the huge fireplace and the sparkling chandeliers afloat with tables and chairs.

"She says most of the city is going to be fine. But remember, the club was in a low-lying area, and a creek nearby went over the banks. Annie, she says the club is talking about shutting down indefinitely."

"Well, tell her not to panic until she knows for sure."

"I did," said my mother. "But we saw the damage on television. They had twelve feet of water!"

Poor Charlotte. Another stress she didn't need.

While I talked to my mother, Nick and I slowly wandered back to the car. By mutual agreement the interlude was over. He opened the back door and placed my camera bag on the backseat before climbing in next to me. We buckled our seat belts while I finished talking.

I hung up and sat staring numbly at my phone. Nick must have seen the panic in my face because he reached over and grabbed my hand.

Had I heard right? Two worlds were on a collision course and I felt helpless to prevent it.

"Oh my God, Nick! My Mom says that if the country club in Atlanta isn't available we should have the wedding at the inn!"

PART II: TRUHART

Chapter 8

I have vivid memories of summer evenings when my father was alive and the inn was bursting with people. My parents would sit hip to hip at the piano, surrounded by a crowd of tipsy singers, while my dad played some well-known tune, and my mother would swing her fingers in midair, prompting the crowd to sing along. My brother and I would watch from our favorite vantage point at the top of the lobby stairs, hiding from Aunt Addie, who had long ago put us to bed. Oblivious to dirty dishes, crumpled tablecloths, and crumbs scattered on the floor, the party went on. My parents made sure that each guest understood that tomorrow was never as important as today.

It was a snapshot in time I will never forget.

Now, three days after I had returned from the long weekend in Atlanta, I collapsed on the couch in the lobby and wondered where my parents had found the energy. I had just finished cleaning up the last of the dirty dishes and stacking the chairs in the corner of the dining room. The pressure behind my eyes reminded me that I should be in bed, and my feet were killing me, even in my comfortable flat-heeled shoes.

We had served over a hundred guests tonight. I knew almost half of them, which made my job harder. Everyone wanted to stop me and talk about Charlotte, or the inn, or just tell me whatever was ailing them. With a smile on my face I had juggled each conversation while keeping an eye on the buffet and the water glasses. I dodged between the tables like an expert in the obstacle course while Aunt Addie managed things in the kitchen and my mother played her role as the master hostess.

The last guest had left an hour ago, and I rubbed the tension from my temples and circled my neck, trying to ease my headache. Behind me, my brother, Ian, rolled the vacuum across the lobby. He was singing a song in a falsetto that was supposed to be either Led Zeppelin or Jack White, I wasn't sure. He had worked behind the bar all night after driving home from Ann Arbor, where his band was backing up some semi-famous indie group.

"Hey, Bump, did you see Mrs. Weideman? Was it just me, or did she drink half the vodka behind the bar? I tried to replace it with water and she laughed at me and served herself when she thought I wasn't looking."

"Well, she just had her last schnauzer put down, and now she is all alone," I said. "Give her a break."

Ian ran his hand through his long sandy-colored hair. "I'm just sayin'." His brown eyes were speckled with hazel, the opposite of my own, which were hazel speckled with brown. Then he put the vacuum in the closet near the front desk and joined me on the couch. Slipping his feet out of his shoes, he lifted them to the coffee table and spread his long, wiry frame into a horizontal position, a typical Ian posture.

"Did you unplug the toilet like your mother asked a half hour ago, Ian?" yelled Aunt Addie as she shuffled into the lobby from the dining room. She spied Ian sprawled on the couch. "Get your feet off the furniture, Ian Adler!"

"What!? I am just taking a break. And I took off my shoes."

It was an old battle between them. I was so used to it I didn't bat an eye, and neither did my mother as she rounded the corner, a dishcloth still over her shoulder. She sat down in the chair next to me and we both ignored Aunt Addie, who had come to stand over Ian, her voice rising to a piercing level.

"That went well, Annie. Thank you so much for all your help. I don't know what we would have done without you and Ian," said Mom.

"It was like old times, wasn't it?" I didn't point out that in old times we would have had the assistance of half a dozen hired wait staff. "I can't remember the last time we hosted over a hundred."

"It certainly has been a while," said Mom with a sigh. Getting tired of the argument next to us, she took the towel off her shoulder and swatted Ian's feet. Immediately he lifted them off the table, which aggravated Aunt Addie all the more.

Placing a hand on her hip, Aunt Addie huffed and hobbled away.

"I'm going to bed. I might still be able to catch tonight's episode of *Murder, She Wrote*," she said.

"Yeah, and I hear there's an episode of *The Honeymooners* at midnight," taunted Ian under his breath as she left the room.

Mom swatted Ian with the towel again. "Enough!"

"She can't hear me," he said, lifting his shoulders and raising his hands, palms up.

"She hears more than you know," Mom chided.

For several minutes we sat silently while the clock on the rustic oak mantel ticked away. The temperature had dipped this evening, so I had turned on the gas fireplace in front of us and we stared at the flames as they danced around the ceramic logs.

My mind wandered to Nick, who had called me only briefly on Tuesday to make sure I had gotten home all right. After Aunt Addie's second phone call, our car ride had been more subdued, as if we weren't quite sure how to act in a world with shifting tectonic plates. And even though he had rubbed the back of my neck with his free hand as we talked about Charlotte and the wedding, there was no discussion about what would happen next.

When I dropped him off at his fancy hotel in Detroit, Nick asked me solemnly if I would be okay driving the rest of the way to Truhart. He went on to ask if I wanted to stay the night. His crooked grin was adorable and sexy.

Was I tempted? Absolutely. The vision of the two of us wrapped in the sheets made heat rush to my face. But I didn't want a one-night stand with Nick. I wanted something more. Something even I couldn't put into words. For several days now, I had tried to imagine what would have happened if I had spent the night. Would we be calling one another every hour and making up pet names for each other like teenagers? Or would we have said good-bye in an awkward moment, too uncomfortable to look each other in the eye? That would have broken my heart.

No. It was better to wait. I had loved Nick for years. If something was going to happen between us, there was no reason to rush. My wisdom surprised even me.

"So, any more news from Charlotte?" asked Ian, yanking me out of my thoughts.

"Yes. I spoke to her before the dinner tonight. And I spoke to Henry this morning," said Mom.

Charlotte had called us half a dozen times to fill us in on the wedding crisis. The country club had announced the need for extensive renovations and canceled all events through Memorial Day. She and Henry were in the process of searching every available venue within twenty-five miles of Atlanta for their reception. Several other areas in the flood zone had been deluged by the storm, but most of Atlanta had escaped major damage. Still, their search had yielded only a few options.

"I've been waiting to tell you all evening, but we've been so busy there just wasn't time," said Mom with a wide smile. I closed my eyes, unable to look at the excitement on her face. "Henry likes the idea of having the wedding here."

A cold sweat broke out on the back of my neck. This was a bad idea.

Ian let out a low whistle. "Are you sure we can't just convince them to go to Vegas? I don't want to witness Charlotte turning into Bridezilla firsthand."

"I don't know what you're talking about sometimes, Ian," my mother said. "This is good news. It would be wonderful to have the wedding right here."

I opened my eyes. "And Charlotte and June are good with this plan?" I couldn't see Charlotte agreeing to this easily. In fact, I was convinced Charlotte would have preferred the tackiest hall available. And June? Well, she was probably thinking it would have been better to wait a year—or ten—before the happy couple walked down the aisle.

"Henry says he can be very convincing. He insists that not only would it be perfect for Charlotte's family and friends here, but the inn would be a wonderful setting for their wedding. He says he loved the stories you told of growing up in Truhart when we were down in Atlanta, Annie."

Why did I ever open my mouth with those stories of growing up? I wanted to kick myself.

My mother continued. "If Charlotte agrees, Henry and I think it should be a winter wonderland wedding. Henry was entranced with the idea of sleigh rides and snow for all the Southern guests. I think it would be perfect for us to show a little Midwest hospitality."

Henry really had no idea.

While he was picturing people bundled in furs riding in horse-driven sleighs like a quaint Currier and Ives print, I pictured unshaved men, and women for that matter, in Elmer Fudd hats and camouflage hunting jackets behind the wheels of SUVs with snow chains and gun racks.

But something else my mother said was making my heart race faster.

"Winter? Snow in April is a little optimistic, even for Truhart."

"No, Henry thinks we should make it a New Year's Eve wedding," Mom said with smile.

"Are you kidding? We can't plan a wedding that quickly!"

"Of course we can. We *are* an inn, after all. Hosting is what we do." My heart was racing in panic. But Mom barely looked fazed. "We are already prepared for guests, and anyone we can't accommodate can stay at a hotel nearby. All the other details are just little things that need to be handled."

Details? I looked around the room at the peeling paint, worn carpet, and frayed curtains and tried to think of them as details. I would die if June Lowell said anything about the way our inn was falling down around us.

I stared at my mother and tried to come up with other reasons to change her mind. What could I say that wouldn't insult her?

"Our band doesn't usually play weddings," said Ian, "But hey! You never know who might be there. Maybe Scarlett will put us on *The Morning Show* if Charlotte won't. And as for wedding music, if they come here I guess the band can start working on the chicken dance."

I nearly fell off the couch at the thought of June Lowell doing the chicken dance.

"You can practice your piano instead, Ian," Mom said. "I didn't pay for eight years of piano lessons just to have you wailing on the electric guitar your whole life. This is going to be classy." I thanked God for small favors. "You can play something nice, like Barry Manilow."

Ian practically choked. "Uh, Mom, leave the music to me, okay? I promise not to play anything that will embarrass Charlotte."

Ian and I exchanged a look, knowing full well how Charlotte felt about our mother's favorite artist.

Mom moved to the edge of her chair and leaned forward, her hands on her knees. "Well, I for one would be excited to have the wedding here. All my life I thought the three of you would be married at the inn. I used to tell your father how beautiful it would be to see him escort one of you girls down these very stairs."

She waved her hands in a sweeping gesture and for a moment I saw what she saw. A grand chalet with cathedral ceilings, pine log trusses, and a massive split-stone fireplace that rose all the way to the rafters, dominating the room. An incongruous vision of my father and a golden haired girl in white, coming down the stairs, sprang forth in my mind, forming a lump in my throat.

Dad wasn't here, so that dream would never happen. But if this was so important to my mother, and if Charlotte agreed, I vowed to make it work. I would simply have to put myself in charge of damage control.

I leaned over and hugged my mother. "It would be beautiful."

"Yes, I think it would," she said after a moment. She put her hands on her knees and rose. Circling behind Ian, she kissed him on the top of his messy head. "Bridezilla. You've been watching too much TV, Ian. Charlotte would never be demanding. Good night, you two. Don't stay up too late."

When she left the room, Ian followed her with his eyes. Once he was sure she had gone, he said, "Hey, Bump, just to be safe, if this thing happens why don't you make sure all the Barry Manilow sheet music is hidden by the time this wedding rolls, okay? Charlotte will lose it if she hears 'Copacabana' at her wedding."

I put my head in my hands. "Oh my God, Ian. Barry Manilow songs are the least of our worries."

"What do you mean?"

I lifted my head and gazed at him. "Ian, you met Henry's family last summer, right?"

"Yeah, I was backing up the Good Fridays in Atlanta and we all went out to lunch before I left town. They seemed nice. What's the problem?"

His feet were back on the table and his lanky frame was horizontal again. I noted the perpetual two-day-old stubble on his chin and his overlong dark blond hair that was the exact same shade as my own. Ian was good-looking in a rocker sort of way. He was bright and creative, and over the years he had been in and out of relationships with various women who, strangely, found him appealing. He didn't have much money, but that never fazed him. His eyes were sharp and his ears could detect perfect pitch. So, as I stared at him, I couldn't help but wonder how he could be so dense.

"Ian . . . come on. Tell me you didn't pick up on a few subtle differences between Henry's family and ours."

Ian's eyebrows rose. He stared at the ceiling. His mouth dropped open as he tried to figure out what I was getting at. "They're Southern?"

"Are you kidding me, Ian? Is that the only thing you noticed?"

"Well . . . yeah." He crinkled up his forehead as if there was something he was trying to figure out. "I mean, they were nice looking—but so are we." Then he laughed at himself. "Well, *I* am at least."

I hit him on the thigh with the side of my hand. My neck was getting sore from looking sideways at him, so I moved to the corner of the couch and faced him, drawing my feet up. "That's not the only difference, you idiot. Didn't you notice the expensive clothes? Did you eat at their club?" He nodded. "They're loaded," I finished.

"Oh, that."

"That? Not only are they really wealthy, but they're snobs. Well, actually, Henry is nice. Charlotte wouldn't be marrying him if he weren't. But June and her friends are really stuck-up. Charlotte is practically a nervous wreck when she is around them. Honestly, Ian, I'll bet they think we sleep in one long bed and wear red underwear with flaps on the back."

"Oh, come on. You're exaggerating." Ian looked at me with narrowed eyes.

"No. I'm not. During the shower I even overheard June talking to one of her friends in the restroom about how concerned she is that Charlotte and her family don't measure up."

For a moment, Ian just stared at me. "So, you think we'll prove them right if we have the wedding here? Sure, Mom has bad taste in music, and Aunt Addie is—well, she's Aunt Addie. But are we that bad?"

"No. No, we aren't. But let's face it, Truhart is a little different than Atlanta. They rub elbows with national news anchors and CEOs of big corporations. They don't think anything of wearing thousand-dollar dresses and driving cars that cost as much as a house in Truhart. No, I take that back—three houses in Truhart."

"Yeah, well, they still pee in the pot."

"That's crude."

"Well, I mean it, Bump. Why should we care what they think?"

"Because Charlotte cares. She was practically in tears last weekend. You saw their club; it's gorgeous. Look around at this lobby. The drapes are so old I think they came from a Montgomery Ward catalogue. This couch was popular in the seventies. The carpet is threadbare, the roof in the dining room is leaking, and the inn is practically empty. The bills are adding up, and we have no employees left—except one part-time housekeeper."

Ian turned back to the fireplace. After a minute, he asked, "Are *you* embarrassed?"

That sounded like something Nick would say. I wished I hadn't brought the subject up. "No. Of course not. But I don't want to hurt Charlotte. And even more, I really don't want Mom to find out how they feel. It would crush her."

I stared at the fire and tried to imagine a wedding at the inn. Was I overreacting?

"Mom keeps joking that she is going to sell to a developer," I said.

Ian took a deep breath. "Whoa. I mean . . . really? I knew things weren't great, but is Mom really thinking of selling?" He shifted his weight, letting the prospect sink in.

"No. She says she won't. But we've lost so many summer regulars over the years, and we never really had a big winter crowd. Fall isn't too bad, but springtime is terrible. Remember? No one comes during the muddy season."

"Well, I can help. I keep bugging Charlotte to do a story about our band on *The Morning Show*. With a few more good gigs we would have enough to—"

"No offense, but your toilet plunging is a hell of a lot better than your guitar playing." I stood up and hit him on the shoulder like old times. Ian and I showed affection by squabbling, tattling on each other, and fighting.

"All right. I'll keep an eye on things, and if we have the wedding here, I'll do what I can to help."

Even though Ian irritated me with his laid-back, scruffy-faced, starving-musician routine, I always knew his heart was in the right place. Together we could keep the seams of this celebration from bursting wide open.

"Thanks, Ian . . ."

"First get rid of Barry Manilow. Then you can thank me."

I was the last to turn out the lights. I passed the plaque that hung near the entrance and straightened it for the thousandth time. *Where There Is Love There Is Life.*

My father was never one to quote sweet sayings like "home, sweet home." He preferred Mahatma Gandhi and Henry David Thoreau most of the time. He had carved the plaque years ago and I thought of him every time I straightened it. Not for the first time I wondered how different things would have been if he were still alive.

Chapter 9

The leaves blew across the road and I skirted the edge of the shoulder just to enjoy kicking them. Someone must have been burning leaves because the smell lingered in the wind. Wisps of my hair caught the breeze and I gave up tucking it behind my ears.

What was Atlanta like in October? Probably as warm and muggy as it had been in August. Did Charlotte and Nick miss days like this? I had spoken to Nick on the phone several times, and he had sent me some funny e-mails. But I was beginning to wonder if I had imagined the episode on the picnic table.

Stopping for a moment, I glanced to my right along a rise that overlooked a large red barn. This was my favorite spot. Even if I hadn't had such a ridiculous childhood crush on Nick, I would have loved it.

Years ago, when Nick's father, Russell Conrad, was alive, a sign had stood in the corner of the barn that read, "Conrad and Sons Construction." It was gone now. Three generations of Conrads had been builders, and if Russell had ever wanted his son to join him in the family business, he had never admitted it. He had been enormously proud of Nick and his career in architecture.

Farther down the ridge, beyond my sight line, was a butter-colored farmhouse where Nick's mother still lived. It was charming as well, with a porch on three sides and a peaked roof. But this view was special. The barn stood like a lighthouse overlooking the point a mile away where both Echo and Reply Lakes framed Truhart. Like a Norman Rockwell or Andrew Wyeth painting, it was pure Americana. Of course, from here no one could see the imperfections.

I raised my old film camera and snapped several good images. I still had a darkroom tucked away in the basement of the inn. But I had no idea when I would have time to develop these photos. Sighing to myself, I swung my camera back over my shoulder and continued toward town.

One of three towns in the county, Truhart was the most developed, which wasn't saying much. In the core of the town, a handful of buildings with false clapboard fronts were a combination of "vintage Midwest" and "cheap 1970s."

Walking at a brisk pace, I was soon in town. I dodged a cluster of painted trash barrels and skipped across the street, making my way to Cookees Diner. The heart of town was what most of us half jokingly called the business district. Everyone passed through here at least once a week and almost everyone stopped by Cookees for coffee and gossip. I pushed open the door of the diner and looked around. Except for a few customers, things were quiet.

In the back of the diner a counter was flanked by swivel chairs and a built-in foot rail. Metal shelves lined the wall next to a large commercial griddle, and an old-fashioned Hamilton Beach milkshake mixer with large metal cups sat near the cash register. It had been used for decades, and I admit that growing up I had consumed more than my share of chocolate milkshakes after school and on weekends.

Mac, the cook, leaned against the counter with his head buried in the newspaper, frowning. I looked around for Corinne, the owner. She huddled by the wall near the restrooms with George Bloodworth, the mayor of Truhart. Her head was bowed as she listened to him with as foul a look as I had ever seen on her face. When he finished, Corinne shook her head and said something, flicking her wrists downward as if to indicate she was through listening. He tried to keep the conversation going, but Corinne saw me and started toward me, with George still talking behind her.

"—not doing any good," he said.

Corinne kept walking as if she hadn't heard a thing. Then she looked over my head at someone in the blue booth by the window. I swiveled to see who it was. Grady Fitzpatrick sat with his back to us, slouching over a cup of coffee and staring out the window. Corinne lifted her chin, seemingly satisfied with what she saw, and shifted behind the counter.

"Hi, Bump, honey." Placing a mug in front of me, she poured me a cup of coffee and then pushed the cream my way. I sat on a stool and prepped my coffee.

George walked over to us. "Hi, Bump. Your mama around?"

"No, she's at home."

"Say hi to her for me. Oh, and make sure you tell your sister that I sure liked her story last week. I really was interested to hear about ways to make a person sleep better. I'm gonna try some of her suggestions."

"A clear conscience makes a person sleep like a baby, George," said Corinne. He ignored her.

"You'll say hi to her for me, won't you, Bump?"

"I sure will, George," I said, forcing a smile.

As he left, Corinne rolled her eyes and put her hands on her hips. "He'd make a great feature story himself: the Grinch—alive and well in the heart of the North!"

"What's got you in such a foul mood?"

Corinne lowered her voice and nodded her head toward Grady. "Seems that some people are complaining about him . . ."

I peeked back to Grady, who hadn't moved a wink as he stared out the window. Five years ago he had lost everything. He had taken a big gamble on an irrigation and sprinkler business and overextended his credit. Unfortunately, the bank reclaimed not only his business but his home. At that point his wife took their kids and moved back to her parents' home in Indianapolis. Since then he had wandered the town doing odd jobs and drinking far too much. He hit rock bottom last winter when he drunkenly entered Ruth Zimmerman's home by mistake in the middle of the night. He crawled right into bed with her and fell asleep. The funny part was she didn't even wake up until the morning. Word was, her curlers practically shot off her head when she screamed and ran to her neighbor's house for help. The police charged Grady with breaking and entering and now no one would hire him.

"He's been going to AA meetings at St. Mike's for the past two months and I'll be damned if I deny him a cup of coffee and a warm breakfast each morning. I swear it's the only meal he gets," Corinne hissed.

"Let me guess. Our esteemed mayor wants him off the streets . . ."

"Can you imagine? This is my diner and I can do what I want."

I reached out my hand and squeezed her arm. With her over-painted eyebrows and her bleached hair, Corinne could easily have played a role in an old sitcom. She was the waitress everyone confided in, and if fairy godmothers existed I wanted her to be mine. Her wisdom was part of the glue that kept Truhart's soul together.

"I'm sorry, Annie. You take on enough burdens these days. You don't need mine."

"Me? Oh, I don't have a care in the world."

"About yourself, that is," she said, looking me in the eye. "Oh well, let's talk about more important things, like the fact that Charlotte has finally agreed to have the wedding in Truhart. It took them long enough to make a decision." And it had. Charlotte had kept holding out hope that they would find something that would work in Atlanta.

Corinne topped off my cup. "I am planning on being at the meeting at the inn next week so we can all help your mama plan this winter wedding in less than three months. Lord knows she'll need a little help," she said, looking thoughtfully at Grady.

An hour later I heard a car coming up behind me as I was walking back home. An older model SUV paused beside me. I heard dogs barking and recognized Mary Conrad's voice.

"Hi, Annie!" she yelled, and shushed three black Labs in the back of her vehicle. Nick's mother was one of the few people who did not call me Bump. "Looks like you could use a ride." She leaned across the front seat and opened the passenger door. "Hop in."

I couldn't say no. Nick's mother was a lonely woman these days. With her children—Melissa, Jenny, and of course Nick—gone, the only companions she had left were her dogs.

As she shifted the car into gear she nodded her head at my camera and said, "You know, one of these days you're gonna have to show me all these pictures you take. How are the wedding plans going? I am so excited they finally decided that the wedding will be right here in our little town."

We passed the creek that meandered toward the swimming pond behind our golf course. It was breathtaking. The trees, burnished in yellows and reds, formed a tunnel over the water.

"Annie, are they disappointed it isn't in Atlanta?"

I looked back at Mary, guilty of daydreaming. "They really didn't want to wait for—"

"I know it is hard to plan things around everyone, but if you talk to Charlotte can you let her know that we are really looking forward to it?"

"I can—"

"It must be so crazy for them to put together a wedding with half the guests in Atlanta. How are they going to get people here?"

"Already taken care of. They are going to charter a plane for the guests."

"I was talking to your Aunt Addie the other day and she said Charlotte said some people don't think they can make it to Michigan for the wedding."

"No. It seems like we are going to have only half the number they were planning," I said. Half the number was still more than we could handle.

"That's what Nick thought too."

I perked up at the mention of Nick's name. "How is Nick?"

"Oh, you know Nick, the same as ever. Burning the candle at both ends. Working too many hours, staying up too late."

Acid ripped through my stomach at the thought of Nick so many miles away. Was Brittany keeping him up these days? What if they were burning lots of candles? As if reading my thoughts, Finn, the oldest of Mary's labs, leaned over the head rest and gave me a slobbery kiss.

"Finn! Get back!" Mary reached into the back seat and pushed him away and the car swerved on the empty road. "It's so hard to handle planning long-distance weddings, I'm sure. It sounds like it is going to be so fancy. All those people from the GATE Network we love to watch. Do you think Scarlett Francis will come? I just love that woman."

I cringed. A vision of Satan with red hair cropped up in my mind. "One can only hope," I murmured.

The next morning was slightly different than our usual Saturdays. There was purpose and excitement in the air. It seemed like every woman in town was gathered in the dining room of the inn.

I pushed open the swinging door from the kitchen, where I had grabbed a cup of coffee, and entered the dining room. I was taking advantage of the fact that the only guests we were expecting this weekend weren't checking in until after 3:00 p.m. I wore no makeup, my favorite old jeans, and an oversized flannel shirt. Finding an empty seat by the window, I watched the chatter volley from one end of the room to the next. Dozens of ladies sat at a large cluster of tables, debating local politics, complaining about the newest under-sheriff, the retirement of the old minister at St. Francis Methodist Church, and, of course, the wedding of the century.

My mother carried a decanter to the table. "Coffee?" she asked Marva O'Shea.

"Oh, for heaven's sake, Virginia. Put that blasted thing down and come and sit. We can all pour our own coffee, and if we need to make more we know where it's stored. That's why we're all here, after all. To make your life a little easier during this time." Marva pushed her pink-rimmed glasses a little farther up her nose and looked around the room. "Anybody got any trouble serving themselves this morning?"

Everyone shook their heads and my mother sat down abruptly. Why Marva was Corinne's best friend was beyond me. Marva was the loudest mouth at any gathering. She prided herself on hearing gossip first, repeating gossip first, and keeping a secret. Despite this, we all put up with her because her heart was in the right place.

"Everybody shut up, now! We've got a wedding to plan and not much time to do it," said Marva. Her glasses sank to the end of her nose on her puffy face and I found myself mesmerized that they could stay balanced as she moved her mouth.

Corinne, who was taking a break from the diner, rolled her eyes. The two friends fought together as much as they laughed together. "For the love of Pete, Marva, would you put a lid on it and let Virginia do this? It's not your wedding to plan."

Marva straightened her shoulders and angled her eyes at Corinne. "I am only helping, Corinne. No need to get testy, here. I—"

"No worries, ladies," interrupted my mother. "I'm grateful to get this meeting started. When I called a *few* people, I had no idea I would get such a large turnout." She fixed her eyes on Marva, who seemed pleased with herself. "I have a list of items I need to figure out here, and since so many of you have already planned a wedding, I was hoping you might give me pointers." She took out a sheet of paper and started to tackle the first item. "Flowers," she began.

"I can get you a real good deal from the Family Fare, honey. We get a truck in every week with fresh flowers and arrangements," said Marva smugly, sitting up straighter and pulling her peach-colored tunic down over her large frame.

"Oh, those are too everyday-like," said a woman whose name I couldn't remember.

"Yeah," piped up Corinne. "She's got a point, Marva. How 'bout the flowers from the wholesale warehouse just across I-75? We can get everything from purple roses to pink orchids there. And the prices are good."

My mother wrote down the recommendation. "Well, that just might work. Charlotte is going with pale pinks and deep blues."

"Oh, that will look so good with her coloring," sighed Mary Conrad. I wondered when Nick's mom had turned into Charlotte's biggest fan. Oddly, it bothered me.

"We can get some vases from the craft store and put together really nice table arrangements, Virginia," said Bridgette Farley in the back of the room. Several ladies from the Garden Club volunteered to work with her on table arrangements and bridal bouquets.

"And I can provide Cozy Candles if you'll host a candle party for me. I'll give you a discount—" shouted Marva, always mindful of her home based businesses.

Corinne rolled her eyes and hit her on the shoulder. "This isn't about you, Marva!"

Mom spoke up trying to stop the fight. "Charlotte sent me some pictures of bouquets and arrangements. I'll get them to you, Bridgette. Just make sure you keep track of how much I owe you—like you did after our Fourth of July picnic celebration last year."

We went through a list of things that needed to be handled. My mother had already found a nice hotel near Gaylord that would be perfect for the extra guests. Everyone agreed that the Red River Lodge would be an ideal restaurant for a rehearsal dinner. It had great steaks and a room large enough to fit the out-of-towners. My jaw clenched at the memory of Atlanta's elegant and sophisticated restaurants. There just were no other options in the county.

"Photography is next," said Mom. Even though I could have handled the photography, my mother felt I should enjoy the wedding. I had helped photograph weddings, but it wasn't something I took pleasure in. I was relieved not to be asked.

"I have a really fantastic photographer you should use. If he is available you won't regret it. He is the best in Northern Michigan," suggested Regina Bloodworth, the mayor's wife. Mom took notes.

Father Bob from St. Francis was happy to officiate the wedding at the inn. My mother seemed stuck on the idea of a wedding in the lobby, but all I could think of were those curtains and the couches. I was searching online for slipcovers and curtains from an outlet website. I just had to figure out how to approach my mother without insulting her. Then she surprised me.

"I really need help getting the inn in order. We have peeling paint and a leak in the dining room roof that I have been ignoring for way too long," she said quite loudly.

"I can do that," said a gruff voice from the back corner of the room. Mom looked toward Grady Fitzpatrick, sitting with his back against the wall, and I wondered at the unlikely surprise on her face. For a moment the room went silent.

Then several women started whispering, and Regina Bloodworth didn't even try to lower her voice. "You aren't going to hire that drunk, are you, Virg—"

My mother interrupted her. "Why, Grady, that would be perfect. Let's talk about that after the meeting." She sent the ladies a withering look and I couldn't help feeling proud. I only wished I could be as gracious someday.

Corinne reached out and rubbed Mom's shoulder. Her back was to Grady, so he couldn't see her lips. "Thank you," she mouthed.

A huge discussion about which beauty parlor to use took up a half hour and almost ended in war. Two beauty parlors graced Main Street in Truhart, and a third was down Crooked Road. Everyone's loyalties were divided. My mother ended the discussion with a simple statement that Charlotte may not even need a beauty parlor because she had learned how to apply her makeup and do her hair from being on TV.

"What food are you going to serve, Virginia?" someone asked.

Aunt Addie had been happily sitting in the middle of her gaggle of friends, enjoying the attention of being in the bride's family and in the know. But now she perked up. I could see the wheels spinning in her head as she thought of all her favorite menus throughout the years.

But Mom rested both hands on the table in front of her and pretended to brush away a crumb. "Well, the food is going to be special." She grinned and I recognized an expression that I had seen before. It was the same look she gave us kids before we opened our birthday presents. Everyone sat forward and waited.

"Nestor is coming up for the wedding. He is going to be our chef!"

Everyone clapped and several women jumped up in excitement.

"But he never comes in the winter," said Corinne.

My mother looked like the cat that swallowed the cream. "Well, he is coming this time."

Nestor Nagel was a summer resident who was a legend in our town. He was the best cook east of the Mississippi in the opinion of many, and a favorite among the women in town. Well past his prime, Nestor had never married, loved cats, and could play a mean game of euchre. He had recently retired from his winter job as the head chef at a famous restaurant in the Keys and had been featured once on the Food Network. But we just knew him as Nestor. His recipes were top secret and he was in demand at every church cook-off or bake sale. My relief was palpable. For the last few days I was trying to picture June Lowell eating baked ziti from a buffet and chicken nuggets with ketchup.

"Oh, this is going to be the best wedding Truhart has ever seen," said Marva, jiggling in her chair. Even Aunt Addie agreed.

"Anything else?" asked Corinne.

"Well, the cake," said my mother, reaching for a binder. Phyllis Gentry, owner of the Log Cabin Bakery, had brought a book to show my mother. It had little tabs for all kinds of occasions, and Mom opened it to the section with pictures of wedding cakes.

"Oh, pick something really fancy, Virginia," said Aunt Addie as my mother pointed to a simple basket-weave design with flowers on top.

"I like this one," said Marva. Her finger rested on a picture of a cake that took up an entire table. It had two massive round bases shaped like islands, a bridge connecting the two, and bride and groom figurines crossing the bridge. Each base was several layers high and was topped by a pagoda with luminescent birds perched on each peak. The proportions were all off. The birds were twice as large as the bride and groom.

"You know, that is really something else, Marva," Mom said with a smile that was as sugary as the cake. "But Charlotte has simple taste. I think the one with fresh flowers is nicer."

Marva turned her large frame around and pointed her finger at me. "Well, when it's your turn, Bump, you take a look at this cake here. Simple is nice, but bigger is better." She laughed.

"When it's my turn, Marva, I'm going to elope!" I said as I flashed her a smile.

"Who's eloping?" a familiar voice from the doorway said.

Every head in the dining room swung toward the sound. It had been more than three years since he had visited Truhart. But by the way he casually leaned against the door frame of the dining room, he looked like he hadn't been gone ten minutes.

Chapter 10

"Nick!" Mary Conrad sat back in her seat with her hand on her chest. She wore her heart on her face. It almost hurt to see her happiness. She rose unsteadily from her chair, still clutching her chest, and enveloped Nick in her arms. I wasn't the only one who'd missed Nick.

If Charlotte was the homegrown celebrity who put Truhart on the map, Nick was the boy wonder who had made it big in the outside world. Now, like a show-and-tell project, Nick was passed around the room as each of the ladies, who had watched him grow from a scrawny boy to a stunning specimen of a man, took turns greeting him. Marva shook like a Jell-O mold as she rocked him back and forth, and Corinne managed to smear lipstick on his chin when she reached up to plant a kiss on his cheek. Aunt Addie just put her hands on her hips and told him he looked like he needed to eat more.

He patted his stomach and then leaned over to give her a hug. "Feel free to help me with that, Aunt Addie."

I remembered how his flat stomach felt with its ripple of rock-solid muscles and the way a sprinkle of hair led up to his chest and down to . . . well, I wouldn't change a thing about him. He was much better groomed than the last time I had seen him in his old jacket, with messy hair and wrinkled clothes. But he was no less handsome. Dressed casually in jeans and a barn jacket, with a tan sweater and blue button-down underneath, he could have been the cover model for *Men's Health*.

While he made the rounds, I crossed my arms in front of me and observed the spectacle. To the average person Nick looked like a bashful schoolboy being fawned over. But it slowly dawned on me that there was something off. It was the stiff way he held his shoulders and the smile that didn't quite reach his eyes. He was holding himself back.

"I'm so sorry, Nick, you just missed Ian," Mom said. "He left for what he calls 'a gig' yesterday."

"I know, I called him while he was on the road," Nick said, looking down at her. He gave her shoulder a gentle squeeze and then turned toward the table in the corner where I sat. Lowering his chin, he headed my way with a smooth gait that parted the sea of ladies like Moses parting the Red Sea. I resisted the urge to meet him halfway. He stopped right in front of me and looked down with a feral gleam in his eyes that could not be mistaken for anything other than lust. For a moment I thought he was going to take me in his arms and kiss me like he had on the picnic table.

"Hi, Annie," he said softly.

Then he reached out to pull me up and plant a kiss on my mouth. Conscious of the room full of some of the biggest gossips in the county, I moved just before his lips landed and he caught the side of my mouth. No one else seemed to notice anything unusual in the way he greeted me. Thank God. I caught a smirk on Nick's face as he stepped back and looked me up and down.

Why hadn't I dressed in something nicer? I had felt so comfortable in my shapeless flannel shirt. But now I just felt like a pillow. Nick's eyes traveled back to my face, and I was spellbound by the heat radiating from his gaze. Thank goodness his back was to the rest of the room.

The ladies returned to their chatter and were now on the topic of groomsmen's tuxedos and bridesmaids' dresses.

Mary Conrad left the conversation behind and walked up to us, putting her hand on Nick's back as if she was making sure he was real. "You should have told me you were coming home, dear. I would have made up your bed and cooked you a decent breakfast," she said.

He put his arm around her shoulder. "I'm only here for a day, Mom. I had a last-minute meeting in Detroit that finished yesterday, and I figured I would rent a car and come up here and then fly home Sunday. Besides, I know old Finn is probably taking my bed these days. No need to push him out prematurely," he said, referring to his mother's oldest Labrador.

"Well this is wonderful, isn't it, Annie? It's been a long time since you've been back, honey." She fondly laid her head on her son's shoulder. "I am so glad all my nagging has finally paid off."

"It's not like we never see each other. We just met up at Melissa's in Chicago last month."

"But that's not home," Mary said.

I walked over to the sideboard and grabbed a mug for Nick. I felt like I was intruding in the conversation, and since I agreed whole-heartedly with Mary, I didn't trust myself to keep my mouth shut. When I returned, I shoved the cup of coffee into his hands. He tasted it and looked down in surprise that I had added just the right amount of sugar. Long ago I had made note of what he liked in his coffee.

"I do it for guests all the time," I said.

He nodded his thanks with that crooked grin I was enjoying more and more, and I wondered how his mother hadn't noticed her son flirting shamelessly with me. She kept talking as she explained her plans for the night.

"The Harrisburg Arts Association is hosting an art show tonight at the St. Francis parish hall. I have several quilts entered. Why don't you come with me? George Bloodworth and Jerry Landry are the auctioneers and everyone would love to see you."

Nick's lips compressed in a thin line. "I'm pretty tired, Mom. I was looking forward to a quiet night."

"Nick, honey, it's been ages since you saw some of those people. They were friends of Dad's and I know they would love to see you."

"That's all right. I can hang out at home. Or better yet, I'll wander around here at the inn. What are you doing tonight, Annie?" His eyes traveled over my face and landed on my lips, which still felt parched under the glow of his stare. I licked my upper lip absently. He stared at my tongue as it finished its journey. I hadn't meant it as a seductive ploy, but based on his reaction, I made a mental note to use it some-time in the future.

Nick cleared his throat, and I placed my hand on my chest to make sure my heart hadn't catapulted out of me. I wished we were back on I-75 and alone in a car. This was too public a place for these emotions.

Mary was saying something and I forced myself back to reality. "We put Annie to work. She is taking pictures at the art show for the newsletter. She won't be here either, Nick. So why don't you come with us?"

Nick looked away from my face and blinked, focusing on the rest of the room. "I'm not sure I am up to a large crowd tonight, but I could help with some of this wedding planning. I'm sure there is something around here that needs to be done." He ran his hands through his hair and raised his eyebrow as he looked back. "That is, unless someone has suddenly decided to elope?"

"Oh, that was just Annie," said Mary, letting the crease in her forehead melt away. "She says she's going to elope when it's her turn."

"Is she?" said Nick with a choking sound.

Was he making fun of me? "Oh, I was just talking off the top of my head. I'm not getting married or anything. I mean, I'm not planning anything, just if it were me and not Charlotte." I stumbled over my words.

"Yes?" Nick prodded, leaning toward me.

"I was just commenting to Marva that I didn't want to have a big cake and all these complicated details if I were to get married. That's all," I said, emphasizing the last two words and daring him to laugh again.

"Well, she'd have to *date* someone first," interrupted Aunt Addie, coming up behind me. "We tried to set Annie up with Sterling Gutman's nephew, but she said he had a fish mouth!"

I put my hand over my eyes in mortification.

"Did she?" asked Nick.

"I'm relying on you to introduce her to some of your friends, Nick. Someone tall enough for her to wear heels around, and smart enough to figure out how to keep her from sticking her foot in her mouth."

Nick laughed. "I don't know anybody that smart, Aunt Addie."

I lowered my hand to glare at him.

The meeting was breaking up and the ladies grabbed their purses and called out their good-byes. I waved to several of them as they hurried out the side exit that led directly to the parking lot.

"Did you drive from your mom's?" I asked Nick.

"No." He turned to Mary. "After the dogs tackled me, I wandered around the house, trying to figure out where you were, Mom. The wall calendar showed a meeting here this morning, so I thought I would walk over and see what was up."

"Well, Marva and Corinne picked me up, so I am sure they can give you a lift home," said Mary.

"No, that's okay. I'll hang out here for a while, then walk back," he said, giving her a quick kiss on the cheek. "We'll catch up at home."

"All right, but I have to warn you, I don't have much in the fridge. If I had known you were coming I would have stocked up." She shook her head as she turned back to Marva and Corinne, who were arguing at the side door. "Oh no. There they go again. They argued the whole way here about which foods cause gas, and I'm sure it will be something even worse on the way home."

Nick watched his mother walk away and shook his head. "Some things never change."

"I guess it seems that way." I wanted to tell him all about the way things had changed since he left. But I didn't.

He took a sip of coffee and I grabbed my own mug as we made our way down the hallway to the front lobby. His eyes wandered from the crack in the ceiling to the worn carpet beneath our feet. Was he remembering the games he played here when he was younger? Or did he notice all the ways the inn was falling apart?

Grady and Mom were deep in conversation in front of the fireplace. She gestured to some of the peeled paint that needed the most attention and he nodded as he followed her pointing finger.

Not wanting to disturb their conversation, Nick and I retreated to the staircase. Like when we were kids, I sat down several steps up from the landing and he followed, sitting one step below me. Leaning against the railing, I asked him, "So, how was business in Detroit? You have been there a few times now."

"It was pretty successful, actually. Our Midwest division has a great new team leader and his concepts on repurposing old buildings are really innovative." He told me about a new start-up division that wanted to convert an old warehouse to loft offices. I watched his eyes light up as he explained how they were using old materials from the warehouse in the new designs. It was disarming to see him so electrified. I asked him to describe the newest project and he put down his coffee mug and painted a picture for me, shaping his hands in the air as they became imaginary office buildings in front of us.

"I know it seems hard to picture, Annie, but imagine this—the third floor conference room will have a wall of glass that will overlook the exposed beams and wood of an atrium on the ground floor." Somewhere in the conversation, Nick had stretched out lengthwise along the step with his back against the wall and I had stretched myself the opposite way with my back to the rail. As we faced each other, Nick's hand rested on my knee. He talked and I nodded, transfixed by the strange and innovative beauty of the building he was describing.

"But that is so different from the high-rise buildings you showed me in Atlanta, isn't it? I mean, those were all new construction starting from scratch, right?"

"Yes. Not many of the architects in the Atlanta office are willing to invest in the urban renewal projects, which tend to be small-scale and less profitable. But, honestly, if you could see them you would love the smaller projects."

"Actually, you did a pretty good job describing them without me seeing them. I think it sounds wonderful, Nick." I couldn't help it. I was gushing like a silly teenager.

We were interrupted by Aunt Addie coming down the stairs with a pile of folded towels in her hands. "Look at you two. Hanging out on the stairs just like you did when you were kids."

"Yeah, except Ian would have run his Tonka truck off a ramp into your potted plants by now, Aunt Addie," Nick said, looking up at her.

"Either that or Annie would have convinced you all to slide down the steps using your sleeping bags like toboggans," she said, sweeping past us as we folded our knees and left her a path between us.

"Aunt Addie, I only did that a few times," I called after her.

"More like a dozen times," interjected my mom over Aunt Addie's shoulder as she grabbed the newel post and looked up at us. "Until you broke that vase. Dad grounded you for a month after that."

"I still think you overreacted." I turned to Nick, wanting to explain further. But what was the point? "This is why middle children have issues, you know."

Mom stood next to Grady, who looked on with interest, and placed her hand on her hip. "Oh, here we go . . . Does this sound familiar to you, Nicholas? How many times has Annie complained about her birth order?"

"I lost count, but I know I'd be a rich man if I had a penny for—"

I kicked him in the shoulder and he grabbed my foot and wouldn't let go. "Hey, that's my golf arm! Be careful," he said.

"Maybe it will help your golf game. It certainly can't hurt it," I said, trying to free my foot.

"Children, children . . . It's a fine day outside," said my mom as if we were five. "Why don't you two go out so I can show Grady the rest of the things that need fixing in this inn."

I opened my mouth, ready to protest, when Nick let go of my foot and abruptly stood up, grabbing my arm and pulling me up with him.

He took my coffee mug and put it on a nearby table. "Come on Annie, let's go out and play like your mom wants us to. I should be getting home soon anyway. I'll race you to the second hole," he said, referring to the old shortcut we used to take that led across the golf course to the Conrads' house.

Minutes later I practically collapsed on the green, as my breath vaporized in the brisk air. "Oh my God, I am way too old for this."

Nick had arrived several moments earlier and barely looked winded. "Not me. I feel great. Most of the time it's too hot or muggy to run in Atlanta. But this is perfect."

"Well, don't forget, it may be forty-five degrees right now, but it will be ten below in another few months. No one will be running then. Skiing . . . or wading through snow . . . maybe. But not running." I was still bent over with my hands on my knees.

"You wimp, Annie. You're panting so hard, you've created a microclimate with your breath."

"Well la-di-da, Mr. Marathon Man! Not all of us can train at some fancy gym with a hulking trainer named Thor."

"More like a cute cheerleader named Trixie. She keeps me in tip-top shape." He patted his chest and posed like an Adonis.

"Well, excuse me," I said as I straightened and walked off ahead of him. Images of a girl named Trixie wearing Lycra on her sculpted body danced in front of me. I would have said more, but I was still out of breath. Nick laughed at my irritation and I buried my hands in the pockets of my old jeans, not only to keep them warm but to keep them off Nick.

Nick drew up beside me and matched my footsteps. "So, are you jealous?"

My heart did a little dance. Being accused of jealousy meant I had reason to feel that way. It was one short step in the right direction, and the first reference he had made to anything that might mean there was an *us*.

"I could never be jealous of a girl named Trixie."

He wrapped his hand around my elbow and tugged until he pulled my hand out of my pocket. Then he held on to it. I rolled my eyes at him, feigning anger just because it felt good to be jealous, and even better to be coaxed out of it.

We were coming up to a copse of trees and the old shack at the edge of the golf course. Above us low clouds moved at a fast pace across the sky. The wind carried a cluster of leaves out of our path and I realized we were close to the shortcut that led to the large barn that had been Russell Conrad's workshop. The trees shielded us from the road and the inn farther away, and we walked more slowly until we stopped and faced each other.

Nick took a step forward and brought his hands up to either side of my face. "I missed you," he said before lowering his head and pressing his lips to mine.

There was no tender beginning to this kiss. Instead we came together, impatient and trembling. My hands ran up the inside of his coat, along his chest and around his back, pressing him closer as our mouths and hands explored each other. Our kisses were anything but neat or careful. In fact, with every powerful moment, I felt myself losing control.

I had been kissed before, and had done much more than that in my life. But somehow I had always been conscious of my body and my feelings. I had known where my lips wandered, where my hands went, and as strange as it sounds, I had always felt like there was a part of me that was detached and looking down at myself from above. A little voice inside would direct me. *Move your hand here. Feel his hand there.*

But this was so much different. I was almost frightened by my lack of awareness of my own body. I found myself with my back against an old pine tree, my legs wrapped around Nick and his body hard and warm, keeping me in place.

A crow cackled above us and we paused to catch our breath. I gazed into Nick's startled face and knew mine was a mirror image. I had no idea how much time had gone by and I could never have drawn a map of the places my hands had been. From the dazed expression in Nick's smoky dark eyes and the shaky way he drew in breath, I could tell he felt the same way.

He raised his hand and ran his fingers along my cheek. His eyes softened and he smiled. "I should have shaved this morning. You're getting red here."

"I don't care." I sighed and reached up to pull his head down to bring his lips right back where they had been. Now he was gentler, taking his time as he kissed each side of my mouth, then down toward my jaw.

"So, how have you been?" he asked into my neck, teasing me with his tongue.

"Good," I said absently as I tilted my chin so he could reach the most sensitive part of my neck.

"You aren't too stressed about the wedding?"

"Well, yes. I'm really worried about it. But we'll deal. I mean, we have no choice, really."

"Well, there is always the possibility of an elopement. Oh, that is for you, I forgot." He was back to my face and kissed me gently on the lips.

I shivered.

"Are you cold?"

"No."

As if answering me, the wind sent a powerful gust our way, lifting Nick's unbuttoned jacket and exposing my hands to the chill.

"Come on, let's get out of the wind," he said as he gently lowered me to the ground. With his arm around me, we scurried over the ridge toward the large barn beyond. I felt a wayward drop of icy rain against my cheek and looked up, wondering if it was cold enough to snow.

I let go of his hand and ran ahead to the large red barn door, where I rattled the padlock. It was locked. I hadn't been inside in years.

"Can we get in?" I asked, wrapping my arms around myself and feeling like a child breaking into a secret fort.

"Ian and I always had a top-secret entrance," he said, looking like he wasn't sure about telling me. We walked around the corner of the barn and his hands trailed gingerly along the boards.

He turned and confessed, "We used to steal beer from the refrigerator at the inn, come up here at midnight, and smoke when we were teenagers."

"Are you kidding me? In your dad's workshop barn? Why didn't you use the golf shack?"

"We were afraid Aunt Addie would spy. Shh," he said, raising his finger to his lips. He pointed to the house a hundred yards beyond, where his mother was probably waiting for him.

I felt like a kid again and clapped my hands in anticipation. "Let's go in!"

"I don't want to, but you can—"

"Oh, come on. Are you scared you'll get caught?"

He was quiet as he concentrated on the wood at waist level and found a loose board. He raised it up to let me in.

I crouched low and kneeled to crawl through, then paused. "I don't want to go in there by myself. There could be all sorts of creepy things inside."

"You'll be fine." He grabbed my rear and practically pushed me into the barn.

I scrambled forward on my knees, making contact with the rough pine floor that was covered in a layer of dust. Once I was clear of Nick's secret portal, I rose to my feet and looked around me. It was like visiting an old friend from childhood. It had changed, but then so had I.

I cupped my hands over my mouth. "Nick!" I screamed.

Within moments Nick crawled through the opening behind me, concern on his face.

I pointed up at the ceiling. "I thought I saw a bat . . ."

He stood up, not sure whether to believe me. But then his eyes traveled around the barn and he was lost in memories.

The inside of the barn had a hollow, abandoned feeling, like an empty church. To the left were two large doors that marked the entrance. They were always padlocked from outside. Above them was a shallow loft with several large windows that tapered down from tallest to shortest on each side. Dust motes danced in the air where the grimy windows filtered light into the rest of the barn. Below the loft was a small office and two restrooms that Nick's dad had used when he employed a dozen carpenters. Above us the beamed ceiling spanned the entire huge interior, and I looked up just to make sure there actually were no bats.

Nick looked down at me and put his hands in his back pockets. "I feel like I should have brought in a six-pack, but I guess I'm too old for that stuff, huh?"

I smiled. "It kind of takes the fun out of it when it's legal, doesn't it?"

We walked through the cavernous space and looked at it from different angles. I was remembering how loud this barn was when Nick's dad was alive. The sounds of power saws and hammers were always reverberating from the open doors. Nick's father had been a large man, almost as tall as Nick, and I remembered how quick he was to smile and even quicker to laugh. His eyes used to crinkle in the corners when he came out into the light and greeted me or my parents.

I looked at Nick now and wondered if his own memories were rattling around in his mind. There was a grim twist to his mouth as he wandered to the back of the barn and lifted a tarp. Underneath was an old machine, and he ran his hands lovingly along the surface.

I moved to stand beside him. "What is that?"

"It's an old Powermatic reciprocating saw. My grandfather bought it and passed it down to Dad. They don't make them like this anymore." He bent down to look around the edges and underneath the machine, tracing the lines of the machine with studied intensity. It dawned on me that here was a man who truly had a passion for the fine details and hard work that went into carpentry and building. He was the third generation of Conrad men who understood the lines of a building and the strength of a power tool.

"So your mother never wanted to get rid of it?"

He looked up at me as if he had almost forgotten I was there. "No." He stood up and reached for the tarp. "This is actually not my mom's to get rid of."

"Oh?"

"No. It's mine." He settled the tarp over the machine and turned back toward me. "My dad left it to me."

I reached out and adjusted the tarp to cover a side he had missed and tried not to look like it mattered to me that a little piece of Nick had stayed right here in Truhart. "So, do you ever wish you could use it?"

"No," he said.

"Well, why not? Wouldn't it be kind of fun to play around with these old tools and do some woodworking? You used to love that stuff. Your dad was the best in the county and beyond . . . I mean, not that you ever wanted to become a builder like your dad. But still."

"My dad worked his ass off, Annie. He gave more of himself to his work and this town than you or I could ever imagine."

"I'm sure he did. More of the buildings in this town were built by your dad and grandfather than anyone else. But that's something I don't understand."

His hands rested at his sides, but I saw them clench into fists as I talked. Perhaps I was pushing it, but there was something that bothered him and I wanted to figure it out.

"What don't you understand?" he asked slowly.

"With all this—your dad's barn, the buildings in Truhart, your mom—why don't you come back? Is it just hard because you miss him? Or is it something else?"

Nick tilted his head.

I put up my hands defensively. "I'm not trying to make you a woodworker. I know you love designing those monoliths. I just wonder if maybe you are the least bit interested in coming back to Truhart once in a while."

"I'm here now. Isn't that good enough?"

"Well, yes," I said, moving closer to him. "Maybe it's just me imagining things, but it doesn't seem like you actually *want* to be here."

"I have changed, Annie. Small town life isn't for me anymore." He grasped my shoulder and pulled me close.

"What is for you, Nick?"

"I've been wondering that."

His lips touched mine. For several minutes he proved just what kind of wondering he was referring to. I let myself melt into him. It wasn't until I heard barking from outside that I realized we had been discovered.

"God, I hate those dogs." Nick moaned as I pulled my flannel shirt back together. My hands shook as I struggled to recover.

"Somehow I don't believe that."

He stopped my hands and buttoned the last few buttons himself. Kissing me on the nose, he said, "Finn, I like. But those other two, especially Lucifer, are obnoxious. I'm surprised my mom hasn't given them away by now."

"They keep her company, Nick," I said, looking him squarely in the face. "She is lonely."

He looked away. "She has friends."

I shook my head and changed tactics. "Are you sure you can't come to the art festival tonight? It doesn't have chocolate martinis, but there will be some wine from Michigan's west coast."

"No."

"Why—"

He shut me up with a firm kiss and then turned back to the secret portal, speaking over his shoulder. "Sometimes you really talk too much, Annie."

Chapter 11

As I drove home from the art show late that night, I stared blankly at the headlights illuminating the empty road ahead of me. I tried to understand why Nick was so reluctant to attend tonight. Earlier, when I'd entered the St. Francis parish hall, Mary had greeted me and said she thought Nick might show up after all. The excitement on her face was so contagious I felt my own spirits rise. But as the night wore on it became apparent that he wasn't going to come. One night home in three years, and he couldn't seem to find it in himself to spend the evening with his mother?

As disappointed as I had been, it was even more pitiful to watch Mary check her phone over and over for a message that never came. Even worse, when her beautiful quilt won first prize in the fabric category, and second prize overall, she had stood by herself while the other award winners took pictures with their families around them. Of course, everyone who loved her made a big deal of her prize, but it wasn't the same.

Tired of small talk and my head throbbing from the flash of my own camera, I had been one of the first to leave the show. It was almost 10:00 p.m. The old SUV ate up the winding state road, and I realized that my hands were clenching the wheel like a vise. I flexed my fingers and tried to calm down, but it wasn't working.

I should have trussed Nick up like a calf and hauled him to the show.

Would it have been so hard for him to make a simple appearance? He had driven all the way from Detroit but couldn't be bothered to drive fifteen minutes to St. Francis?

Things had been so good this afternoon. We were so hot and heavy we might have generated enough electricity to use that old reciprocating saw in a whole new way. And then when the dogs had followed our trail and erupted in a frenzy of barking, we had split apart as if the saw had done its job. Mary's confused expression as she stood on the front porch and watched us crawling around the side of the barn on our hands and knees would have been funny if it hadn't been so embarrassing.

When we righted ourselves and brushed off the dirt, Nick cupped his hand over his mouth and called out, "Annie just found a loose board, so we were trying to secure it."

Mary had crooked her head sideways and given us an odd glance. She was still giving me strange looks at the art show, but if she had figured anything out, she hadn't said a word.

Turning into the long driveway that led to the inn, I noticed a sedan with a rental agency tag on the license plate in the visitors' parking area. I parked across from it and grabbed my camera equipment from the backseat.

Opening the front door, I was momentarily blinded. The room was uncharacteristically bright and the smell of turpentine and paint hung in the air. I looked around with curiosity at the work lights, tarps, and ladders by the front desk. A pile of boxes and books were gathered in the center of the room and I heard the sound of scraping nearby.

"Hey, Annie, how was the show?"

Nick appeared around the corner by the front desk and I took a step backward. He wore an old pair of jeans with rips in the knees, and a faded Lions T-shirt with paint smeared on it. He was so adorable I almost forgot my irritation.

"Fine," I said weakly.

"Did you have any photos in the show?"

"No." I hadn't entered any shows or contests in years and had no intention of doing so again. "Your mother won an award in the fabric division and second place for best overall. She would have really appreciated it if you had been there tonight." He needed to understand how he had hurt her.

His smile faltered. "Whatever my mother is feeling, I am sure she will be fine."

"But I don't understand why you couldn't just come to the show, even for a short time."

"I don't really want to talk about it right now," he said as he wiped his hands with an old rag. He closed the gap between us and lowered his head to give me a light kiss. As kisses went, it wasn't as life altering as his others, but it still had that goosebump quality to it. "I was happy helping out right here and waiting for you to get home." He smiled with huge charm, and for a moment we were nearly back to where we'd left off in the barn.

He walked toward the pile of boxes in the middle of the floor. "Grady and I decided to get started on the lobby tonight, while things were quiet."

I didn't see Grady, only cans of spackling compound and painters' tools at the top of the stairs.

"Well, that was nice of you," I said, wondering what he was looking for in the pile in front of him.

"We were clearing out some boxes by the reception desk and I came across this." He turned around with a smile, and held his hands up.

I felt a chill run up my spine. He was holding one of the photo albums I had worked on this past summer. Not wanting anyone else to see what I had been doing while I spent long hours at the front desk, I had tucked it away in a back closet, thinking I would put it in the attic later. Inside the book were photographs I had taken of the back-country roads and small towns I had traveled last spring. They were marked with comments, the names of the towns or roads, and random titles that held more personal meaning than I wanted to share. Each sleeve in the book held pictures of life in struggling towns throughout our county. In many ways they were a departure from my simpler, off-the-beaten-track images. They were edgier and bleaker.

Nick turned a page to a photo of an old woman wearing a man's hat, sitting on a porch next to a young girl in a torn dress and bare feet. *Crooked Porch* was scrawled in pencil next to that photo along with questions I had wondered about. *Whose hat is that? Where is the child's father?* He turned to the next page and I already knew what was on it. An old Chevy truck with no wheels parked behind a gas station. *Going Nowhere.*

A sour taste formed in my mouth as I watched Nick leaf through the pages of the album.

"These are great, Annie. You should do something with them." He sounded as casual as if he was looking through a cookbook.

I walked over to him and held my hands out for him to pass it back to me. "I didn't want anyone to see them."

He closed the book, held it to his chest, and gave me a tentative grin. "No, I mean it. These are really great! You should get them published. Or even consider displaying them in a gallery. You could create an entire show with these."

"I'd rather not." I continued to hold my hands out. I heard my voice speak calmly and clearly, but inside I was shaking with emotion.

He frowned. "Are you mad that I looked at them? I know that art is really personal, but you have talent."

I lowered my arms and took a deep breath. I was overreacting. Why shouldn't I be proud of my work? I knew in my mind that it was silly to feel so agitated. But the book was as personal as a diary to me. It was strange to know that he had just looked at the photos and notes without my consent. I felt exposed, as if my clothes had been ripped off.

Nick sensed my mood and put the book back down in the pile, and I resisted the urge to snatch it up.

"It's personal, that's all."

"You seem mad. I'm sorry. I couldn't help myself. You really need to show that book to someone. Brittany has some friends—"

"I wasn't ready for someone to go through it," I interrupted. The image of Brittany looking at my book made me nauseous. "Was there anything else you went through behind the desk? Feel free to look at my checkbook while you're at it."

"Whoa," he said as if I were a wild horse. "Sorry to upset you. I won't do it again. Look, I appreciate art. I thought the photos were beautiful and had no idea you would have a problem sharing them."

His tone sounded patronizing to me. "If you're so into art, you should have gone to the art show." I couldn't hold it in any longer.

"I was helping out here."

"We are fine without your help. Next time help your mother. She is lonely and misses you. It was just one night, Nick. You couldn't give that much?"

Nick's eyes darkened and his body tensed. "Stay out of it, Annie."

"Oh, so it's all right for you to go snooping through my photos, but I can't discuss something that is right in front of us. Like the way you treated your mother tonight."

"I don't want to talk to you about that," Nick said, turning his back on me.

"Why not? Are you afraid you'll sound as stuck-up as June Low-ell or Scarlett Francis? Go ahead, Nick. I am a big girl. I can take it."

"Say what, Annie? You're so good at reading people. What is it you think I am going to say?" Nick bent his head and stared at the floor. I couldn't see his expression.

"Tell me how much you hate this town. How much better Atlanta is than Truhart."

"Oh, are we back to that? Is that you what you think?" His voice was flat and ominous.

"Well, you won't tell me what's going on. I have no idea what you are feeling half the time, so it's easy to think you hate this place."

He swung around to face me, his cheeks mottled red and his eyes black. "You want to know what I feel? You have this naïve idea that just because this is a small town with people who go to church and play bingo together, nothing is ever bad. Big cities are bad. Right, Annie? Atlanta. New York. Evil places. But Truhart, well, it is just full of good citizens who would never harm a soul."

I stood rigidly.

"Well, guess what, Annie. All isn't perfect in Mayberry." I could see a vein clearly throbbing at the side of his neck.

"What are you talking about?"

He opened his mouth and closed it several times. I waited for him to say something. He stared at me, but he wasn't seeing me at all. He was lost in a place I couldn't begin to picture. Around us the room was silent except for the sound of the clock above the mantel.

Finally, he lifted his chin and narrowed his eyes. "You couldn't possibly understand how I feel, Annie."

"That's because you won't tell me. I'm not a mind reader." I swallowed before adding, "I just don't think you should punish your mother by running away from your hometown and abandoning her. It isn't her fault."

"Abandoning her? Is that what you think I've done? You don't really know me at all."

"Well—"

"You know, I can't believe you're talking to me about abandoning things. That's ironic. It really is. You're the expert at running away, not me. You ran away from your dreams a long time ago."

I tried not to let his words twist in my gut. "I don't have any dreams, Nick. I am perfectly happy." I was surprised how feeble the words sounded as soon as I said them.

Nick pointed to the photo album lying nearby. "That's not the story those pictures tell."

I stared at the book, speechless. I was happy, wasn't I? The book was full of images of lonely roads and decaying buildings. And sure, the pictures were sad, but it wasn't like they were a Rorschach test. The other albums I had created were stuffed with pictures of life off the main interstate, too. Even though I knew my photographs were growing increasingly glum, they were a reflection of the times. They were a part of the backdrop of my life. Not some deep subconscious neurosis.

I was so lost in thought that it took me a moment to realize Nick was holding his coat and looking up the stairs with a stony expression.

"See you later, Grady," he said. I looked up at Grady, who was standing at the top of the second-floor landing looking like he wished he was on the other side of the planet.

"You're going? Just like that?" I asked.

"There is a fundamental problem between us, Annie." He put on his coat, painstakingly adjusting the collar while the silence grew. Then he stared me in the eye. It felt like he could see through my skin and I wanted to look away. "You want to stay in Truhart. You want nothing to change. And I don't."

I couldn't believe what I was hearing. Was this over before it even started? I thought we had begun something special. I knew the reality of loving Nick was different than my dreams—but everything had been coming together.

I couldn't get enough air. Nick blurred in waves as he walked away from me.

"You know, Nick, I may still be here in Truhart, but at least I don't let anything get in the way of what I care about. Whatever feelings you may have for this town, you're letting them get in the way of coming home, and you're hurting the people who care about you."

He froze for a moment.

I blinked furiously and walked over to him. "This little town didn't seem to bother you so much when you were a kid," I said, grabbing his arm.

Nick pulled his arm away from my grasp and stepped around me. He walked out the front door without looking back. I stood in the doorway for a long time and watched his car drive down the road until his taillights faded in the distance.

A part of me wanted to pick up stones and throw them at his back windows. *Good riddance.* The cold wind did nothing to cool the anger that washed over me. Good thing we figured out how incompatible we were now, before anything else happened.

I stepped back inside and slammed the door.

Chapter 12

"Are you sure you don't regret it, Annie?" asked Mom.

I nodded my head and thought for the millionth time how much I regretted it. The trip to Atlanta in August, and even Nick's visit in October, seemed years ago.

Bing Crosby crooned "White Christmas" on the radio and I stared out the picture window in the dining room at a winter scene that was anything but white.

For the first time in recent history, Northern Michigan had just celebrated a snow-free Christmas. Although the sky had been overcast all week, nothing white and fluffy fell from the sky. The ground was frozen solid in gray and brown hues, making the landscape look like a dirty filter over a camera lens.

As I looked at the barren scene before me, branches swaying in the December wind like skeletons, I could barely make out Mary Conrad's rooftop. Her house had been empty all week while she spent Christmas in Chicago, which meant Nick hadn't come home for the holidays. Again. But this year Nick's absence was my fault.

Actually, no. It was his fault.

Dozens of times I had replayed the night of the art show in my head. I should have kept my feelings to myself. I could admit that much. If I had just said nothing about Mary and the show, if I had hugged Nick and given him a kiss and kept my big mouth shut, everything would have been fine.

"Annie?"

I looked down and realized I was stabbing the table with the tines of one of the forks we were polishing. I turned toward my mom as she stared across the dining room table at me, a worried frown on her face. She had been looking at me like that a lot lately. I tried to smile, but my lips twisted into a messy contortion.

Why was she asking me about regret? I stared at her, wondering if Grady had mentioned the horrible scene in the lobby. He had never brought it up to me, but I caught him studying me as he did odd jobs around the inn. His solemn eyes looked as if he wanted to say something, but whatever it was, he kept his mouth shut.

"What do you mean, Mom?" Maybe I hadn't heard correctly.

"Do you regret not going to Las Vegas with the other girls in the bridal party?"

The day after Christmas the entire bridal party had taken a flight to Las Vegas, where they were celebrating a bachelorette weekend. While Charlotte, Bebe, Patty, and even Brittany had enjoyed the shows and been pampered at one of the ritziest spas in Vegas, the boys had celebrated their own way. Aunt Addie was very concerned about this, but Charlotte assured us it would be tame. On the final night in Vegas, both bridal parties met up and celebrated together at a chic French restaurant at the Bellagio, a place I had only read about.

I could only hope that Nick woke up next to a fat Elvis, discovered a bad tattoo on his chest, and suffered a hangover the size of Texas. It would serve him right.

"I don't regret staying home, Mom. I'm not much of a bachelorette-party person. Besides, Ian and I want to help get the inn ready for the wedding." I didn't tell her that Ian and I had sunk a large chunk of our savings into getting the inn in decent shape. *The same amount Nick probably tipped some long-legged waitress in Vegas.*

"Well, Charlotte felt really bad about the fact that you couldn't go to Las Vegas. You should have taken Henry up on his offer to fly you and Ian out there." Neither Ian nor I wanted to be Henry's charity-case future in-laws. "You and Ian have put a lot of work into this wedding, Annie. I can't tell you how much I appreciate everything. But sometimes I feel like you are giving up too much for this."

If only she knew how much this wedding was costing me.

"Actually, Mom, you're kind of my excuse. I don't think I would like Las Vegas much," I said as cheerfully as I could.

My mother grunted. "Well, I don't think I would either. But I would be interested to see what all the hype is about. And I would love to see a show and maybe that handsome single magician . . ."

"Well, I can't argue with you there." I wasn't about to tell her he was gay.

It was three days before the wedding. Charlotte, Henry, the wedding party, and the immediate family were set to arrive tomorrow afternoon. That meant Nick would be back as well. Unless, of course, he had decided that he couldn't handle Truhart anymore. Stupid man. I jammed the rest of the utensils in the drawer and tried to keep from chipping off a piece of wood in frustration.

"Hey, it finally came, Bump!" Ian walked into the dining room with a large box in his hands.

"What's that?" asked my mom.

Ian put the box down on a table and grinned at me. For the last few weeks we had found ways to slowly improve things at the inn. The trick was not letting Mom know how much money we had spent.

Ian pulled out his pocket knife and began cutting open the box. "When I was playing a gig in Columbus last month, I mentioned to a production assistant that we owned an inn. He said that occasionally they get promotions for special beauty products in trial sizes for the bands he manages. He had a whole lot of extra products and was hoping to unload a few on me." Ian finished cutting and peeled open the top of the box.

"Check this out," he said, throwing aside a clump of the packing material. He picked up several small bottles of shampoo and soap. The brand was far more luxurious than we had ever been able to afford, and my mother placed her hands on her throat.

"Ian, I can't believe you were able to get this!"

Ian grinned. "And you always thought I'd amount to nothing . . ."

She cocked her head at him. "It's all very strange how we're suddenly finding all these connections for fancy hotel goods. If I didn't know better—

"Hey, I have never actually tried before. I guess that's what a little effort can do."

She laughed as she held up a shampoo bottle. "Well, Ian, fancy shampoo won't help pay off our bank loans. But it sure makes me feel better about this wedding."

Ian stopped smiling and I saw concern in his hazel eyes. The truth was, everything we were doing was nothing more than a Band-Aid on an open wound.

Now it was my turn to ask about regrets. "Do you regret having the wedding here, Mom?"

She placed her hands on our shoulders and shook her head. "No."

I had the feeling there was something she wasn't saying. She had been working hard managing things too. Hopefully no one would notice the patch job on the roof or the duct tape holding the tables together under the tablecloth. Grady had patched the walls and Mom had bought slipcovers and pillows at an outlet store. Ian and I had pooled our money to buy new linens and sheets as well. Ian even revamped our tired old website. Of course I made him remove the massage package he had built into the website. I don't know who he thought would handle that, but there was no way I was rubbing oil on some old man's back.

Charlotte was clueless about our efforts. She had stayed in Atlanta for Christmas. We had watched her on television making gingerbread houses from milk cartons, decorating Christmas trees with origami, and reporting on the experiences of the department store Santas. We missed her but loved seeing her growing success.

We talked on the phone several times a week, making sure the details of the wedding were in place. She assured us that everything would be wonderful no matter what, but I could still hear anxiety in her voice when she talked about Henry's family.

I couldn't blame her. June wasn't exactly making things easy.

June had overruled our choice of photographer, insisting that the one Scarlett recommended would be more appropriate. She was flying him up from Atlanta on the chartered plane with the guests. Then, after we negotiated a deal and reserved almost three dozen rooms for extra guests in Gaylord, June had left a long message on the answering machine explaining that she had reciprocal club privileges with the Grande Lucerne Resort and Spa across I-75. It was a little farther away than the hotel we had booked, and much more expensive, but she felt her guests would "appreciate the amenities."

"I am totally going to use the bubble bath tonight," Ian said, holding up a blue miniature bottle.

Mom snatched it from him. "Oh no, you're not. We need to make sure there are enough for the guests."

"How many guests do we have now?" Ian asked.

We all turned our heads to see a huge pile of unopened presents on the buffet that the mail carrier had delivered. Next to them was a stack of RSVP cards we had been marking off.

Charlotte and Henry had printed the most elaborate wedding invitations I had ever seen. They popped up like picture books with little white shapes of a sleigh and snow-capped hills beside the words *"Charlotte Adler and Henry Lowell invite you to share in their union, December 31, New Year's Eve."* Of course, June Lowell must have had a hand in it. And even though I wanted to say something snarky about everything June did, I had to admit the invitations were beautiful.

"We are at seventy-one out-of-towners and eighty-two locals." Mom said it with pride. The number was nowhere near the original four hundred or more guests who might have attended in Atlanta. Still, with every RSVP I felt a sense of panic.

"Well, I'm guessing that by now that is all we will get?"

"It should be," she said. "But you know how the cousins on your dad's side always plan at the last minute. I have a feeling they'll show up with kids and dates we don't know about."

"Hopefully we'll meet the dates we don't know about before they have the kids we don't know about," said Ian, wagging his eyebrows.

"You know what I mean, Ian."

"Well, I guess we could just put them up in the golf shack."

"Don't worry. June made sure to book extra rooms at the Grande Lucerne for her group. I am sure we will be fine either way. I just hope Nestor has planned enough food. Speaking of Nestor, don't forget to pick him up at the Traverse City airport. You should be leaving soon, Ian."

Ian patted his stomach. "Nestor is one person I would never forget."

Aunt Addie pushed open the double doors of the kitchen with enough force to make the walls shake.

"I still can't find them! I've looked everywhere!"

"What is that?" asked Mom.

"Those blasted Christmas decorations. I can't believe we misplaced them this year. Of all times to lose them."

Ian and I sent each other a stealth look of relief.

She still hadn't found them. Thank God!

The lost decorations included dozens upon dozens of figurines made of pasta, courtesy of Aunt Addie's "food craft" phase years ago. Macaroni reindeer, spiral swirl Santas, and even a crèche of penne, spaghetti, and shells, had been on display at the inn every Christmas since I could remember. They were so hideous that when Aunt Addie was gone one Saturday morning in November, Ian and I had snuck up into the attic and grabbed them out of the Christmas decoration bins. Now they were hidden where we hoped she would never find them.

Right now the inn was perfectly decorated. A giant white fir from a Christmas tree farm down the road dominated the main lobby. A smaller tree stood in a corner of the dining room. Garlands of pine and spruce draped over almost every imaginable doorway and the large stone fireplace. A new centerpiece rested on the table in the lobby, a Christmas gift for Mom, purchased from one of the fancy decorating catalogues she always admired but never ordered from. Even the grounds of the golf course were adorned with twinkling lights, thanks to Grady.

Ian and I were calling the tragedy of the missing decorations "Pastagate," which Aunt Addie said was insensitive.

"Maybe someone got hungry and cooked them," said Ian.

Aunt Addie put her hands on her hips and snarled, "That is not funny, young man! Do you know how many hours I put into making those? They've been a part of our Christmas for over twenty years, now."

She started on a familiar tirade about the importance of Christmas traditions and how our generation never appreciated them.

Ian looked at her with a straight face and interrupted. "Well, have you asked Al?"

"Al who?"

"Al Dente!" he said, lowering his eyebrows.

Aunt Addie reached out to hit him on the behind. He ran out of the room, giving her a wide berth. "I'm off to pick up Nestor. See you later," he called as he left.

Mom had a hand over her mouth, trying not to laugh. I had already given in. Aunt Addie swatted me on my backside since she couldn't reach Ian.

"You should never have been so easy on him, Virginia. That boy needs taking down a notch or two."

"Don't worry, I'm sure the decorations will show up next year," said Mom. As Aunt Addie turned away, Mom looked to me and mouthed "thank you."

The next day, clattering and banging came from the kitchen as Nestor organized himself. He had been busy prepping the kitchen since he arrived. Aunt Addie was yelling at Ian about the music blaring on the speakers in the dining room. And above it all, my Mom was shouting into the phone to her cousin who was on a runway in Chicago.

It was zero minus two days. Just in case I had forgotten, the calendar behind the desk reminded me that soon my little sister would become Mrs. Henry Lowell. I was looking forward to everything about as much as a root canal. I was going to smile and be the good hostess, but I dreaded the possibility that June and her friends would judge us. And even more, I couldn't help but feel that I was losing a little sister. Suddenly it all seemed so permanent.

And then I thought of Nick.

In my dreams last night, Nick had turned into the preacher marrying Charlotte and Henry. When it came time to read their vows they had pledged never to return to Truhart ever again. The wedding guests had cheered and laughed while Aunt Addie sat with the dogs on boxes of macaroni and cried.

I had to get out of the inn. Grabbing my old camera, I pulled on my coat and gloves and escaped the lobby through the back door.

Walking briskly, I made my way over the back nine and past the old golf shack. The frozen brown grass crunched under my feet and a few stray snowflakes drifted in the wind. I slowed as I passed the copse of trees where Nick and I had made out. I tried to find the exact place where he had pinned me against a tree, but it was impossible to remember. Taking my hand out of my glove, I ran my palm against a nearby tree. Sadly and irrationally I felt like the lack of evidence meant nothing had ever happened. We should have carved a heart into the bark and written our initials.

With no warning Lucifer, Mary Conrad's mischievous dog, appeared at my side. I reached down to pet him with my bare hand and he snatched the glove right out of my other hand.

"Lucifer!" I yelled. But he pretended he didn't hear me and ran up the slope toward the old barn.

I followed him up the ridge until I reached the barn. By then he was out of sight.

I looked around for Mary, the one person with any control over the mutt. She was nowhere to be seen. Distracted now, a curious impulse took over. A pile of firewood rested against the side of the barn next to the secret portal. I moved several logs out of the way. Then I kneeled down, lifted the loose board, and crawled through the opening while I awkwardly clutched my camera to my chest.

Once through, I stood up and let my eyes adjust to the light. Because of the low winter sun, the barn was darker today than it had been several weeks ago. Taking the lens off my camera and changing the settings, I aimed it up at the row of windows above the door. For several minutes I walked around the room taking pictures. Finally, I moved to the old saw. I removed the tarp and thought how depressing it looked sitting alone in the massive space, like a forgotten friend. It was beautiful in a vintage industrial kind of way. I shot it from several angles, trying to capture the dim light from the windows and something I couldn't quite describe. Rejection? Neglect? I guess I would have to wait until I looked at the way the photos turned out.

When I was finished I pulled the tarp back over the saw and made my way to the opening with a sigh. Charlotte and Henry would be arriving soon. It was almost show time.

I was on my hands and knees with my head through the opening when I stopped cold. Two black shoes appeared in front of me. With a sense of dread I felt a stab in my chest. I knew who the owner of those shoes was before I even looked up.

Chapter 13

"I had no idea there was a Masters of the Universe meeting today," said a deep, sarcastic voice.

I didn't even bother responding. Instead I scooted backward into the barn, hearing the bang of the loose board swinging into place. Damn.

I waited on my hands and knees. But there was only silence from the other side.

After a moment I lifted the loose board again, hoping by some miracle he had disappeared.

"Still here," Nick said. I couldn't see his face but I could see his shoe tapping the earth. His voice was drenched in ridicule and it fueled my anger. Was he going to make fun of me now?

Fine.

"Why don't you just go on back to that rock you crawled out from and leave me alone," I said loudly before slamming the board back in place.

"Excuse me, but isn't this Conrad property? Forgive me if I'm wrong, but I thought the person caught trespassing was the one who was supposed to leave," he yelled through the pine boards.

"I will leave if you go first," I shouted.

"No."

"What?"

"I said no. Look, Annie, you are acting like a child. Why can't we talk this out?"

"Spoken like someone who won't talk. You didn't even call."

"Call? Was that my job?"

"What did you want me to do, grovel over voice mail?"

I crossed my arms and leaned against the wall beside the opening.

I could outlast him. At least I was warm. He was outside in the bitter wind. Silence stretched between us. I could hear the muffled sound of him pacing back and forth.

"Oh, for God's sake, Annie. Get out here."

I said nothing.

"I really don't feel like getting down in the dirt and coming in after you."

Well, la-di-da. "Do you think it will make you look like a small-town hick if you get dirty?" I yelled.

Nick swore from the other side of the boards. Then I heard a shuffling sound and the board was lifted. His dark head appeared in the opening and I tried not to smile at how silly he looked trying to fit his big frame through the little opening without getting himself dirty.

When he was finally through, Nick stood up, brushing his clothes. I didn't feel the least bit guilty seeing the dust on his khaki pants and dark-colored sports coat.

"Are you happy now?"

"Yes," I said, crawling toward the opening. I sent one last glance his way and saw his mouth drop open in astonishment right before I edged out of the barn. I was much quicker than he had been, and when I reached the other side I grabbed one of the logs in the pile of firewood and jammed it up against the loose board, making it impossible for him to get out.

"Annie! Annie? What are you doing?" I heard him yell. Damned if I knew what I was doing. But it felt really good, whatever it was.

"This is silly, Annie. We need to talk!"

If we could get through this weekend without killing each other, I would be happy.

"Annie, are you just going to leave me like this?"

"You want to talk? That doesn't make sense since I'm the only one who ever does it. I'm tired of doing all the talking, Nick!" I yelled through cupped hands.

Then I turned and left.

I guess maturity had never been something I had excelled in.

I was out of breath and blowing steam from my mouth and nose by the time I reached the back patio of the inn. Just as I was about to open the door, Lucifer came tearing around the side of the patio wall with my gnawed-up glove in his mouth.

"It's too late to get back on my good side, Lucifer." He cocked his head and wagged his tail. Before I could grab my glove, Mary Conrad appeared from behind me with the other dogs. They barked and pushed each other out of the way in an effort to get my attention.

"Calm down, gang," said Mary as she reached the patio steps. "Finn, down!"

The senior member of the pack of black Labs wagged his tail and obediently sat in front of me. "Good boy," I said. The others followed suit, hoping to get praise as well, although not quite as calmly. Lucifer dropped the glove, expecting a treat.

"Don't open that door to the inn, Bump! Oh my gosh, your aunt would have a heart attack if these dogs got inside."

I moved forward and hugged her in greeting, trying to figure out the best way to tell her she needed to retrieve her son from the old workshop.

"Melissa and Jenny say hello, Annie. They'll be here Saturday. How was your Christmas?"

"Cold and snowless," I said. I stepped back and rubbed my hands together, stalling for time.

"I made the last few adjustments on your bridesmaid's dress and left it with your mom. Let me know if you need anything else," she said.

"Thanks. Uh, Mary?"

She went on speaking. "Well, the weather report says Chicago is supposed to get snow today, so I'm guessing it'll be here by Saturday. Charlotte will get her white wedding, I hope."

I reached down and patted Finn on the head and then shrugged my shoulders, "That would be nice . . . Say, Nick is back in the old workshop."

Her eyes grew big and she looked at me strangely, as if I was speaking a different language.

"What?"

"Well, he is in the old workshop . . . you know, the barn."

She put a hand to her lips. "He never goes in there anymore. I couldn't believe it when I saw him there a couple of months ago," she said in a soft voice.

I paused. Did Mary have the answer to the puzzle I had been trying to understand?

"Why?" I asked slowly.

She placed her hand on the small of her back and backed up until she was sitting on the low wall of the patio behind her. "Oh, Annie. It's a long story."

I moved to sit beside her. The dogs became restless and found their own entertainment in the bushes nearby.

"Nick would probably hate it if I told anybody."

"Well, I don't understand why he seems to hate coming home," I said.

She gave me a sharp look. "I didn't know anyone else even noticed."

"I sort of mentioned something about it to him in October."

"I'll bet he didn't like that," she said with a grimace.

"No. Not at all. We had a slight argument."

"I suspected something happened between you two. He was in a horrible mood after the art show." She looked at me with a strange gleam in her eye. "You always have managed to get a rise out of Nick."

I clutched my hands together, feeling my spirits rise.

She put her hand on my knee. "Russell dedicated his whole life to Truhart, you know, Annie. He worked night, day, and even weekends to build this town into what it is today."

I stayed quiet, hoping to understand where she was going with her thoughts. She looked up at the sky for a moment and sighed.

"Several months before Russell died, George Bloodworth promised Russell his biggest contract in twenty years. He and the city council commissioned a new project on Main Street. They called it the New City Commons. George and the rest of the county commissioners promised him that the project would be the showpiece that would get the economy and the town moving again.

"So, for the last few months of his life, Russell dedicated himself to a project that, as you can guess, never happened. I tried to tell him to stop working so hard, but you know how much of a workhorse he was. His blood pressure went up, he lost sleep, and he let himself go. By the eve of the project he had excavated the land, framed-out parts of several buildings, and hired ten new men. He ordered enough material to complete the job. Then the commission started changing their minds. Russell was in debt up to his eyeballs at that point. But he still didn't complain. Every phone call, every new meeting, brought a change from the commission. And then they canceled on him."

"I didn't know . . ."

"Nick was busy with his new career at the time. Russell would call him, but it seemed Nick could never talk. He had his own life, Annie. Russ never blamed Nick for that. But unfortunately, Nick blames himself terribly. We never talk about it, but I know he thinks he could have prevented Russell's stroke."

"I am so sorry."

"It was awful at his funeral. I knew Nick was eaten up by guilt. He blames himself for not being here, for not warning Russell not to get so involved in that damn project." Her voice shook on the last words and she lowered her head. The wind whipped across the patio and blew the last few brittle leaves of autumn into a corner near the door.

"You know, Nick still hates to come back home. I try not to give him a hard time about it. Maybe someday he'll find it in his heart to forgive George and the other commissioners . . . and himself."

"Don't you miss Nick though?"

"Oh, Annie. I see Nick all the time. That's not a big deal. We went on that cruise at Thanksgiving, and then Chicago at Christmas. In February he is flying with me to Phoenix to visit my sister."

"Really?" My face felt hot and I must have shown some discomfort because Mary put her hand on my forearm and laughed.

"Why, of course. I know he doesn't come back to Truhart, but he is so generous in other ways. He is renting me a condo in Phoenix for a month and even flying this brood out to join me," she said, gesturing to the misbehaved pack of dogs she loved so much. "Of course I won't see him more than a few days, but it will be so nice to be with my sister this year. Last year Nick sent both of us to a quilting convention in St. Louis. He teases me about my quilting, you know. But that's just for show."

The youngest dog was starting to dig in a dormant flower bed. "Get out of there, Lucifer!" she said, clapping her hands. But the rascal only put his ears back and wagged his tail. As Mary marched over to reprimand him I shivered and let her words register.

It must have been so hard for Nick to be home. Now that I thought about it, I remember how tortured he had been when we first entered the barn, and the look on his face when I had uncovered that old saw.

Mary was back, clutching Lucifer's collar and handing me the frayed glove. "I'm going to run the energy out of these guys, Annie. Tell your mom I'll call her. Don't hesitate to let me know if you need anything at all! It looks like I am going to have a full house. Not only will Nick and the girls be staying with me, but I am making room for any extra Adler cousins, just in case. Your mother put me on standby."

"Thanks for that, Mary," I said absently.

"No worries, we can put someone on a couch if we have to."

I was still lost in thought when Mary brought me back to the present. "So Nick is in the workshop? Well, that's actually a good sign, Annie."

I put the glove in my pocket, avoiding eye contact. "Well, he didn't exactly get there on his own."

"How's that?"

"I kind of, well . . . trapped him in there?"

"You what?"

I looked up and met her questioning eyes.

"Well, he followed me through that opening where a board was loose, and I used a log to block him from getting out. He's still in the barn. And I don't think he's too happy either."

For a moment she just stared at me, blinking. Then a slow smile spread across her face as she looked beyond me to the ridge. Snapping her fingers, she walked away with the dogs at her feet. Her laughter was lost in the wind long before she was out of sight.

Chapter 14

"Charlotte's here. She's here!"

After locking Nick in the barn, I was taking out my frustration on a pillow in room 204 when I heard Aunt Addie's voice calling out from the lobby. I flew down the stairs, and my heart lifted at the prospect of welcoming home my little sister. I wasn't the only one who was excited. Mom turned the corner from the kitchen, a dishrag still in her hands, and joined Aunt Addie in the doorway. Even Ian had picked up the pace from his usual lazy amble.

I passed the plaque on the wall that said *Where There Is Love There Is Life*, and quickly straightened it. *You would be so happy today, Dad.*

A shiny rental sedan sat in the circular driveway in front of the inn and we all cheered as Charlotte uncurled herself from the front seat. Henry held the door open for her and waved to us. They looked like movie stars with their chic sunglasses, leather coats, and their golden Las Vegas tans.

Aunt Addie clapped her hands and ran to embrace Charlotte. Her backside bounced up and down as she jiggled with excitement.

Mom waited patiently for her turn and she finally enveloped Charlotte in her arms. "Welcome home, honey."

Aunt Addie reached for Henry next and shook him up and down in an affectionate clinch. His lips looked like they were moving but his voice was inaudible.

Ian leaned against the opposite side of the large doorway from me, smiling at the expression on Henry's face.

"Should we rescue Henry?" I asked.

"No, he'll have to get used to it sometime," Ian said with a nod.

I stepped away from the door to greet Charlotte just as two luxury

SUVs pulled up behind the smaller rental. Through the glare of the low afternoon sun, I saw Scarlett Francis lean forward and look up at the inn. She said something to someone behind her and shook her head.

Kevin was behind the wheel of the third car and honked the horn as he pulled behind Travis. I could hear laughter and shouting from where I stood.

"Well, well. This is about as pretty as a picture, y'all," exclaimed Travis as he opened the car door for Scarlett. She paused, wrapping her arms around herself at the blast of cold air.

Charlotte helped June Lowell out of the car. How June could travel on a plane and still manage to look that way was beyond me. She was as elegant as the last time I'd seen her. With her high-heel boots, tight black pants, and midlength white-and-black leather coat, I had to wonder if the woman actually owned a pair of jeans. She shivered and raised her eyebrows. "Charlotte, honey, I don't know how you could stand this cold growing up."

Charlotte nodded. "Sometimes it's hard for me to believe it myself."

"Now, you aren't a Southerner yet, young lady," said Aunt Addie, clapping her hand on Charlotte's shoulder.

As Charlotte laughed and explained to June how cold things could really get, I was struck by her expression. She pointed to the inn, smiling as if she hadn't a concern in the world. But her smile was the same smile she used for the camera. Not the one I was used to.

The younger crowd—Bebe, Patty, Richard, and Kevin—greeted Mom and Aunt Addie. Brittany even seemed excited. With her hair slicked back in a ponytail, a red leather jacket, and dark denim jeans that fit her like skin, she reminded me of NASCAR Barbie. When Ian grabbed her suitcase she tried to hand him a dollar bill and he laughed in her face. She sucked in her breath and stood with her hand on her hip as Ian walked away with her luggage.

Most of the guests on the charter flight had gone ahead to the Grande Lucerne, while the immediate family and wedding party had driven to the inn. The ladies stood together, listening to Charlotte point out the landmarks, so I gave up on getting a word in edgewise and helped unload the suitcases from the trunk of Travis's SUV. I felt like the doorman.

"Oh no, wait a minute. Careful with that. Only me, please, only me," said a man I hadn't noticed, peering at Ian over the SUV's third-row seat as he tried to grab a large metal suitcase. *"Faites attention, s'il vous plaît."*

Ian stared with his mouth open as the red-faced man tried to wrestle the case from his grasp. Letting go, Ian looked to me for an explanation. The man with the strange accent clumsily grabbed the luggage as Ian and I stood uneasily, trying to figure out what to do.

Scarlett Francis stepped forward. "Only Alain handles his equipment. He doesn't want you to touch it."

Ian backed away from the overweight bald man and mumbled, "I don't want to touch his equipment, believe me."

Scarlett ignored Ian's comment and put her hand on the man's shoulder as he exited the car. "We will make sure they don't touch anything, Alain. *Ne t'inquiète pas.*"

He put a hand on his chest and leaned down to pull his cases forward. Now I realized who he was. I should have known by the accent and the freakishly pretentious attitude.

When Charlotte introduced him to us my suspicion was confirmed. "This is Alain, our wedding photographer." Charlotte turned to me and smiled enthusiastically. "Scarlett pulled all sorts of strings to get him. In fact, Alain rarely even shoots weddings. He is sought after for his work in the fashion and portrait industries these days." Charlotte put her hand on my arm and drawled, "He comes highly recommended."

Her words hung in the air and I did a double take, thinking Charlotte might have been using the words as a joke. I heard a snort nearby and knew Ian was thinking the same thing. He stared at her as if he was trying to figure out if she was still related to us.

Alain opened a metal suitcase and checked each piece to make sure we hadn't damaged anything. I watched him inspect each bag. Even from a couple of feet away I could tell that his photography equipment was top of the line. I felt the tips of my fingertips tingle at the thought of getting my hands on what I saw in those cases.

Charlotte introduced us as he continued to scan his precious lenses.

"And this is my sister Annie," she said as she finished up. "She studied photography once and she can help you with anything you need."

I doubted he even heard her. With my hands full of luggage now, I nodded. But Aunt Addie walked up and gave Alain a hearty pat on the back.

"Nice to meet you, Alan," she said.

"Alain, madame," he said, looking up for the first time.

"That's what I said, Alan. Welcome to the Amble Inn."

The man seemed to think better of correcting her and pursed his lips before closing his suitcase.

"Where's all the snow?" asked Jessica.

I had been wondering when someone was going to get around to that little detail.

"Well, honey, I know it looks kind of gray and cold right now. But the weather report says there is a front coming from the west. I'm sure there will be snow soon," said Mom.

"It was supposed to be a winter wonderland. It's almost New Year's and there's nothing? I can't believe it. I can't imagine what everyone will think when they show up for a winter wonderland and have this . . . this . . . gray, brown cold," said Charlotte with her bottom lip out. She looked just like she did when she was a little girl and didn't get the last Twinkie in the package.

Henry came up behind her and grabbed a suitcase from my hand. "Charlotte, I don't care if we have sleet, rain, snow, or sun. This wedding is going to be perfect," he said. I sent him a grateful look and he winked at me.

Mom ushered the group up the front steps and into the main lobby. Those of us who were porters followed. I put down the brown leather luggage and stared at the words "Louis Vuitton" written on the label. The piece looked bizarre sitting on our cheap green commercial-grade carpet.

June, Scarlett, and Travis looked around them in curiosity and I could feel the hair on the back of my neck stand up.

"Well, this is as cute as a button," Travis said. I tried not to flinch at the word *cute*. He raised an eyebrow. "Is that a golf course I see?" I slumped behind the luggage to avoid his gaze. I suppose I should give him back his hundred dollars. Richard laughed from the corner.

"What a lovely view," said June politely. She walked to the windows behind the open stairway and looked out at the back nine.

"I like those, uh, slipcovers," Brittany said before joining them at the window.

Aunt Addie watched her and then whispered in my ear, "That

girl's jeans are tight enough to see Lincoln smiling on the penny in her pocket."

I nodded and glanced around. For a moment it was just family standing together in the corner of the room. Mom, Charlotte, Ian, Aunt Addie, and me.

"It all looks like I've never been gone," Charlotte said, eyeing the room.

"Well, not exactly. There were a few changes," I said. "We spruced up the paint, and we have new curtains and a few other things."

"Oh, I didn't notice, Annie. It just always seems like nothing ever changes here." To Charlotte we must seem like figures in her old dollhouse. We were still in place right where she left us.

"Mom, you still have a towel over your shoulder." Charlotte laughed.

Mom looked down absently, "Oh, well, I guess it's always part of my wardrobe."

Charlotte walked over to her and took the towel. "You look like the maid," she said, shaking her head and throwing it behind the front desk.

"Well, are you ready to tie the knot? It's hard to believe you will be an old married woman," said Ian.

Henry overheard and walked toward us. "Don't give her any reason to change her mind. I can't believe she ever said yes. It took me months just to get a date with her and even then I needed help."

"Just another thing you owe me for!" a voice called from the doorway.

Nick.

Well, I suppose I should be glad about two things. He was out of the barn. And he wasn't carrying any lethal weapons. He stood in the doorway, outlined by the daylight behind him. As Ian and Henry rushed forward to greet him, I hung back, pretending to organize the luggage.

He greeted everyone in the room and never once glanced my way. Heat bloomed in my face as I realized that Nick was purposely ignoring me.

As I stood at the side of the lobby with my insides in a knot, Mom explained to everyone where they would be staying and how the rooms were arranged. June and Jessica, and then Scarlett and Travis, had the two largest guest rooms. Everyone else would be in rooms on the second floor. Tomorrow, when my cousins and aunts and uncles arrived, they would take the rest of the rooms on the first floor. That would make us full to the brim.

"Charlotte, wait until you see all the wedding gifts stacked in the dining room," added Aunt Addie.

"Oh, let's see," said Jessica excitedly, tugging on Henry's arm.

"Is it rude to open them now?" asked Charlotte.

Aunt Addie laughed. "It's rude if you keep me waiting."

I lifted Alain's extra camera bag off the floor just in time to avoid Aunt Addie's foot as she ushered Henry and Jessica down the hallway. Charlotte trailed behind.

"I suppose it would be all right if you could *aidez-moi*, mademoiselle," said Alain, pointing toward the largest piece of luggage in his pile.

I helped Alain gather his bags and tried to keep my pathetic gaze off of Nick. He and Ian had collapsed on the sofas by the fireplace.

"Gentle, gentle . . ." Alain said as I swung a camera bag around my shoulder. "*Doucement* . . . let me show you how to carry theez," he wheezed.

"Say, what language is that, Alan?" Ian taunted from his horizontal position.

"*C'est français*," said Alain.

Ian stared blankly at him and from the corner of my eye I could see Nick put a fist over his mouth. We both knew Ian had taken four years of accelerated French in high school and had spent a summer in Paris playing in cafés around Montmartre.

Alain looked down his nose at Ian and said, "French." Only the word sounded suspiciously like it was said with an American twang.

"You're from France?" asked Ian.

"No, but the language is like my own native tongue. It just spills from me and I don't even know I have shifted from English."

"Spills from you?" Ian looked at Alain's pants and then down at the floor.

"I have spent so many years there that it has become part of me," Alain corrected in a haughty voice. Then he turned and said, "*Ici*, mademoiselle."

I watched his back as he walked up the stairs, trying to remember from my own limited French what the word *ici* meant. Ian snickered as I trekked up the steps with the heavy bag. For some reason helping this pompous man as Nick watched from below made me feel lower than the day I'd had to caddy for Nick's senior prom date.

Ten minutes later I left Alain in his room, fretting in French over his equipment. I returned downstairs and helped Travis find the old ice machine and grabbed extra towels for June. I rounded the corner to the dining room, and stopped. Nick stood by the table stacked with presents, his head down as he said something to Ian. I hadn't had a chance to really look at him since he arrived home. Of course part of that was my own fault since I'd locked him in the barn. But now that he was busy, I could finally steal a moment to drink in the sight of him without being noticed.

Like the rest of the wedding party, his face was tanned from the Vegas sun. He wore an untucked light blue button-down and jeans. The stubble of a beard darkened the lower half of his face and I guessed he hadn't shaved since the day before. His hair was tousled, as if he had been caught in the wind or had run his hands through it repeatedly. If I had just met him I'd think he was relaxed and enjoying himself. But something in the clench of his jaw told me differently.

Nick looked up from his conversation and spotted me. He narrowed his eyes and a muscle in his cheek twitched. He took a deep breath, then blinked and looked back at Ian. I felt like nothing more than a smudge on the wall.

"Look at this, Annie," said Charlotte as she spotted me. She held up a large crystal bowl and Henry grabbed it from her.

"Charlotte and I think it would be great for popcorn. Hey, we could use it for the bowl games that are on during the reception. It's fancy enough for a wedding football game. What do you think? Right in front of the TV in the lobby, Annie?" He held the bowl out for me.

Ian spoke up, his voice tinged with familiar sarcasm. "You might want to keep it away from Bump, Henry. Ever since she cracked Aunt Addie's antique Waterford vase, she isn't allowed near anything fragile. I had to put the angel Gabriel and the shepherd on the mantel this year."

Ian and Charlotte laughed. That hurt since she knew the full story. Nick put his hands in his pockets and looked at the ceiling. In the old days he might have defended me against the two of them when they ganged up on me. Now, he just stifled a yawn.

Nestor had worked his magic and the aroma of veal scaloppini and morel mushrooms drifted from the kitchen. It was a special meal to welcome the arrival of Henry and his family.

Ian ignored the gifts Charlotte had unwrapped and was preoccupied with the food. "Hey, you've been helping Nestor in the kitchen, Bump. Ten dollars if you steal me a small plate. Charlotte was going to, but he won't suspect you."

I shook my head and declined. On any given day I was up for that kind of bribe. In fact, I made twice my allowance on Ian's bribes when I was growing up. But now I couldn't bring myself to take the bait.

"Since when do you refuse a challenge, and cash, Bump?" he asked.

I sent him a withering look. I wasn't in the mood for his games today.

Looking beyond Ian, I could see Nick leaning against a table, his gaze resting on me. Expecting to be confronted with his indifference again, I realized I had been mistaken. His dark eyes bore holes in me and I took a step back.

Nick wasn't just trying to avoid me. I was pretty sure he hated me.

I opened my mouth to say something, but realized Ian was still talking. "What's wrong, Bump? Changing your mind? Nestor won't care." He pulled a bill out of his pocket and dangled it in front of my face.

I shifted my gaze to Ian. Then I looked back at Nick. I couldn't stand the thought that he detested me. I didn't know what to say.

"I'm so sorry," I managed.

Nick pressed his lips together and looked away.

"I don't blame you for hating me." I couldn't swallow past the lump in my throat.

"It isn't that big a deal, Bump," said Ian quickly, panicking at the tears in my eyes.

I gulped, trying to keep myself from falling apart.

I couldn't see Nick's face anymore, but I heard him. "Annie . . ."

As an awareness of my actions this morning sunk in, something else inside me was taking shape. I was beginning to understand the full impact of my mistake.

Ever since the weekend in Atlanta I had hounded Nick for answers about why he never visited Truhart. I had accused him of ignoring his mother and caring more about himself than her loneliness. I had baited him. I had teased him. And I had locked him in the old barn. A place that haunted him.

Like an imbecile, I hadn't thought past my own worries. I had failed to recognize that this wonderful, caring man would never be cruel to anyone, especially his family. A sheet of icy perspiration grew at the back of my neck and I rubbed it away. I was too ashamed to stay.

I turned and rushed through the kitchen and out the back door to the annex. When I reached my bedroom I flung myself on my bed and curled into a ball. As I sat there surrounded by my old pastel wallpaper and sentimental belongings, images of my childhood rose before me.

I remembered all the times Ian and his friends had called me annoying names, broken my toys, and made fun of me for being a pesky little sister. But not Nick. If I fell off my bike, he had been the first to pick me up off the ground while everyone else laughed. When the boys stole my doll to use as Queen of the Damned in their superhero games, he had wrestled it away from them. Even if Aunt Addie was about to yell at me for using her curlers to build ramps for our Matchbox cars, Nick would say it was his idea.

But instead of thanking him for his protection, I had done things like throw sticks at him, or chase him when we played tag—even if I wasn't "it." I had spied on him when he swam in the pond, and stolen his towel before throwing it up to the highest branch of a tree.

I had stood near him at his father's funeral and watched a war I didn't understand play across his face. And then I had harassed him about not coming home, failing to recognize that his war was right here.

And now, I had accused him of being coldhearted. Of caring more about granite than his mother.

The truth was, even though I loved Nick with all my heart, I hadn't been kind to him.

Chapter 15

As the winter sun sank lower in the sky, I helped in the kitchen, hiding from the guests and Nick, and tried to pull myself together. I had been through worse. I had seen death and sickness and sorrow. Hell, I had photographed sorrow.

And Nick had never really been mine.

Somewhere in my girlish crush, I had failed to realize that he was more than just a hero on a pedestal. He was a man with complications and fears and all the messy things that people had in their lives.

I loved him even more for that.

But I didn't deserve him.

I stood at the sink and smoothed the apron at my waist. I took a deep breath. My sister was getting married in two days and there was so much more to think about than myself.

As if my thoughts had conjured her up, Charlotte swung open the door to the kitchen.

"Have you seen my wedding dress?" she asked. Her hair hung down over her eyebrow as if she had been pulling at it, and her eyes were round with panic.

"Your wedding dress?" I asked dumbly.

"Yes. My dress."

"You mean you can't find it?"

She turned from me in exasperation and I followed her as she ran to the lobby.

"Annie hasn't seen it. But it has to be here! Are you sure you didn't unload it somewhere?" she asked Ian, who was looking down at her warily. "Ian, my God, if this is your idea of a joke, I'll kill you. This isn't funny!"

Ian put his hands up. "I haven't seen it."

I looked out the open front doors and saw Henry and Nick searching through the backseat of the SUV. All the doors of the cars were open and Aunt Addie was yelling at them from the front bumper.

"It was in an oversize black bag with Bellasposa written on it," Charlotte said through the doorway.

"Maybe with that fancy French name the French guy thought it was his," said Aunt Addie hopefully.

"Bellasposa is Italian, Aunt Addie," said Charlotte, rolling her eyes in exasperation.

Mom entered the lobby, a worried look on her face. "Grady hasn't seen it. Charlotte? Didn't you see your dress at the airport?"

"Yes. They let me carry it on the plane for an extra fee. And I carried it off the plane."

Scarlett and June hurried down the stairs. "I've checked with Alain and he hasn't seen the dress since we were in baggage claim."

"Well, I know I saw it when we picked up the rental cars," said June.

"Me too," added Charlotte.

"Okay, that's something," said Mom, who stood with her arm around Charlotte. Charlotte had begun to breathe in frantic gasps and I reached out and rubbed her back to try to calm her as well.

"Where was the last place anyone saw it?" Mom asked.

The wedding party arrived in the lobby wearing looks of concern. They had searched their rooms and found nothing. Everyone agreed it had been on the curb when they were loading the rental cars. Nick and Henry returned from the cars empty-handed and shut the front doors. Nick cast a glance in my direction and I turned my head away.

"Charlotte," said Henry. "Did you put it in the SUV or the car?"

"I didn't put it in anything. I thought you did," she said.

"I didn't see it at all. I assumed you took care of it."

"It was by the car, Henry. You were handling the luggage. That was your job!" Charlotte's tone had reached a fevered pitch as she looked at Henry accusingly.

"You had been guarding it with your life the whole trip. Why would you just assume I was going to handle it because we were standing by a car?"

"Oh my God! I can't believe this is happening."

"It's okay, Char," said Nick in a soothing tone he might have used on me not too long ago. "We can call the airport and see if anyone has claimed it."

"That's right," said Travis Hartwick. "This kind of thing happens all the time. They have a place for unclaimed luggage and I am sure even wedding dresses end up there sometimes."

"We can even ask some of your cousins who are flying in tomorrow to double check when they get to the airport," said Henry.

"Tomorrow?" Charlotte looked at Henry like he'd lost his mind.

Charlotte, June, and Mom spent the next half hour making phone calls. "We will find it, honey. Don't worry," Mom repeated over and over.

I couldn't stand to watch Henry and Charlotte continue to blame each other, and it seemed neither could anyone else. We drifted away to various parts of the inn, occupying ourselves before dinner.

By the time we gathered at the table, everyone's good spirits were returning. Bebe, Patty, Kevin, and Richard joked about their trip to Vegas. And Henry teased a glazed-looking Charlotte about her sorry gambling skills.

I helped Nestor serve the meal. Earlier we had pushed several tables together so that we could sit at one long table, family style. It seemed like the right thing to do since this wasn't supposed to be a formal meal. Even so, Nestor had outdone himself.

Kevin closed his eyes after his first bite. "Wow, I'm in Nirvana. Thank God we didn't get delayed on our flight to Traverse City or we would have missed this."

"It's too bad we don't have a closer airport," Mom said.

"Hey, Nick," shouted Aunt Addie from the end of the table. "George Bloodworth has been talking about an airport for years. If we built ourselves something here nobody would have to use Traverse City's airport. You should talk to him about a design."

I was still putting plates on the table and as I passed her I put my hand on Aunt Addie's wrist. "Nick doesn't do that kind of thing, Aunt Addie." I could feel Nick's eyes on my face.

"Well, he might—

"No, I don't think so, but tell me—does Corinne's nephew still have a plane?"

Aunt Addie was easily rerouted as she talked about our local daredevil.

Finally, I sat down at the end of the table next to Jessica and opposite Alain and Aunt Addie. Between Jessica's lack of conversation and the way Aunt Addie seemed to enjoy mispronouncing Alain's name, I felt like I was sitting at the kiddie table. At the other end, Henry and Ian entertained everyone with their views on football while June and Scarlett name-dropped. Nick and Brittany sat together, their heads bowed in conversation. It must have been riveting, the way Nick nodded his head and gazed at her so intently.

The more lively the other end of the table grew, the quieter ours became. Aunt Addie seemed to have decided Alain wasn't worth her time because she turned her back on him and asked Nestor about morel mushroom hunting.

As for me, I barely had a chance to eat. Every time I raised my fork to my mouth someone needed something. I had just returned from the kitchen with a third helping for Travis, when Charlotte asked, "Can you get us some more water since you're up again, Annie?"

I moved to the sideboard and grabbed a pitcher. Making my way down the table, I refilled glasses while everyone continued their conversation. From the corner of my eye I caught Nick frowning down at his plate. Maybe he was finally bored with Brittany's chatter. Just as I approached him he put his hand over his glass.

"I can do that for myself, Annie," he said quietly, still staring at his glass. Brittany kept talking, but he didn't notice her.

"Sorry," I said, and moved on. Evidently just my presence in the same room irritated him. If this was the way he was going to be for the next few days, I didn't know how I was going to keep myself from falling apart.

By 11:00 p.m. only a handful of people were still awake. Earlier, Ian and Nick had taught the guys how to play euchre. Now Kevin, Ian, Henry, and Nick sat around the game table in the corner of the lobby and argued about their cards among empty beer bottles and cookie crumbs. Travis Hartwick and Scarlett Francis had signed on to WiFi and I was glad that a friend of Ian's had finally fixed it last month. They were buried in their laptop screens.

The shrill sound of the lobby phone made Charlotte jump. She answered it before the first ring ended. It was the airline. We waited impatiently for the news.

Two minutes later, she hung up the phone and clapped her hands. "They found my dress!"

A collective cheer went up around the room. In a bizarre turn of events, her dress had ended up in Houston, of all places. The airline was flying it back to Traverse City and it would be in Truhart by tomorrow night.

"Damn! I was looking forward to seeing you in Annie's ugly old prom dress," said Ian. Charlotte threw a sofa pillow at him. Nick caught it in midair as it missed its mark and re-aimed, hitting Ian on the head. I tried not to stare like a sick puppy as Nick laughed at Ian. It was one of the few times he had smiled since dinner.

"Well, it looks like you might have some more luck, Charlotte, honey," said Travis, staring at his computer. "The weather report says Michigan is going to have a little snow tomorrow."

Scarlett laughed. "If that's the weather report from the GATE Network, they always get things wrong. It will probably rain."

"That means there could be ice," said Mom as she rose to go to bed. "Ian, did you get the new bag of sidewalk salt out of the golf shack like I asked?"

"Mom, I'll do it tomorrow. I'm beat," said Ian. The game had just finished. He threw his cards on the table in defeat. Losing always made him crabby.

"I asked you three times—"

"I'll do it," I said. "But you owe me, Ian."

I could use the cold air and a good walk.

"See you all tomorrow," said Nick as the rest of the card players said good night. He flung on his coat and found his keys in his pocket, not once looking my way. He bent down and kissed Charlotte on the cheek. "Glad you found your dress, Char."

When Nick closed the front door, the remaining group needed little encouragement and trudged off to bed. It had been a long day for the weary travelers, and tomorrow was a big day, with the rehearsal dinner and last-minute preparations.

Slipping into my coat and gloves, I grabbed the keys to the golf shack and flipped on the outdoor lights to help me see my way. It wasn't far from the house. But the moon was behind the clouds and the night was darker than usual.

When we were little, we always begged my parents to let us host sleepovers in the golf shack. My father would guide us to the shack with a flashlight and make sure we were settled before heading back to the inn. One of our favorite pastimes was to play truth or dare. The most terrifying dare was to run back and forth between the shack and the house in the dark of the night without a flashlight.

When I reached the shack I pulled my hands out of my gloves and unlocked the door. I flipped the light switch and the bulb flickered and cracked before it went out. Great. I felt my way to a low table in the corner and turned on a small camp lamp. Its dim glow cast shadows in the room that reminded me of all the nights we had conjured up shadow monsters on the wall with our hands.

Two old couches sat across from each other with a low table between. Near the doorway was an old refrigerator where we kept sodas and beer for hot days on the golf course. I moved a pile of boxes in the corner and cleared away the extra golf clubs and shoes that were piled up. I searched until I located several bags of rock salt tucked between a box and the refrigerator. I grabbed one that was half empty. I hoped we would need it. With its rustic charm, the inn looked its best in the winter. A pretty snow would be perfect for Charlotte's New Year's Eve wedding.

I turned to leave and bumped into a dark form.

I screamed.

Or at least I thought I did. What came out was more like a hiccup. It took me a moment of hyperventilating panic to realize who stood in front of me.

Chapter 16

The dim light cast a glow on half of Nick's face, making him look like a character in an old B horror movie. His shadow lurking on the wall was twice as large as my own and his hand was braced on the wall in front of me, blocking my path to the door. The half of his mouth I could see was turned up in the corner. He was obviously amused at my funny scream.

"You scared me to death, Nick."

"Really?"

I waited for an explanation, but he said nothing.

"What are you doing here?"

"Wondering if I should lock you in and leave. Would that make us even, Annie?"

I looked beyond him to the doorway. Would he be that vindictive? He tilted his head and crossed one leg in front of the other as if he was enjoying my fear.

"Only if you tell my mom about it," I said. "I mean, that's what I did. Told yours you were locked in . . . so . . . so, you should be fair." I clutched the bag of salt to my chest, wondering halfheartedly if it would be a decent weapon. Nick would never hurt me. But he was mad at me, after all.

"Hmm. You know, I would hate to wake up your mom," he finally said.

He stood up straight, removing his hand from the wall, and took a step forward. Feeling like a stalked animal, I took a step backward.

I juggled the bag in my arms and held up a hand. "Okay, I know I deserve your anger. In fact, I have a lot to apologize for."

"Why does it seem like you are always apologizing, Annie?"

"Because I feel like I do a lot of stupid things."

He took another step toward me and grabbed the bag from my arms. Putting it on the floor, he straightened up and asked in a soft voice that sounded like a caress, "Why is that?"

Without my salt-bag shield I felt defenseless. I crossed my arms and tried to figure out how to explain myself. He reached out and ran his hand down my shoulder until he reached my elbow. Then he grazed my forearm and tugged until my arms loosened. He was closer now, so close I could feel his breath on my face. His eyes glittered like black diamonds in the lamplight and I couldn't look away. His fingertips stroked my limp arms and moved to my waist. I was having trouble concentrating.

But what I had to say was important. I couldn't be distracted.

I raised my hands to his chest, which was a big mistake. It was the only enticement he needed to wrap his arms around my back.

This wasn't what I expected. Was he actually trying to seduce me? "Hang on a minute, I thought you were mad."

He bent his head until his mouth nuzzled my neck. He smelled of pine and soap and something else. I breathed deeply and tried to collect my scattered thoughts. But with the prickly feel of his chin against the soft skin of my neck, I couldn't concentrate.

"I decided to forgive you . . ."

"Nick, wait, I have so much I want to say . . ."

"Shit, Annie, why are you always talking?" He moaned, and then he bit my ear.

One hand moved away from my back and brushed over my chest. I could feel my nipples responding. His hand at my back pulled me close.

Then he lowered his head and kissed me. But the word *kiss* was a feeble description. The moment his lips met mine was pure combustion. Every touch, every kiss, was like a rocket blast. I would have screamed if my mouth wasn't so busy trying to breathe in between kisses.

I fought to get to his skin as my hands traveled under his shirt and tried to pull it off. What started out eager turned frantic. Our hands tangled as we fumbled to remove each piece of clothing. We couldn't stop. His touch was like a drug that magnified my sensitivity. I wrapped my legs around him and pulled his hips closer. He lifted me toward him and groaned.

His mouth trailed down my body, scorching a path along the way.

I ran my hands through his hair and he looked up at me, his hair mussed and his eyes unfocused.

"Annie, I don't know if I can stop . . ."

"I don't want you to."

I pulled him back and shivered as his tongue flicked across my nipple and then tugged harder. Nick mumbled against my breast, "Are you cold?"

I shook my head. It wasn't the cold that made me shiver. But he slowed his pace for a moment and lifted me up, placing me on the couch and covering me with his body. I arched against his weight, wanting him closer, and smoothed my hands over his shoulders as my tongue explored his mouth. His smooth chest with its thin layer of hair rubbed against my wet nipples, making me crazy. I bent my head and bucked, pushing him up so I could trail my mouth down his body. He froze and then shuddered. I kissed his nipples and I heard him gasp, trying to catch his breath above me. He pressed his lower body into mine and I opened up to him.

I reached down and ran my hands around him, overwhelmed with anticipation. He took several jerking breaths, "God, Annie, that feels so good, but you have to stop or I'll—"

I stroked him again, loving the fact that I could make him lose control. He tried to pull my hand away.

Giving up, he moved his fingers lower, sliding them up my leg until they were inside me, making me cry out and loosen my hold on him. My teeth sank into his shoulder. He kept teasing me with his fingers, lightly stroking and then plunging. When he finally removed his hand, I protested. But he kissed me and slowed his pace. He took a deep breath and propped himself on his elbows, positioning himself between my parted thighs until he was pressed against me. His face glowed above me in the low light. Our eyes locked and I clutched both of his hands in mine. He moved forward slowly. Like steel on velvet, until he was all the way inside me.

I sighed just a little at how exquisite it felt to be connected like this. But then he ground against me, making me cry out at the explosion of pleasure that radiated through me. I smiled up at him an answered invitation and he looked down, surprised at my response. Every thrust, sent me into a sensual haze.

Finally we reached the peak together. Clinging. Sweaty. Struggling for breath. And calling out each other's names in wonder.

I lay in the crook of Nick's shoulder, one arm draped over him, watching the rise and fall of his chest. Our breathing had returned to normal and Nick gently caressed my shoulder. His eyes were closed and I smiled as his hand moved slower. He was falling asleep.

"I know you don't want me to talk, Nick. But there is something I have learned about you and me that I want to say."

"Annie, every time you open your mouth I'm afraid."

"But that's just the point. I realized today how terribly I've treated you."

"Trust me, I don't even notice it anymore," he mumbled.

"Nick, this is important." I took a deep breath and started. "I was always chasing you and bugging you when we were growing up. And you were always so nice to me. I still don't know why. And since this whole wedding between Charlotte and Henry, I've been even worse. I didn't understand how upsetting it was for you to come home. When I ran into your mom this morning she told me how guilty you felt about your father's death and what happened with the county commission."

"She shouldn't have said anything to you."

"Well, I forced her into it. Don't blame her. I was trying to understand why you never came home—and I get it, Nick. I mean, I would be totally pissed at George Bloodworth and everyone else in this town too, if I were you." I reached up and traced my finger along his brow. "I'm sorry. I really didn't have a clue what was going on."

"Well, how would you? In case you didn't notice, sharing my feelings isn't exactly my strong point."

A gust of wind rattled the windows. Nick leaned down and grabbed our coats from the floor nearby and draped them across us. I wasn't cold, but it felt nicer under the coat. Like a glowing ember after a bonfire. He was silent as his gaze strayed to the ceiling. He took a breath. I lay my hand on the side of his head and stroked his temple.

"Dad must have called me a dozen times that fall and winter to talk to me about the project, but I barely listened. I was wrapped up in my own career and all the projects our firm was designing. Truhart's buildings seemed so insignificant compared to all the skyscrapers we were working on." He turned to me. "So you weren't wrong when you accused me of caring more about granite than my own family. I treated my dad like that."

I hated how he turned my words back on himself. I wished I had never said them. Burrowing underneath the coat, I sank back and sighed. "Oh, Nick, don't—"

He moved his lips to the corner of my mouth and hushed me. His lips traveled toward my ear and then the tender skin of my neck. I savored the feel of them.

Then he said into my neck, "Don't think you're off the hook now, Annie. Especially after locking me in the barn."

I closed my eyes as Nick ran his tongue along my collarbone.

"Was it awful? Being in there so long?"

"No." He lifted his head and I saw a smile spread across his face. "Actually, I ended up wandering around checking out the old equipment again. Did you know the heater and the plumbing in the bathrooms are still working? Nothing has been running for years in that barn and everything just started right up as if it had been turned off overnight. That place is more solid than most new buildings. Damn, my dad was a great builder!"

"Like father, like son."

I climbed on top of him, ran my hands up his chest and pressed my hips against him. "I just noticed how good you are at keeping your equipment running too."

It was a while before we were able to talk again.

I would never think of the golf shack in the same way.

Much later, we were back under the mound of coats.

"Annie?"

"Huh?" I had collapsed on top of him, too exhausted to move.

"I was just wondering . . ." he said in a groggy voice, his mouth buried in my hair.

"What?" I could barely keep my eyes open.

"Is that a box of macaroni reindeer next to the couch?"

Chapter 17

My bedside alarm clock went off at 6:00 a.m. like it always did. But this morning felt anything but normal. I lay in my bed, holding my old camera, and stared at the faded floral wallpaper and discolored pictures taped to my headboard. I was tempted to pinch myself but afraid I might discover I had been dreaming. Everything was where it had been the day before, yet the world had shifted. In the dim light before dawn, I touched my face and trailed my hand down my body. My lips felt swollen. My body seemed new to me. My skin felt as if a new layer of nerves had been added overnight. I moved my hand back to the familiarity of the camera. I couldn't seem to wipe the smile off my face.

In the early hours of the morning, Nick had walked me back to the house. A gentle snow had started to fall and we lingered over snowflakes and kisses. When I finally fell into bed I slept like a baby. I might have had only a few hours of sleep, but I didn't feel it.

Little girls dreamed of princes in white gleaming castles. Big girls dreamed of passionate kisses, candlelight and roses. But I had always just dreamed of Nick. Last night as we made love for the first time, spread out on an old plaid couch in the golf shack, I realized that reality beats dreams any day.

As much as I wanted to linger and relive last night in my head, I knew Nestor and Mom would be working on breakfast. I showered and dressed, trying to focus on the busy day ahead. But all I could think about was the night before. Taking one quick look in the mirror, I stopped and stared.

At five foot ten, I had always felt like an awkward stork. But this morning, as I looked closely, I saw a different person reflected in the mirror. My wide hazel eyes and arching brows seemed more exotic.

The color in my cheeks emphasized high cheekbones that I never knew existed. There was no need for lipstick on my bruised lips. Even my hair, which was always just dark blond to me, came alive in burnished honey tones. For the first time I felt, well, beautiful. I turned my head back and forth and wondered if this was what Nick saw.

A smile still lingered on my face as I entered the kitchen.

"Is Charlotte up yet?" asked Mom, her back to me as she poured water into the coffeemaker.

"No. Her door was still closed. You know she can sleep forever," I said. I waved at Nestor, who was swirling a crepe in a pan. Beside him was a stack of crepes he had already made and two large bowls of berries.

"Well, I guess she needs her sleep."

"You never say that about me," said Ian as he opened the door from the dining room. His hair stuck straight up and once again he hadn't shaved. Of course, it made no difference to his looks. For some reason, dishevelment suited Ian.

"Because you sleep all the time," Mom answered. "Charlotte has to get up for that morning show every day at four."

"That's bedtime for me when we've got a gig. So my sleep is important too. I sleep during the day to catch up for *not* sleeping at night."

"Stop whining, Ian. It makes you sound like a wimp," I said. He picked up a strawberry from the bowl on the counter and threw it at me.

"Virginia, if you don't keep this young man out of the kitchen, I'm going to hop on the next plane to Key West," said Nestor.

I was pretty sure he was only half joking. So was my mother, because she threw Ian a frown. "You better get the shovel out and start working on the steps. I have a call into Don Cooly to make sure we get the snow plow down our road and up the driveway several times today. This snow makes me nervous."

For the first time I looked out the window. My curtains had been closed this morning and I had been too lost in my own world to notice the weather. The sky was still dim, but there was a glow on the horizon and I could see the reflection of white on the ground. Last night's gentle snowfall had turned into something else entirely. I moved to the kitchen window to get a better view while Mom and Ian trailed behind me.

"I guess Charlotte will get her wish," Mom said.

"She might get more than that," said Ian.

Thick flakes of snow the size of cotton balls fell at an alarming rate. A blanket of snow already coated the branches of the blue spruce trees next to the inn, and as I looked farther toward the front parking lot, I realized that the snow completely covered the rental cars that had arrived yesterday.

My mother shook her head. "The weatherman on the GATE Network says this is just a dusting of snow. They should fire that man."

"What do the local guys say?"

"The local radio station says this is the first winter storm of the season. It's moving slowly right now. But the worry is that if it stalls over the state, we're going to get a lot of snow."

I turned to my mom. "How much is a lot?"

"Two feet or more."

"Don't tell Charlotte!" Ian and I said in unison.

Not much later, as I set out breakfast dishes, I heard a commotion. The sound of the front door opening and closing and men talking drew me to the lobby. Ian stood in his snow-caked boots and coat just inside the front door, looking puzzled. Two men were in the process of shaking the snow from their hair and coats as they stood, surrounded by cases and bags.

I almost swore out loud.

She didn't!

"We're staying at the Grande Lucerne and we thought we would come out here early this morning to film some of the pre-wedding activities." I couldn't remember the man's name, but I remembered his face from the bridal salon. He turned, recognizing me as well. "That snow is falling like crazy. We almost ended up in a ditch."

My heart dropped to my feet and I clutched a chair. Ian looked at me with concern. The crew introduced themselves and shook Ian's hand. Ian still looked perplexed as he put his gloves back on. I pulled myself together and took their coats.

"It looks like the wedding is going to be part of *The Morning Show*," I said through gritted teeth.

Ian grinned. "Really?"

Of course Ian would think this was great. I wanted to kick some sense into him, but he was already busy telling the guys where to go. "Go get yourselves some coffee. Everyone will be eating in the dining room and you can set up there. Later we'll be enjoying some of the local talent."

Oh great. I knew what he was thinking. When they were out of earshot I pointed my finger at Ian. "This is *not* fun and games, Ian. I can't believe Charlotte would allow her wedding to be broadcast on TV."

"Why not? Everyone does it these days. What's the big deal? I kind of like the idea. America can watch a wedding on TV and eat their cornflakes at the same time. Cool." He put his hands up in the air and started singing as he made his way out the door and back into the snow.

While the camera crew set up in the dining room, I found my mom standing in the kitchen talking on the phone. "Let's just hope they're wrong, Mary. If you don't mind, maybe Nick can come over and help with things."

I listened with one ear as I helped Nestor finish breakfast. Thinking of Nick made me daydream all over again. I wondered if we would ever wake up together and do the kinds of things couples did, like sipping coffee in bed, reading the paper, and then, well . . .

"Oh my God! Have you seen it out there?" My dream bubble popped the minute I heard Charlotte's high-pitched voice.

"Charlotte's up, I gotta go," Mom told Mary.

When she hung up, Mom smiled. "Hi, honey. It looks like your wish for snow is going to happen," she said too brightly.

"But there's so much. Is it going to slow down?"

Mom walked over and hugged her. "No worries. The weather report says this is just a dusting." She turned the volume up on the old TV in the corner on the kitchen counter so Charlotte could see the weekend edition of *The Morning Show*. Not a single snowflake showed up on the brightly colored weather map. The weatherman finished his report and smiled before the map faded from the screen.

Mom placed a cup of coffee in Charlotte's hands. "See," she said.

Charlotte didn't look overly convinced as she watched the weatherman join the weekend anchors on the couch. "'Don't forget, next week we'll bring you Charlotte Adler's wedding highlights from the great North. Sorry there's no snow up there for New Year's after all. I guess it won't be a white wedding . . . ahem.'" He laughed at his stupid pun. "'But we wish you the best of luck anyway, wherever you are, Charlotte!'"

Mom put her hand on her hip and turned to Charlotte. Charlotte took a long sip of coffee.

"I was just going to say, uh, it looks like your camera crew is here," I said, breaking the silence.

Charlotte sent us a guilty look. "I guess I forgot to tell you." She had forgotten to tell us many things lately.

"Why would you do this?" Mom asked.

"The network thought the wedding would be a great story. It's not a big deal, really. There are two cameramen who will be filming. It's really no different than having someone videotape the wedding. People do that all the time." She saw the way my mom clamped her lips shut and rushed to explain. "It's an idea Scarlett has been really hot on. You know, small-town girl comes home and gets married. Scarlett says that since my name and face are becoming more and more recognizable as part of *The Morning Show* team, this would be a great way to promote me. She told me this could even get me a spot as a substitute anchor."

"Televising your wedding will promote your career?"

"No. It's not like that, Mom. It's just part of the television personality thing. The audience relates to me. Everyone wants to feel part of the wedding."

"But you didn't even talk to us about it."

"I—"

She was interrupted by the voice of June Lowell. "Good morning." June stood by the swinging door of the kitchen. She took in her first glimpse of the kitchen and looked around with interest. "Well, isn't this just the homiest place?"

Mom turned to her with a smile pasted on her face. "Well, it's not as fancy as most big restaurant kitchens, but it has everything we need." She gestured around the room to the large industrial stove, the eight-foot counter, the farmhouse sink with the large picture window framed by cheery yellow curtains, and raised her chin.

"Will you be able to handle all the wedding food tomorrow night?" June looked a little panicky.

Nestor turned from the sink. "We might be busier than a stump full of ants, but we don't need no fancy kitchen."

I tried not to laugh at the alarm in June's eyes.

"Don't let Nestor fool you, June," said Charlotte, ruining Nestor's fun. "He is going to have plenty of people and some extra equipment to help. We employ lots of local aspiring chefs for special occasions like this." The words rolled off her tongue, sounding as convincing as a veteran politician. Our local aspiring chefs were teenagers and a few bored grandmas who needed extra spending money.

Charlotte escorted June into the dining room and I knew her well enough to recognize a retreat. It was obvious she didn't want to explain anymore about the filming. When the door swung closed I put my hand on Mom's shoulder and looked closely at her for the first time. She was pale and there were circles under her eyes.

"Are you okay?" I asked.

She ran a hand over her eyes. "I'm fine. Absolutely fine." Then she turned away. Something in the way she carried herself worried me. My memories of the weeks after Dad's death came back to me. I hadn't been able to get her out of bed, much less eat.

This wedding was putting too much stress on her. I clenched my fists and vowed to keep things running smoothly for the next two days.

The guests gathered in the dining room while we served a light breakfast of crepes, fruit, cereals, and breads on the long buffet. By the time the last of the wedding party was finished eating, the camera crew was set up in the corner. I was too busy to worry about the snow, or the film crew, or my mother's tired eyes as I ran plates back and forth to the kitchen and tried to make sure coffee was flowing hot.

"Hello, everyone!" said a familiar, piercing voice. "We rode over to see how things were going."

I looked up to see Marva and Corinne standing in the doorway of the dining room, their snowsuits on, their snowmobile helmets in their hands, and big smiles on their faces. They hugged Charlotte with gusto, then looked around the room, zeroing in on Scarlett.

No one was fooled. This wasn't a casual drop-in. They gazed at Scarlett Francis with fanlike adoration in their eyes.

Mom introduced them to everyone and after quick nods they dumped their helmets, tore off their suits, grabbed seats across from June and Scarlett, and made themselves comfortable. June and Scarlett's eyebrows were almost lost in their hairlines as they stared at Marva's green sweater covered in cherries, and Corinne's penciled-in black eyebrows and over-bleached hair.

"So, what was Tom Cruise really like when you interviewed him last winter?" I heard Corinne ask Scarlett.

"He's old news, Corinne," Marva interrupted. "I want to hear about that actress who had the wardrobe malfunction at the Academy Awards. Don't you think that was a publicity stunt?"

Mom and I were clearing the last of the serving dishes when Charlotte walked over and put her hand on Mom's arm. "Mom, isn't there some way you can get rid of them?"

"Now, honey, they're harmless. Just let them get it out of their system. Scarlett must know how to field those types of questions, after all. Why don't you relax?"

Charlotte shook her head and frowned. "I can't." She moved closer to the table and hovered, wringing her hands. Several times she tried to change the subject and failed miserably.

Alain stopped me as I poured him more coffee. He had just started his third pastry. "I will need some extra help today and tomorrow. Your sister says you will be a good assistant."

"Of course. Just let me know when you need me." I tried to be polite.

"*Merci*, mademoiselle."

I turned around and bumped into a broad chest. The room fell away from me.

"Good morning," Nick said. His cheeks were red and I could still see snowflakes on his eyebrows. I felt heat rush to my face and wondered if he could feel it where he stood. The gleam in his eyes made me want to run my hands along his naked skin all over again.

"Good morning," I said. For a moment we just stood there grinning. Travis Hartwick walked up and slapped Nick on the back.

"Pretty as a picture out there, isn't it? But colder than a witch's tit, I'll bet. Heh, heh. Gotta say, I am glad we don't have to deal with this kind of weather in Atlanta."

Aunt Addie rose from her seat at June and Scarlett's table, where she had been listening to the gossip. "It might be a little cold here, but I'd rather have snow than deal with your hot summers. Honestly, Atlanta was hotter than a goat's butt in a pepper patch when we were there," she yelled across the room.

Alain choked on his pastry. Moving faster than I thought possible, Aunt Addie rushed up to him and whacked her hand on his back. "You okay, Alan?"

You could put Aunt Addie in the palace with the queen and she would act the same way she did in the grocery store.

The sounds of a piano chord filled the room and I stifled a moan. The crew finished running sound and light checks, and as if on cue, Ian tried to make the most of it. When he opened his mouth to sing Charlotte flew across the room and grabbed his wrists.

"Not now, brother dear," she said through gritted teeth.

"But I'm just warming up," said Ian.

Henry and Mom pulled them off each other and the morning went downhill from there.

I barely had a moment to speak with Nick as I found myself running races around the inn. I cleaned up breakfast, double-checked the details for tomorrow's wedding meal, helped our two temporary housekeepers find extra linens and supplies, and trailed after Alain as he scouted out backgrounds for wedding pictures. At one point he and I trudged through the snow and wind, trying to get the right angle on the back of the inn, which he wanted to use as the background for some kind of artistic pose he had planned. I didn't know how he thought he was going to get the ladies to stand in the snow in three-inch heels, but every time I made a suggestion, he shook his head as if I had no idea what I was doing. After a while I kept my mouth shut. My feet were getting numb and my arm ached from holding his clear umbrella over his head to keep the camera dry. I rolled my eyes later when he said "*Voilà!*" to my original camera angles as if he had figured it all out on his own.

When we returned to the inn and shook the snow off our coats, we found Nick and Travis Hartwick sitting in the lobby surrounded by paperwork. Brittany sat beside Nick on the couch. She was so close that I wanted to pry her off with a crowbar. She looked glossy and fresh in a white ribbed turtleneck, black jeans and boots. Her perfectly plucked eyebrows rose as she looked me up and down.

I was pretty sure my earlier glow had worn off hours ago. I pulled off my old knit ski hat and my static-filled hair clung to my face. My armpits were moist from trudging through the snow and my nose was wet.

Nick frowned at me. I must have looked like his mother's dog, Lucifer, after a romp in the pond. I shook out the umbrella and Alain handed me his coat before collapsing on the couch.

"*Je suis fatigué!* Can you dry off my camera bag and make sure to put my equipment someplace safe, mademoiselle? I don't want anyone playing with it while I rest," he said.

"Annie—" Nick said. I looked over, but before he could finish, Travis interrupted him with a comment about the building codes in some business district. Whatever they were discussing, it sounded important. Nick was pulled back into the discussion. I hung up the coats and decided to take the camera equipment into the back office where it would be away from Aunt Addie and Marva's clumsy feet.

The office was dim when I entered and I didn't see the pile of boxes near the desk. I tripped over them, almost dropping my precious cargo. Setting the equipment down, I let my hands linger over the camera case. With reverence and only a little guilt, I opened the clasp and lifted the lid. For a minute I just ogled. I used to dream of lenses and filters like these. I lifted the camera from where it was nestled in gray foam and slowly brought it to my chest, measuring the delicate balance in my hand. The Nikon was first-rate and one of the most expensive on the market. I removed the cover and lifted it to my eye. Pleasure passed through my pores at the power I felt, holding that beautiful piece of equipment in my hands. But something akin to torment got the best of me. I set the cover back on and tucked the camera away. I would never own anything like that in a million years.

When I turned to leave I stopped to pick up the overturned box I had tripped over. Still thinking about the way the camera felt in my hands, I almost missed the words written on the pages in front of me. "Terms of Sale."

I looked more closely. There must be some mistake. I flipped on a light switch and looked again. All of a sudden my legs gave out and I sat down on the floor to reread the page. It took a while for the words to sink in. I couldn't believe it. Feeling light-headed and short of breath, I rifled through the rest of the documents.

Inside the box were bills and notices warning of a possible foreclosure on the inn. Paper-clipped documents on top outlined the terms of sale to a commercial real estate agent whose name I recognized. The agent was known around the county for reselling property to bargain-basement land developers. That explained the surprisingly low price. It was a steal by any measure.

I knew I shouldn't be surprised. This was what my mother warned me could happen. But somehow I hadn't expected it to be so soon. Our home—our livelihood—was being sold right out from under us. And what was worse, the foreclosure notices pointed to the fact that Mom had little choice in the matter.

No wonder Mom looked ten years older this morning. The dates on the documents indicated they had all been drawn up in the past week. She had been keeping this a secret in order to spare us the worry during the wedding celebration.

As Ian and I had been buying bedsheets, centerpieces, and designer shampoo, thinking we were helping, Mom had been dealing with a landslide of bills.

How could I have been so naïve?

I looked around me and felt an overwhelming sense of helplessness. For Mom, Aunt Addie, and our family—this was everything. The inn had been owned by Adlers for four generations. It was our home, our livelihood. And for me, well, I couldn't imagine life without it.

As a child I took my first steps behind the front desk, played tag down the hallways in the winter, and chased geese along the links of the golf course. I knew the inn like the back of my hand. I had committed to memory the trademark cookie and pastry recipes we prided ourselves on baking fresh every weekend morning. Like Aunt Adelaide, I could make a bed in thirty seconds flat, and sanitize a bathroom in less than ten minutes. Most people would have thought that was a pitiful thing to be proud of, but Aunt Addie actually timed me one summer.

I wanted to grab the documents and throw them outside in the snow. I couldn't let this happen. This would have killed my father.

Chapter 18

As I tackled the endless list of tasks for the wedding it seemed like I was dragging a hundred extra pounds around my neck. I felt like I was looking at everything through the wrong end of a telescope and I found myself unable to focus.

Suddenly the wedding details seemed unimportant. Trivial.

But conversations about the snow and the wedding dominated the day. In light of the snow, it was decided that the flowers and cake should be brought to the inn earlier rather than later. Fortunately the cake was ready to be transported to the inn. It took a while, but with the help of two men from the bakery, we were able to set the cake up in the corner of the dining room. It was simple and elegant. Charlotte worried it was too small, but Mom assured her there was plenty to feed an army.

When the van with the flowers arrived, Ian, Nick, Kevin, and Richard helped unload. Mom stood at the door, opening and closing it on the gusting snow.

"Oh, they look beautiful, don't they?" she said, clapping her hands. I could only nod, afraid my voice wouldn't make it past the permanent lump in my throat. I couldn't look her in the eye. She knew me so well she would guess what I knew.

"What do you think?" she asked Charlotte, who stood beside us.

"Are we going to put anything else around them, like candles, or are they just going to go on the table with nothing?" Her words woke me from my haze. I looked at Charlotte and wondered if she knew how she sounded.

Mom didn't even notice. "We'll have tea lights around them."

"Oh, that will be nice," Charlotte said. But she sounded disappointed.

I turned away, hating the direction my thoughts were taking. I began to understand why Mom didn't want to tell us anything until after the wedding. We would never be able to muddle through all these insignificant details if we knew. What was a centerpiece compared to the loss of the inn?

The flowers were carried to the storage room in the basement, where they would stay cool. I volunteered to count them, taking advantage of any opportunity to be alone. When I finally finished I wandered to my tiny darkroom under the stairs so that I could be alone. I crossed my arms and hugged myself, taking several deep breaths. We needed to get through tomorrow and then we could worry about the future. This weekend was about Charlotte. I said that over and over in my head. But it was a mantra that grew weaker and weaker the more I repeated it.

I had just turned to go upstairs when I felt a hand on my waist, yanking me toward the dark landing. I barely had time to protest when my mouth was covered by a very warm set of lips. Despite my earlier worries, my body reacted instantly and I threw my arms around Nick's shoulders and clung to him. I responded to Nick's kisses with such intensity that I think I surprised him. After a few minutes, a rising panic inside me threatened to surface and I found myself gulping for air. I ripped my mouth away from Nick's and buried my head in his neck.

I refused to cry. If I repeated that to myself maybe it wouldn't happen.

Nick held me close and ran his hands along my back. "Annie? Are you okay?"

I gripped his shoulders until I realized I was going to leave a mark, and broke away. I paced back and forth along the back wall of the alcove, trying to compose myself.

Nick watched me and I could feel the intensity of his stormy gaze. "You're working too hard, Annie. Let the rest of us do more."

I laughed bitterly. "If only it were just that." I turned my head away. "This wedding is suddenly the least of my problems."

He put his hand to my chin and turned me toward him, studying my face. "You've been running yourself ragged for this wedding."

I debated whether I should keep my discovery from him, but this was Nick. The man I loved. And besides that, I felt an overpowering need to confide in someone.

"My mom is selling the inn," I blurted out in a shaky voice.

It wasn't what he thought I would say. He blinked. "What?"

"I discovered a pile of foreclosure notices in her office. We are up to our ears in debt. I found a signed document outlining the terms of sale to a land developer." I remembered how she and I had joked about the inn being turned into a landfill or a parking lot and felt my stomach churn.

It really was happening. Reality hit me. What would Mom do? Where would she live? And Aunt Addie? She had spent most of her life here.

"Annie, are you sure? Your mom never said anything about it to you before?"

"We joked about it. I knew the bills were coming in and we were having trouble. But somehow I never thought it would really happen. If only I hadn't lost my teaching position, I could have helped her out. I could have at least paid some bills off. I can't believe she never even told me, Nick."

Nick pulled me toward him, where I could rest my head on his shoulder. "You've done so much to help your mom. Don't feel guilty about losing your job. Your mom wouldn't want you to use your paychecks to keep this place going."

"But—"

Nick stopped my words with a tender kiss on the top of my head. His hands cupped my face and forced me to look at him. "We'll think of something. After the wedding we'll talk to your mom about it. Okay?"

He kissed me again and put his arms around me. I didn't think there was anything he could do, but somehow I didn't feel so alone anymore. It was enough for the moment.

Chapter 19

When Nick and I returned to the lobby, we found everyone standing in front of the television in the corner. Mary Conrad had arrived and she sent Nick and me a curious gaze before turning back to the TV. We watched as the weatherman from the local television station pointed on the radar behind him to a solid pattern of dark blue covering the northern part of the state.

" 'Almost thirty inches of snow has fallen in some parts of Northern Michigan and there is no end in sight,' " he said.

Charlotte put her hand to her forehead. "This can't be happening."

"It's okay, Charlotte," Brittany said. "This guy might be wrong. Look, his tie doesn't even match his suit. What does he know? The weatherman on the GATE Network is sure this is no big deal."

Behind her, Ian smirked. "Hey, you know you're right. A guy with a fifty-thousand-dollar wardrobe *has* to know more about weather than the local dude who buys his clothes from Kmart. I'll remember that the next time I need a proctologist. Go for the guy with the Gucci tie."

Brittany didn't know what to make of Ian. She blinked several times, opening and closing her mouth before turning back to the TV.

"Hey," said Ian, leaning closer to her ear. "Who wants to play snow golf?"

"What's that?" asked Kevin with interest.

Ian described a game we played with golf clubs and an orange plastic ball in the snow. Kevin, Richard, and Jessica thought the game sounded like fun. They convinced Henry, Bebe, Patty, and even Brittany to join them. Ian narrowed his eyes at Brittany as she put on her designer ski jacket and boots. He looked like a wolf getting ready to gobble up Little Red Riding Hood. I supposed I should have warned her about Ian, but then again, maybe not.

Several minutes later, I closed the back door on Bebe and Patty, who had just finished bundling up. I shivered from the gust of wind that invaded the inn and watched as they leaped through the snow to join the gathering crowd on the back nine. They were covered in white in no time and started throwing snowballs before the golf game began. I was pretty sure I saw Ian teach Brittany how to make a snowball. He threw back his head and laughed when she sprayed him with a poorly packed first attempt. I was glad they were having fun. Someone had to lighten the mood.

Nick stood next to me, watching the scene outside. "Are you going too?" I asked. He might at least keep Ian from being overly vicious.

"No, I'll hang out here," he said. "Grady is setting up some tables, and I thought I would help."

In the lobby, Charlotte sat on the couch next to June and Scarlett and called the airline. Her voice rose as she demanded to know when her dress would arrive. The longer she talked the redder her face grew. Eventually, June and Scarlett grabbed the phone to yell at the poor clerk. The snow had put a major snarl in travel up and down the Mid-Atlantic and the odds of the dress arriving before tomorrow looked bleak.

Meanwhile, Mary, Aunt Addie, Marva, and Corinne huddled together discussing a plan. They pulled me into the conversation hoping I would support them. But I already knew what Charlotte's reaction would be.

"You want me to wear what!?" she said when she heard their proposal.

"We can fix it up—it won't be that bad."

"Mary, there is no way Aunt Addie's dress will even fit me."

I stared at the floor, wishing I was outside with everyone else. The idea of redesigning Aunt Addie's dress was crazy, but then again, what else could they do? My mom had borrowed her wedding dress from her cousin all those years ago, so using hers was out of the question.

"Well, Mary is a wonderful seamstress, and with the help of a few people we could make the dress look like new," explained Corinne.

"I would be happy to do whatever I can. I have loads of prom dresses that I've made, hanging in the girls' bedrooms," Mary said. "They seemed to like them and you know how picky Jenny used to be about her clothes. I am sure we can figure out a way to make the dress look more updated."

She was trying to be diplomatic, but I could read doubt in her eyes. Aunt Addie fished her wedding album from the annex. She proudly showed the dress to anyone who would look. It was made of lace and satin in a style that covered her from head to toe. She had been large even then, when she married my uncle at the age of forty-two. I couldn't imagine how it would work.

June and Scarlett were weighing in on the dress situation as well. Their ridiculous idea involved flying another dress into Truhart on a special plane. I wondered if they had already dipped into the liquor cabinet. All the money in the world couldn't fly a wedding dress into the middle of a snowstorm.

"Once I cut the material I can make it look very pretty," Mary explained, grabbing the album out of Aunt Addie's hands. "Actually a wedding dress is one of the simpler styles to sew. I can make it look like one of those beautiful dresses in your magazine. I'll cut off the arms and the neckline, and then I'll reshape the bodice and pinch in the waist. You won't even recognize it."

Aunt Addie looked at Mary like she had grown two heads. "You will do *what* with my dress?" She put her hand on her hip and glared.

Mary waved her hand in the air, dismissing Aunt Addie's concern. "Oh, come on, Adelaide. It's not like you are going to wear it again. You have to agree it is a little . . . well, dated."

"What do you mean, dated? That dress is absolutely beautiful. I thought you were going to resize it, not chop it up."

"Well, you can chop mine up," said Marva, thinking she was being helpful. "I'd be happy to go home and bring it over. The taffeta would shine real nice for your video cameras."

"God almighty, Marva, your dress is worse than Addie's!" declared Corinne.

I escaped the room as it erupted into loud bickering.

"Well, it looks like that's the last car that's going to make it on the road tonight," declared Mom. Mary's Jeep carried my cousins to her house. It crept down the driveway, the headlights engulfed in white before they turned onto the county road.

The day had gone from bad to worse when the last of the Adler cousins arrived. As usual, they had failed to give us a final head count, and Mom had had to scramble to get several cousins a bed at Mary's. It took them forever to decide who would stay at the inn and who would go to Mary's. I was so confused I still didn't know who was staying where by the time they finished talking.

There was no question that the rehearsal dinner at the Red River Lodge should be canceled. The roads were too dangerous. Even the camera crew had decided to stay put and camp out in the lobby. There seemed little point in rehearsing without the minister. Ian kept the wedding party and the camera crew entertained with a card game. Alain finally woke up from a long nap. He stared morosely into the fireplace, muttering something about a weekend in Palm Beach he had passed up.

Travis, Scarlett, and June fretted over the guests who were stranded at the Grande Lucerne. And Jessica looked miserable. She had passed up the card game to sit next to her mother. With her head down and her hair straggling over her face, I wondered if she was wishing she were back at school with her friends.

Marva and Corinne had left in their snowmobiles hours ago, before the snowdrifts grew deeper. Earlier, they had helped Mary measure Charlotte and cut and baste a rough template for a dress using an old sheet. No one agreed on exactly what the dress would look like or be made of, but everyone agreed that plan B was a necessity. Charlotte held out little hope that her original wedding dress might arrive by tomorrow, especially after the evening forecast.

Grady made several trips out into the snow. He tried to shovel a pathway around the inn, and the snowplows had been nice enough to visit our stretch of road several times. But the wind and drifting snow won the battle by late afternoon. With the exception of the snowmobile paths that were barely visible from the lobby window, we were well and truly cut off. Almost three feet of snow had fallen by the time the sun set.

That was when Charlotte's tears started.

She sat on the couch in front of the fire with Henry's arm around her and clutched a tissue. The silence in the room was cut only by Charlotte's occasional sobs. Unable to handle it after the first few minutes, Ian hastily made everyone drinks. When Brittany asked if he could make her a Truhart Twister, he looked at her like she was crazy. I remembered the story I had told at the Double Olive in Atlanta and wondered if I should explain. But Ian squinted his eyes and left the room. When he returned he held a tray of drinks that looked lethal. After one sip Brittany declared her love for it. Henry forced Charlotte to drink two. This earned him a censorious glare from Aunt Addie, but a thumbs-up from Ian.

Nestor was the only one unfazed by the situation. He heated up the meal he had planned for New Year's Day and said he could make things work no matter what. Mom and I helped him in the kitchen, glad that his famous venison chili was already made. Even June would be impressed by that.

Nick had decided to stay at the inn through dinner and avoid the bedroom shuffling that was still going on with my cousins. He said he would borrow one of our snowmobiles if he couldn't make it to his mother's on foot. I felt his gaze on me as I moved around the inn, taking care of details. I helped prepare dinner and finished a few last-minute tasks in the guest rooms. It helped me forget my worries if I kept busy and tackled one task at a time.

When I entered the lobby to tell everyone that dinner was ready, I found Brittany staring at me. She took a sip from her tumbler and giggled. I wished to God that I could grab the drink from her hand and swallow it, but a drink would put me over the edge right now.

Nick walked over and stood next to me as everyone filtered into the dining room. "You have flour in your hair," he whispered. No wonder Brittany had laughed. I didn't even care. He kissed me on the tip of my nose when the last person left the room. "Annie, why don't you just sit down and enjoy your meal? We can all lend a hand later."

I shook my head. Somehow I couldn't see Brittany with her hands buried in dishwater. Nick reached out and massaged the back of my neck. I leaned into him. For the first time in a long time, I was too tired to talk.

"Does the minister have a snowmobile?" he asked.

I nodded.

"Well then, this wedding will happen no matter what."

I suppose there was a simple comfort in that thought. If only a minister could solve our debt problem too. I walked over to the desk and grabbed my dad's old camera.

"I guess we'll all laugh over these pictures someday, huh?"

"You know, I can think of a lot worse things than being snowed in with you," Nick said. He kissed me again.

A commotion in the dining room caught my attention. What now? I pulled away from Nick to see what was happening and ignored his protest as I left the room.

Charlotte and Aunt Addie stood inside the dining room doorway, arguing loudly while Mom hushed them and glanced nervously at the guests gathered near the table. But it was too late for good manners. June, Scarlett, Travis, and Brittany were focused on the doorway above us. They stared with mixed expressions of amusement and horror. I looked up to see what they were looking at and my heart sank. Macaroni reindeer dotted the garland that framed the room.

"—I've been looking for them for weeks," Aunt Addie was saying. "Grady found them in the golf shack and was nice enough to put them around the room for me. What are you so upset about?"

Charlotte's face was purple in the low light of the dining room. She pointed up and stamped her foot. "Mom, make her take them down!"

"Now, Charlotte—"

"Mom! This is so embarrassing!"

"Let's take this into the kitchen," Mom said as she coaxed Charlotte and Aunt Addie through the swinging doors. I put the camera down in the corner and followed Ian, nodding and smiling sweetly at the table of guests as if this happened all the time.

The door had barely swung closed when Charlotte started talking. "I can't believe you are going to let her keep them up. You have to take them down before the wedding."

"Why? I thought you liked my pasta ornaments," said Aunt Addie, stricken.

"Why would you think that? They are the tackiest decorations I have ever seen," Charlotte declared loudly.

Ian stepped forward. "Look, let's leave them up for now. They're kind of fun and part of our tradition." Aunt Addie's eyes were filling with tears and he put his arm around her shoulders.

"It's great that Grady found them, Aunt Addie," Ian continued softly. "I was really missing them." He looked over Aunt Addie's head at me and we exchanged guilty looks.

"Of course you don't care how this looks! You and your card

games and snow golf . . . and your music! Ian, all you seem to think this wedding is about is you and your chance at fun and fame! Well, all of your lame attempts to get on *The Morning Show* aren't going to work. I swear to God, Ian, if you so much as try to embarrass me I am going to cut you out of every part of the video we air, especially the parts where you play music."

Ian's expression turned cold. He clenched his jaw as if he wanted to say something but didn't trust himself. I watched him stalk off to the sink and pour Aunt Addie a glass of water. When he returned he shoved the glass into Aunt Addie's hands and glared at Charlotte.

"We are all going to remain calm here, okay, everyone?" Mom said, looking at each of us and enunciating each word. Her voice shook as she spoke. "This is not a disaster. Do you hear me? We are going to remain calm and go back into that dining room and show those people that Adlers are not people who let things like snow-storms get the best of them. Is that understood?" We all recognized her tone from childhood, the *don't mess with me* tone. But I saw her shake.

Even Charlotte knew not to cross the line. She glared at Ian before stomping out of the room. Ian shook his head and turned to guide Aunt Addie into the dining room. I stayed behind to make sure Mom was all right. Her eyes glittered and her chin wavered as she stared at the swinging door.

I reached out and touched her arm. She put her hand on top of mine.

"I just wish your father were here, Annie. He would know what to do at a time like this." She was thinking about more than just the wedding, I knew. There was so much that I wanted to say.

"I love you, Mom."

"Oh, Annie. What would I do without you?" Nodding her head toward the door, she said, "Come on, let's try to make the best of this."

When we sat down to eat, the tension in the air was so thick you could cut it. Henry must have read my mind because he tried to lighten the mood.

"Well, that cake is so beautiful I wonder if anyone would notice if I cut into it with a knife and stole a piece right now."

"It certainly is beautiful," chimed in Travis. Even Brittany nodded her head and smiled nervously at the strain in the air. Everyone, including my cousins, looked toward Charlotte for confirmation, but she stared sullenly at the ornaments around the room and said nothing. Aunt Addie blotted the corner of her eye with a tissue and Ian's frown deepened. He set down his napkin and rose from the table, heading over to the piano. He nodded toward the video crew to come closer as he fished out a sheet of music from the piano bench and turned on the microphone nearby.

Sitting down, he flexed his fingers.

"Uh-oh," I heard Nick say from the other side of the table. He realized what was happening before I did.

Ian's fingers flew over the keys as he started playing. Charlotte's water goblet was halfway to her mouth and froze in midair as Ian began to sing the sappiest song Barry Manilow had ever written.

He was only halfway through the first verse when Charlotte slammed down her glass and stood up. Stomping across the room, she grabbed the lid of the piano and tried to slam it shut.

Henry jumped out of his seat, but I was closer. I put my hand on the lid before Charlotte broke Ian's fingers.

"Hey," Ian said. "I was playing a song."

"Stop it!" she hissed.

I pushed Charlotte away from Ian. "That's enough," I said in a low voice.

She opened her mouth to say something but stopped. A rumbling sound caught our attention. The roar grew louder until it shook the walls. From the corner of my eye I caught a flash of white out the window. Was that snow cascading from the roof? It sounded as if a freight train was racing above our heads. The chandelier shuddered. I looked up, wondering what was happening.

Suddenly, a sharp crack of splintering wood ripped through the air.

Then a chorus of cries erupted from the table. I could hear Alain yelling above the din, "Avalanche. Everyone run!"

Most of us were too shocked to do anything but stand with our feet glued to the floor as dust poured from the ceiling. When the noise finally ended we still felt the echo vibrate through the room.

It took me a moment to realize two things. One, the ceiling in the corner of the room was completely open to the night sky. And two, it wasn't dust falling down. It was snow. My eyes followed the shower to the floor. Where the cake once stood, a pile of snow and frosting lay in a rubble on the floor. A sickening heap of white on white.

Oh my God!

A rush of cold air swept through the room and I realized in astonishment that the years of patching the roof hadn't worked. The wood must have been rotting in the rafters.

A crowd of people stood in the doorway where they had been cowering and stared at the wreckage. Mom put her hand on her chest and moved toward the pile of debris. She crouched down in shock and reached for a piece of wood as if she thought she could salvage something. Aunt Addie followed her, holding her arms up to protect Mom from the falling snow. She realized the futility as she looked up at the gaping hole and tried to pull Mom away. But Mom resisted. She knelt in the layer of rubble and tried to put things back together.

A sense of loss hit me. My old camera lay under a pile of wood, broken into pieces.

I looked back at Charlotte, who still hadn't moved. She stared at the spot where her wedding cake had been. Her face was drained of all color. Except for her eyes. They were on fire.

"My wedding is completely destroyed!" Her voice broke and she balled her fists at her sides. Henry put his arms around her, but even he looked scared at the sight of her unraveling right in front of us. She turned to him with wild eyes, "We should have stayed in Atlanta. Even that wedding hall with the pink fountain and bubbles would be better than this . . . this catastrophe!"

Then she twisted toward my mother and screamed, "It's ruined. You have all ruined everything!"

Without thinking I stepped toward Charlotte and drew back my hand.

"Annie!" Nick grabbed my arm.

"Stop it, Charlotte! Just stop it!" I said. My voice was low and harsh. I barely recognized it. "Stop thinking about yourself and grow up! You and this wedding—you aren't the center of everything!"

Charlotte stepped back, startled by my outburst.

"Mom has been doing everything she can to make your wedding special!"

"Annie—" Mom said in warning behind me, but I ignored her.

"Did you ever consider what this has cost her? You and your expensive dress and your trip to Vegas could have paid off half of the bills in Mom's office. They could have kept us from losing the inn. Did you even know about that? Or were you too busy telling the world about origami ornaments on that phony morning show to figure out what was going on in your own family?" My voice rose as I spoke.

I felt a hand pull on my arm and I shook it off. I was trembling with anger. "There is a lot more going on here than your wedding, Charlotte. But you wouldn't notice because you're so busy trying to be perfect for everyone else, you never considered your less-than-perfect family. Your wedding is a day in your life. Just one day! But this family has been there for you your whole life. Does that count for anything?"

I stopped for breath and became painfully aware of the hush in the room. Even the snow coming from the hole in the roof was falling in silence.

"Well, the viewers will love this segment with their morning coffee," Ian said, breaking the stillness in the room.

I turned around and saw the cameras pointed straight at me. If they kept this segment, my tantrum would give *The Morning Show* a ten-point boost in their ratings.

Chapter 20

All at once everyone began to talk. I stood, unable to breathe, wondering if I was going to faint from lack of oxygen. A pair of strong hands grabbed my shoulders and steered me out of the room. I wasn't aware of where I was going or how my legs were holding me up. A door closed behind me. Then I heard Nick saying soothing words that didn't register.

I felt cold all over. He propped me up against a wall and ran his hands along my arms, holding me as I tried to stop my body from shivering. When I could stand on my own, everything started to come back into focus. I looked up at him and realized we were in one of the guest rooms.

My mouth was dry. "Did I really just do that?" I put my fingers up to my lips, hoping that he would tell me I had imagined everything.

Nick smiled and he tilted his head sideways. "I'm afraid you did, sweetheart," he said gently.

"Oh my God. I can't believe I said all that. I just yelled at Charlotte. And everyone heard . . ."

"Well . . . yes."

"How could I? I completely lost it. Everyone must think I'm terrible for yelling at her."

"Well, actually, several people were cueing up behind you to do the same thing. I kind of think you were just the first in line."

I couldn't believe he could joke at a time like this.

"Nick! I almost slapped her."

"Well, I felt compelled to stop that one. I remember too many of your fights when you were little. You have a pretty vicious punch."

I lowered my forehead to his chest. The gravity of the situation began to sink in. "And the roof. The cake . . . What are we going to do?"

"Who cares about the cake? I may only be the best man, but it seems to me that there is a hell of a lot more to a wedding than the cake. And a lot more that needs to be fixed than a roof."

True. My sister probably hated me. My mother must be mortified. Aunt Addie was doubtlessly still crying over her macaroni ornaments. And Ian? God knew what Ian was thinking, but I couldn't imagine he would be smiling as Charlotte walked down the aisle at this point. As for the Lowells and the rest of the guests, they probably thought we were all crazy.

I looked up at Nick. A light by the bed cast a dim glow on his face as he gazed down at me.

"Nick, why are we in a guest room?"

"Never mind about that. You're still shivering. Come on. Let's get you warm."

He guided me to the bed, lifted the comforter, and sat me down. Then he kneeled down and removed my shoes.

"I'm not a child," I complained.

"Oh, come on, Annie." He sounded mildly irritated. "Just let someone do something for you for a change."

I squeezed my lips together. Well, okay. If he insisted.

He lifted my legs up to the bed and tucked the covers around me.

"Tell me this isn't Scarlett's room."

He chuckled and put his hands on either side of my hips. "No. Some of those Adler cousins wanted to stay together. My mom has the whole Chicago contingent at her house tonight. So I gave up my bedroom and switched with your cousin who was in this room." Then he leaned forward and kissed my forehead. "I'll be right back, all right?"

I hid my smile when he smoothed my hair and turned to leave the room. Despite all my worries and the gravity of what had just happened, a thought intruded in my head.

I had just been tucked in.

Nick would make a great father someday.

On a snowy winter afternoon when I was ten and Charlotte was six, we were given permission to take a freshly washed sheet off the housekeeping cart and turn it into a fort using chairs as stanchions and a broom as the center pole.

Aunt Addie and my mother were hosting a church luncheon and I was put in charge of Charlotte and told to stay out of trouble. Mom said she was going to give me this one chance to redeem myself. Just the week before I had discovered how fun it was to slide down the stairs in my sleeping bag and had been scolded by my dad when Charlotte had copied me and we had been caught. I was determined to prove I was responsible and could be a good babysitter.

Charlotte and I lay underneath our white 250-thread-count roof in our sleeping bags, pretending we were safe from the wilds of the jungle outside. We played for almost two hours, reading books and drinking pretend tea at our tea party. I was so proud of myself, and I couldn't wait to tell my dad.

When I took myself off to the bathroom it never occurred to me that Charlotte would return to our toboggan game. I came back to our fort and realized she was missing. Then I heard a gigantic crash. I ran to the lobby to find Charlotte sprawled halfway down the landing beside the shattered remains of Aunt Addie's favorite crystal vase.

"Run!" I whispered to her before anyone found her.

Aunt Addie and Mom discovered me next to the smashed vase and it hadn't occurred to me that I should tell the truth. Aunt Addie cried over her loss and Dad was furious when he found out. I took my punishment and did odd jobs for Aunt Addie after school for the next month. I even accepted a lifetime of teasing for my crystal-smashing ways, never saying a word in my own defense.

Neither Charlotte nor I ever talked about that incident. But I couldn't help but think about it now as I lay in bed and stared up at the ceiling.

Why didn't I get mad at Charlotte all those years ago?

I tried to remember everything I said during my rampage in the dining room. But my memory was one big blur. I had trouble distinguishing between what I had been thinking and what I had actually said out loud.

Images of all that led up to my meltdown flashed before my eyes. The look on Aunt Addie's face when Charlotte demanded her macaroni menagerie be removed, the controlled anger that burned behind Ian's eyes before he unleashed his revenge with the Barry Manilow firebomb, and the despair in my mother's eyes as she watched her family fall apart.

I thought of Charlotte's reaction to the roof cave-in and realized that tonight was the first time in my life I had felt pure anger toward my little sister. I had let Charlotte have the full brunt of my fury. And I had done it in front of my family, her friends, and her future family. Oh yeah, and perhaps even half of America.

I was a walking disaster.

I threw back the covers and swung my feet over the side of the bed. I was just starting to put on my shoes when I heard Nick return. He stood in the doorway holding a bottle of wine, a corkscrew, and two glasses. He shook his head at me.

"You never could follow directions, Annie."

"I can't sit here while all hell breaks loose. We're in the middle of a wedding crisis and I have to help figure out what to do. I can't imagine what my mom is dealing with."

He shut the door with his foot and leaned back against it as if he would physically bar me from leaving the room. "For once, just let it go and take care of yourself," he said.

"Take care of myself? Why would I do that? I'm fine. It's this wedding that's in trouble. I just screwed up everything." My voice wavered and I blinked away the moisture that had invaded my eyes. This was not a time to wallow in self-pity.

Nick walked across the room and sat down next to me. He placed the bottle and glasses on the nightstand and put his arm around my shoulder. "Your mom is fine. She and Charlotte are tucked away in the annex having a mother-daughter conversation. I didn't hear any yelling or sobbing, so I figure they're working things out."

I took a shaky breath. "My poor mom. I feel like I made everything so much worse."

Nick's hand moved to the back of my neck and he massaged the muscles I didn't even know were tense. He touched a particularly sensitive spot in my neck and I almost purred. Then he kissed my brow. "Henry is pacing outside the kitchen, but he says he has Charlotte handled. Ian and the guys are working on covering up the hole in the ceiling. Travis is giving orders to your cousins as if he has a degree in roofing. He says he shingled roofs one summer when he was in college and he knows all about them."

"What?"

"Yeah, I know. I find it hard to believe too."

"Is the hole in the roof very bad?"

He paused. "I think so."

"Dad always wanted to build a bigger dining room for banquets. He had all these ideas about rustic pine planking and big windows. I can't imagine what we are going to do now. The church basement is pretty small and I can't think of any other place nearby that could hold everyone."

Nick turned his head and looked at the swirling snow against the windowpane. He seemed to be considering something.

I interrupted his thoughts. "I'm afraid to ask, but what about June and Scarlett?" I didn't even want to ask about Brittany. Nick should understand that even with her movie-star physique and her Hollywood wardrobe, she was far less drama than me.

"June and Scarlett opened a bottle of champagne and have coerced Aunt Addie to drink it with them." I opened my mouth, speechless. But Nick just smiled back at me. "Really. It's the funniest thing, but the three of them are trading wedding horror stories like war vets."

I wondered if he was lying just to make me feel better.

"So"—he reached for the corkscrew and opened the bottle of wine—"you don't have any reason to leave this room for a very long time."

I looked sideways at him. His words were one hell of a prelude to seduction.

He poured the wine and handed me a glass, watching with hooded eyes as I raised it to my lips. My hand trembled.

"Come on, sit back and relax." Nick shifted and ushered me backward until we were sitting against the headboard. For several moments I just enjoyed the feel of Nick's arm around me and the trail of warmth the red wine left down my throat.

"Tonight was the first time I can remember getting mad at Charlotte," I finally said.

"Well, usually it was you and Ian who battled. You two fought all the time, but never with Charlotte. Why was that?"

"She has always been everyone's perfect little girl . . . everyone's blond-haired, blue-eyed angel." I sighed and took another sip. "It was never like having an annoying baby sister at all. She was like my baby too."

I thought of all the things I had done for her growing up. The times I sat on the edge of her bed and watched her model her new school clothes. When she landed her first job at a TV station in Michigan, I taped her reports and we watched them over and over. Actually, Aunt Addie and Mom still did that. We had all been so proud of everything she did.

"When she was little I remember begging my parents to let me read her bedtime stories. It made me feel so proud, as if she were my own little girl. I can still remember how Ian and I used to fight over who would hold her hand when we crossed the street."

"Charlotte was the proverbial golden girl," Nick said, reaching for the bottle and adding more wine to my glass.

I thought about that for a moment. "But the Charlotte who arrived here yesterday was someone I didn't recognize. She was so distracted by the wedding details that she barely noticed us running around trying to make her wedding perfect."

"I noticed," Nick said. "I watched you lugging that damn photography equipment through the snow, taking care of luggage, serving meals, and running laps around the inn. It made me so irritated to see you work that hard. This whole weekend has been crazy for you."

It *was* a lot of work. But what else could we have done? It was Charlotte's wedding.

"It wouldn't have been so bad if things hadn't started going downhill. The dress, the storm, and those damn ornaments. I don't know what happened, Nick, but suddenly it was like Charlotte was replaced with her evil twin."

"My father used to say that a man isn't measured by how he handles his successes, but how he handles his failures." He said it softly, as if he was afraid the words might shatter my image of Charlotte. But the fact was, the words sounded like something my father used to say too. Charlotte had been in high school when Dad died. I wondered if she had been listening when he had explained his philosophies on life. Or was she still playing dress-up back then?

"It's not like she actually failed, Nick. I mean, none of this was her doing."

"That's true." His words hung in the air as though he wanted to say more.

"Oh God, Nick. Did I really call *The Morning Show* phony? What will Scarlett think?" I was back where I started. "I made things so much worse with my crazy tirade."

Nick squeezed my shoulder and got up from the bed. "Lie down on your stomach, Annie. I've ordered a massage to go with this wine."

I rolled my eyes. "You know that was just a stupid thing Ian put on our website. I thought he removed it."

"This is a special package deal." He took my glass and put it on the nightstand.

"I can't do this right now. I have to go help."

He ignored me and turned me over on my stomach. He pulled me down on the bed with strong hands. "Shut up, Annie."

I felt guilty. I could only imagine the crazy things happening in the rest of the inn.

"There is nothing you can do tonight," Nick said. He turned off the bedside lamp and flicked on the clock radio to a local public station that played jazz.

It seemed so decadent and self-indulgent to be getting a massage an hour after ruining my sister's wedding. But I lay there anyway, anticipating the feel of Nick's hands on my body again. I felt a tingling sensation wash over me at the mere thought of spending the night with him.

He disappeared for a moment and reappeared with lotion from the bathroom. Opening up the miniature container, he smelled it. "Mmm. This stuff smells great."

Thank you, Ian. Who knew I would get to use the lotions his friend had given us in this manner?

"Let's get this shirt off," Nick said. I raised my arms and let him pull it off. "That's better," he said in a low voice.

I smelled the lotion and felt the smooth texture as his hands began kneading my tired muscles. His hands worked their magic and he coaxed my shoulders to relax. I felt as if I were sinking into the bed as his thumbs and the heels of his hands ran up and down my back. I hadn't realized just how tense I was. Then he unhooked my bra and pulled it away from my shoulders. I had a fleeting regret. Somewhere in the back of my drawer was a black thong and lacy bra that had cost way too much. Why hadn't I even thought about putting those on this morning?

He must have sensed my worries because he pushed harder. "Relax," he said slowly.

For once I listened to him and let go of my concerns. I became a melting stick of butter under his fingertips. By the time he moved lower and eased me out of my jeans, I felt moisture between my legs. I waited for him to take off my panties. But he waited, sparking a new tension inside me. He straddled my legs next, gliding his fingertips down my spine and outward toward my hip. Then he dug his thumbs in the small of my back and pushed upward, smoothing out any lingering knots.

After several minutes he lightened his fingers and caressed my spine from my neck all the way down. Snagging a finger in the fabric, he drew my panties down my legs.

My limbs were like lead and my mind lost all ability to focus. I was just a living, breathing mass of nerves. Every touch, light or firm, soothed my troubles. I was at Nick's mercy. He knew that— seemed to relish it. His soothing words were like warm honey and I felt the tender caress of his lips as he trailed them up my body. My legs fell open and he delved in between them to my moist center.

But he didn't stop there. I felt myself being turned over and began to protest. "Sssh," he soothed me. "This service provides frontal massages for free."

My erotic meter entered the red zone and I looked down my body to catch a wicked gleam in his eyes in the dim light. His fingers repeated their pressure as they made their way up my body. He steered clear of my more sensitive parts and laughed softly when I cried out in frustration. When he finally arrived at the tips of my breasts he stopped and squeezed my nipples playfully.

"Hello, Bump," he said.

I started to giggle. I would have kicked any boy who said that when I was younger. But coming from him, it was like a shot of sex adrenaline.

"I used to think of doing this and I would get hard."

I opened my eyes wide, startled that he had ever thought of me this way before.

"Don't look so surprised," he said. "Ever since you were almost seventeen I've wanted to touch you like this." He kissed each breast. I thought I would explode from the pleasure he was giving me. I reached out to touch him, but he stopped my hands.

"No moving. This massage isn't over."

He drew his fingers over my body as if I were a piano. I lay open to him and bit my lip to keep from moaning. When he finally dipped his fingers in between my legs and into me, I let out a small scream.

He increased the pressure and I gasped as one hand caressed my breast and he moved his head lower to touch me in the most sensitive spot with his tongue. I lost all pride and begged for more. But he forced me to wait until I pleaded with him for release. I reached for him, but he pulled back.

"No, Annie. This is for you," he whispered.

His tongue and fingers moved faster. A moment later I cried out as I came in a spiraling, out of control, mind-blowing explosion. It went on and on as Nick coaxed everything out of me until I lay in an exhausted heap.

The night was young, and I was determined to give back what I had taken. I turned the tables and gave Nick the massage of his life. We ended up upside down on the bed, with the sheets strewn on the ground and his clothes scattered across the room. I had no idea how much time had passed, but the rest of the inn was quiet around us.

"I hope no one heard me a moment ago," I said as I lay on top of him.

"Me too," he said with a chuckle. "The last thing we need is Aunt Addie storming in here to save you."

"She would probably bring a shotgun and force you in front of the preacher."

"Hmmm."

Several minutes later I brought us both back to reality. "I guess we Adlers will never be the all-American family. I can see the title of the segment on *The Morning Show* now: Hole in the Roof, Symbolic of Flaws in the Family."

Nick ran his hand through my hair at the back of my head. "I'm sorry, honey. It was a pretty bad day, wasn't it?"

It wasn't the worst day of my life. Not by a long shot. The day my dad took his final breath was worse. The day we found out he had inoperable cancer was up there too. Seeing my mother fall apart after Dad died was awful. And then of course there was the girl on the ledge.

Nick had been right when he told me earlier that there was a lot more to fix than a roof. Maybe we all needed a reality check. I guess that was what I was thinking when I lost my head with Charlotte. I just wish I had found a less public way to point that out.

I rested my head where Nick's heart was, ran my hand along the stray hairs on his chest, and thought about all the times I'd said stupid things. And all the times I kept my mouth shut when I shouldn't have.

"I love you, Nick."

His hand stopped and I didn't want him to feel obligated to say anything, so I continued. "When I was growing up, you were my hero. I swear I thought you lived on a mountaintop. But I was, well . . . a little brat. I wanted your attention, so I did everything I could to get you to notice me. I was your worst nightmare, I'm sure. But lately I realized that all my attention-getting antics had another purpose."

He grunted and I figured that was good, so I kept talking. "Super-heroes are always too busy saving the world. They never get the girl." I moved my head forward and kissed his neck as I continued. "So I tried to drag you down, sometimes quite literally, so you could be closer to me."

He was quiet, letting my words sink in. After a moment, his arms closed around me. I felt a low rumble in his chest. "So, have I fallen far enough?"

"Well, I love you. I will never be good enough for you. But for some reason that doesn't seem to bother you. So it's all good."

"Why do you say that?"

He sounded annoyed. Maybe I shouldn't have told him I loved him. "I'm sorry. I just wanted you to know how I feel."

He rolled me over and propped himself on his elbows as he took my wrists in his hands. "No. Not that. I know you love me. And I always knew you had a crush on me when you were growing up. It was never a secret." Well, that was a little embarrassing. "But, Annie, why do you say you will never be good enough for me?"

I stared up into his beautiful brown eyes. "Well, because it's true. You know me, I always screw things up."

"Sometimes you are so stupid, Annie." He looked angry now. "The only person here who isn't worthy is me. You are the most unselfish, loving person I know."

I didn't know what to say to that. My heart caught in my throat as I looked at him.

"Listen to me," he continued. "I have known you your whole life, and I've never seen you do anything selfish."

"Right," I said with sarcasm.

"It's true. Even when you hustled people on the golf course, you did it for more than the money. You knew those old guys were lonely. They didn't care if they lost ten bucks. They had fun playing with you and talking about their lives, and you knew it. Annie, you are the kind of person who cares deeply. You would give anything to make the people you love happy. You would even give your last penny for this inn because of your mom and Aunt Addie. In the past few months you have sacrificed every last minute of your time just to make sure your little sister has the wedding of her life."

"A lot that did for her. I pretty much screwed things up," I said sarcastically.

"Are you kidding me? Charlotte made you choose between her wedding and defending your family. That was an easy decision for you."

"Oh yeah. Right in front of Henry's family and their guests. Oh, and I almost forgot, next week's *Morning Show* audience."

His brown eyes gazed at me with intensity. "Annie, you care like no other person I know. Don't make light of that. That's why I love you."

His words made me speechless. And of course they made me cry. But these tears were good tears. As Nick smiled at my blubbering and drew me into the hollow of his shoulder, I welcomed them with all my heart.

Chapter 21

The sun was still sleeping below the horizon when I felt Nick's warmth leave the bed. I reached for him and he bent over me, kissing my cheek.

"I have to see about some things. Stay here and rest," he whispered in my ear.

The clock on the nightstand read 5:45 a.m. and I wondered what he had to do that was so important. "Where are you going?" I asked.

"Just checking on my mom and seeing if I can help get this wedding back on track."

I rolled on my back and rubbed my eyes. "Do you think anyone will miss me if I stay in bed all day?"

"I will, for one." He pulled on his pants and I watched in appreciation as his muscles flexed while he dressed. I found myself unable to stop smiling. He was mine.

Once he finished dressing, he sat next to me and ran his fingers through my hair. "Annie," was all he said. It wasn't a question. It was a statement. *You're mine too.*

I kissed the hand that trailed down to my face and he frowned. "I know it is going to be hard for you this morning. Why don't you wait here until I come back? We can go talk to Charlotte together."

It was a wonderful gesture, and so typical of Nick. But I was stronger than that. I would have to get up soon to see about breakfast anyway. Even with a hole in the dining room roof, people would have to eat. Although I cringed at the thought of having to face everyone, I didn't need Nick to protect me from my own family.

"It's okay. I can do it."

"Yeah, I always remember when you had to face your mom or

Aunt Addie after getting in trouble. While Charlotte would hide and Ian would complain that nothing was his fault, you just held your chin up and took the punishment."

"Yeah, but I wasn't quiet about it."

"No. You had a word or two to say about the situation. I always admired your reasoning. So, no, you were never quiet about it . . . and you shouldn't be now either."

When Nick left the room I stared out the window next to the bed and watched the sky brightening in slow increments. Sunrise wouldn't be for a while, but I could see the red glow on the horizon and wondered if the fact that the snow was falling more lightly meant the storm was almost over.

I washed up and dressed, thinking of how to apologize. Nothing seemed to fit. When I finally stepped into the hallway, I was relieved to see that all was silent.

I walked past the main stairway and the camera crew asleep on couches in the lobby. Once I was in the doorway to the dining room, I flipped on the light switch and surveyed the room. It was empty, but I felt a rush of cold air coming from the corner. The cake and snow had been cleaned up but I could see the stains on the carpet.

I walked over to the corner and looked up. A tarp was secured over the hole by four long two-by-fours that were nailed to the ceiling. The temporary canopy sagged from the weight of new snow. A breeze blew through the tarp, making me shiver.

"Annie?"

I turned around to see my mom standing by the kitchen door. She looked tired. But the light in her eyes and smile on her face were reassuring. She opened her arms and I went into them like I was five again. We stood together for a long time and I suspected she needed the hug as much as I did.

"I'm so sorry, Mom," I finally said.

"Oh, honey. I didn't want you to know about the inn. How did you find out?"

I pulled away from her and looked down. Even with my height I had always felt smaller than my mom. But this morning I was more conscious of her petite frame and the wrinkles in the corners of her eyes.

"I saw the papers in your office. Mom, you should have told us earlier. We knew things were bad, but we could have found a way to help. All the bills and the notice of foreclosure, you shouldn't have had to deal with all that alone."

"Why? This inn isn't your burden. You and Ian and Charlotte—you all need to live your own lives. I don't want you worrying or sacrificing your dreams for this crumbling old pile of wood." She laughed when she said the last few words.

"We love this place as much as you do, Mom. Why wouldn't we want to help?"

She shook her head and hugged me again. "Oh, honey, this weekend was supposed to be about Charlotte and the wedding. I feel terrible that the roof caved in like that."

"Well, it was a lot of snow. Even people with new roofs worry about that in a snowstorm." I patted her back and put my arm around her as we stared at the mess in the ceiling.

"Well, now we have to figure out what to do," said Mom. Eventually we turned and walked toward the kitchen. "Grady says he can try to crawl up there and see if he can fix it from the top, but I worry it will cave in more when he puts his weight on it."

"I know I made things worse by yelling at Charlotte like that last night. When she started yelling at you, I just lost it."

"Well, perhaps you should discuss it with her," said Mom as she swung open the kitchen door. I took a step into the kitchen only to come face-to-face with my little sister.

She stood in the middle of the room, staring at me with red-rimmed eyes. Her hair was pulled back in a ponytail that was uncharacteristically loose and messy. She wore a shirt that was two sizes too big for her and sweatpants. I looked over her shoulder to where Henry sat at the kitchen table. He held a cup of coffee and rose from his chair when he saw me, giving me a partial wave.

Mom poured coffee into a handmade mug and nodded toward the door. "Henry, let's go out to my office and have a cup of coffee while these two talk." He nodded and I saw him brush Charlotte's back with his hand as he passed. The door swung back and forth on its hinges as they left the room. When it finally stopped it left a thick silence.

Charlotte and I avoided eye contact. I didn't know how to start, so I walked to the other side of the room and grabbed a mug from the cabinet. "Do you want any coffee?" I asked.

"Sure," she said as she followed me to the coffeemaker. I poured her a cup. She clutched it to her chest and took a deep breath while I finished pouring my own. Then we looked at each other and started to talk.

"Annie—"

"Charlotte."

We both spoke at the same time.

"Jinx," we said together, a habit that never died.

I was glad for the icebreaker and shook my head. "You first."

She sat down on the stool at the counter. "Annie, I am so sorry. I have been acting like such a jerk. From the moment Henry and I got engaged I have had only one thing on my mind. This wedding."

"Well, I made things so much worse by losing it in front of everyone. And I know the Lowell family hasn't been the easiest."

"Don't do that, Annie. You always make excuses for me when I behave badly. I'm not a little kid anymore."

"I'm not saying you are. It's just that I know Henry's family has high expectations of you."

"But that is just the problem, Annie. I got so full of this image of a fairy-tale wedding that the Lowells, and what they thought of me, became more important than my own family. It's ridiculous. I need to grow up and face the fact that nothing is perfect. So what if June doesn't like me? It wouldn't be the first time a bride didn't get along with her mother-in-law. And who cares if we get snowed out the day of my rehearsal dinner, and the dress goes missing . . ." Her voice trailed off and I knew she was thinking about the roof caving in. Things *had* been pretty bad.

"We just wanted this wedding to be so special for you."

"You guys are my family. What happened isn't your fault. But at the same time it kind of is." I raised my eyebrow. "You should have been the ones to bring me back down to earth long before last night. That's what families are supposed to do. I don't know why, but for some reason you treat me differently than you treat each other."

"What?"

"I've always been a little bit jealous that you and Ian act like you want to kill each other half the time."

I almost laughed.

"No, really, Annie. Ian would never have let you get away with the prima donna routine I pulled."

I sat down on the stool at the end of the counter and let her words sink in.

"I know I am much younger, but most of the time you guys treat me like a piece of fragile glass. I can handle being teased and told to get over myself. I can handle being yelled at. I just can't handle it when no one stops me from turning into a royal bi—"

"Stop it! You are not that bad! This has been a rotten twenty-four hours, you have to admit."

"It is no excuse for the way I have been behaving. I should have known this wedding would put a strain on things. And how could I miss all the clues that we were having financial trouble? I don't like the thought that I was giving Mom a hard time about the flowers, and threatened not to let Ian be on the video tape, or told Aunt Addie to remove all those thingies she likes so much."

"You mean the macaroni reindeer?"

"Were those reindeer?"

I nodded my head.

Her eyes opened wide and she covered her mouth. "I always thought they were gargoyles."

I almost spit out my coffee.

We talked for a long time after that.

Charlotte said that she and Mom stayed up late going over what had happened. Henry stayed up with them and held her hand through it all. He was upset to learn that Charlotte felt so much pressure from June. Henry told her the reason June was so obsessed with her image was due to her own experience fitting into the high society of Atlanta. Evidently, June came from a small town in Alabama. I guess Charlotte and I had misjudged her.

"I didn't realize that the reason you didn't come to Las Vegas was because you were busy here trying to pull this wedding together. How could I be so stupid?" Charlotte said.

"We didn't want you to know. But I didn't know Mom knew. I swear sometimes she has a crystal ball."

We moved to the table and put our feet up on the chairs like we always used to do when we were younger. "Anyway, in the end it was for nothing," I said. "We had no idea there was a possibility of foreclosure. So all the little things we did for the wedding didn't help the inn at all."

Ian wandered in toward the end of the conversation wearing ratty old jeans and a ragged purple sweatshirt. He looked like he could use another five hours of sleep like the rest of us. He grabbed himself a coffee. When I explained Charlotte's feelings about how we had been treating her, he vowed to make up for lost time by teasing her and torturing her for the next twenty-four years.

"You might regret this new attitude from us, Charlotte," I warned her. "But personally I'm relieved to send some of Ian's annoying sarcasm your way." Mom and Henry returned and joined us at the table. Even Aunt Addie, in a purple paisley housecoat and fuzzy slippers, wandered in. She sat next to Ian. The two of them surveyed each other and nodded. For the first time I realized how alike the two of them actually were.

Nestor must have decided that the family wasn't going to murder each other after all, because he snuck in through the dining room and started cooking pancakes and sausage on the griddle. While he worked, we discussed ways to deal with the roof damage and the impassable roads.

Then the door swung open. "Did I miss breakfast?" Nick stood at the kitchen door still wearing his coat, his cheeks red from the cold.

"You better double that batch, Nestor. Nick is a garbage disposal," said Ian. Nick ignored Ian and took off his jacket and threw it over a bench by the window.

"I think the snow is finally stopping." He walked over and pulled out the empty chair next to mine. Then he leaned over and gave me a cold but solid kiss on the lips.

For a moment the room was silent. Mom and Aunt Addie sent each other a meaningful glance, and Charlotte leaned toward Henry, giggling behind her hand. Ian was the only one who seemed completely surprised. He stared at us for a moment and then turned to everyone else for an explanation. No one said a word. Still trying to figure things out, he looked back at me.

"Is something going on between you two?" he asked.

"Yeah," said Nick. "Is that okay with you? Not that I'm asking permission."

Ian's face darkened. "Not that you're asking? You're my best friend. Don't think for a moment that trumps family, you ass. You sure as hell better be careful with my little sister. She's not some kind of fling."

"Ian!" I put my hand out toward him. He seemed serious for once.

"I know that," Nick said to Ian, ignoring me.

I rolled my eyes as the two of them stared at each other in a standoff. It didn't last long. As soon as the pancakes arrived and the conversation around the table started up, they were talking again.

All the chatter and rattling of the pans must have made a racket because it wasn't long before June and Jessica opened the kitchen door.

"Mind if we join you?" asked June. She wore no makeup and was dressed in slim black pants and a black sweater. A rather simple look for June.

"Is anyone else awake?" asked Mom.

"Just us so far," said June.

Then the most surprising thing happened.

Mom waved her hand. "Feel free to drag in chairs from the dining room if you and Jessica want to join us." She didn't insist on serving them in the dining room and she didn't ask Ian to carry in the chairs for them. She would never have treated a guest like that. I saw her eyes twinkle as June and Jessica struggled with the chairs and the door. Even Henry stayed seated as they yanked the chairs to the table.

"There's coffee in the pot near the sink, help yourself," Mom said, turning back to the family around the table.

Henry picked up Charlotte's cup. "Can you get Charlotte some more coffee, Mom?"

June looked surprised by his request, but picked up the cup and did as he asked. I understood what was happening now, and I approved heartily. Perhaps it was time we stopped coddling June as well.

For so long I had wanted us to be together again. Mom, Aunt Addie, Ian, Charlotte, and me. Now, as everyone ate pancakes and talked, I was struck by the fact that we finally were. Nick was practically family and blended right in, like the old days. And it wasn't so awkward to have the Lowells gathered with us. We continued to discuss the snow and the roads and what we could do to get the wedding back on track. I was relieved that no one said a word about my meltdown yesterday.

When he finished the last pancake, Nick spoke up. "I have been checking around and I think I've found a place where you can have the reception. It's not perfect, but it will hold all the guests. You won't have to worry that any snow will fall from the ceiling, and it will be warm."

"Thank the Lord," said Aunt Addie. "But where?"

"Why don't you let Ian, Henry, Grady, and me handle that little detail? Think of it as a surprise. The road crews are going to get the snowplows out to Winding Road first thing this morning. We should be able to set up by midafternoon."

"Do they think the roads between here and I-75 will be open?" asked Henry.

"I talked to several people who said they'll make sure to clear the main roads after they finish Winding Road. And if this snowstorm is actually finished, we might be able to get your group from the Grande Lucerne here by sunset. So, you ladies need to figure out the wedding dress and the cake plans. And we'll do the rest."

I felt like we were a football team, huddling together for one last play before the end of the game. It might be a Hail Mary pass, but we clapped our hands together and started planning.

June was still optimistic we could get the dress to Truhart by sunset. She left to make phone calls in the lobby. And Aunt Addie was racing from her end. She picked up the landline in the kitchen and dialed Mary Conrad, discussing the plan-B dress in coded terms none of us understood.

As we rose from the table, I looked out the window. The sun was finally up. The snow had tapered to a gentle flurry and I could see breaks in the clouds revealing a blue sky.

Suddenly what had seemed like an impossible situation last night was doable. In twenty-four hours we had gone from planning the perfect wedding to the terrible possibility that there would be no wedding. Now, even though it was obvious that nothing was going to happen as planned, for some inexplicable reason Charlotte seemed happier. Nobody had a clue if any of the guests from the Grande Lucerne would be able to make it to the wedding, where the reception would be, or if Charlotte would have a wedding dress. But she was relaxed, almost jubilant.

"Do you want to help us?" Nick asked Jessica, who was the only one who still looked depressed.

"Can I help you in a little while?" she asked. "I need to do something first."

I wondered just what Nick was up to, but I trusted him. If he wanted to turn the gas station at the corner of M-33 and Winding Road into a wedding hall, I would be happy.

As I started to leave the kitchen, Jessica put a hand on my arm and said quietly, "Can I talk to you?"

I nodded and let her lead me out the swinging door to an undamaged corner of the dining room. She sat down at a table and hooked her ankles around the chair legs and wrapped her arms around herself, shivering at the draft of cold air.

"What did you want to talk about?" I asked.

Shifting a little, she said, "I know I should say this to Charlotte and Henry, but I'm pretty sure Henry will kill me when he finds out."

"Why would Henry be mad?" I had no idea what she was talking about and why she was telling me.

"Well, I kind of did something I shouldn't have. I figure that you already know what it's like to do something stupid when you're mad, so you might be able to help me with this."

Great. I was hoping everyone had forgotten about last night. I guess I was going to be the new poster child for outrageous behavior.

"I'm the one who lost Charlotte's wedding dress," she said.

"What!"

"It was my fault the dress went to Houston. Actually, I did it on purpose."

I had been standing, but now I reached down and pulled out a chair. I sat down next to her, waiting for an explanation.

"I was just so . . . so angry. Henry used to talk to me, and play video games and stuff like that, all the time. But when he started dating Charlotte it was like he never had time. When I was home, they were always kissing and hanging out. And he just forgot about me.

"So I thought if I could stop this wedding, or delay it or something . . . I mean I really didn't think it all the way through. I just wanted to hurt Charlotte. When we were standing out by the curb at the airport, there were people nearby checking their bags with a Skycap guy. I stole a tag off a piece of their luggage and put it on the dress bag. Then I shoved the dress toward a pile the guy was loading on the belt. No one even noticed."

I looked at her in horror. "Uh . . . that was really, really stupid, Jessica."

"I know. But I figured you would understand and help me decide what to do."

I took a deep breath. "Did you tell anyone yet?"

"No."

I thought for a moment. "Well, you know you're going to have to come clean."

She nodded her head miserably.

"How about we wait until this wedding is over before you and I tell Henry and Charlotte?" It wasn't the most straightforward thing to do, but I didn't think Charlotte or Henry could handle another family drama on their wedding day. It looked like we weren't the only family that needed a little time to regroup and heal.

"You know, I was really mad at Charlotte last night," I said. "But most of the time we get along very well. I think you are going to find you like her a lot once you give her a chance."

"I know. I heard some of the stories about growing up here yesterday. Anyone who comes from a cool place like this can't be that bad."

"You like it?" I hadn't realized she was having fun.

"Yeah, Ian says I should see it in the summer."

Oh, how I wished she would have that chance.

Chapter 22

"Are you ready yet?" Aunt Addie yelled.

"Almost," answered Mary from behind the bedroom door. Mom, Aunt Addie, Marva, and Corinne sat on the couch in the annex and waited for Charlotte to appear in Mary's secret creation. Surprisingly, Jessica had offered to help. She and Mary were in Charlotte's room putting the finishing touches on the dress. I stood by the door, on call in case they needed me.

Despite all of June's phone calls and Scarlett's bribes, the Bellasposa dress was lost somewhere between Houston and Truhart. Charlotte had been a good sport, telling Mary that she would have been happy to wear jeans at this point. Mary had smiled and said she didn't think it would come to that.

"Hang on another minute," Mary called. "I need to adjust something . . . no one told me that Charlotte was going to have three helpings of pancakes the morning of her wedding."

I heard a strangled laugh from the bedroom and knew it was Charlotte's. Mom and Aunt Addie shook their heads and glanced at each other.

"You did that too, Virginia. I remember it perfectly," said Aunt Addie.

"It was French toast, but yes, I did. I guess that's the way my side of the family handles wedding nerves."

The sun was lower in the sky and the afternoon was more than half finished. The men had been working all day. The chairs, tables, and flowers had been loaded on several trucks and were in place wherever the secret reception was to be held. Nestor had managed to load his food and barbecue equipment on a truck as well. He laughed that at least there was natural refrigeration this time of year.

The roads were declared moderately passable by early afternoon and the guests planned on leaving the Grande Lucerne within the hour. We decided that the wedding was still going to be held in the lobby. The piano had been pushed to the corner for the wedding processional and the furniture had been moved back for a standing-room-only crowd. Father Bob had promised a short service, but we had placed a few chairs around the room for some of the older guests.

All at once I heard excited cries and the tramping of feet as the doors to the back annex burst open.

"It's here. Finally! The dress is here!"

I rolled my eyes skyward. Of course it was. Nothing about the last twenty-four hours was timed right. Why wouldn't the race to dress the bride be anything but a photo finish?

June and Scarlett marched in triumphantly, holding a large black bag high. They were followed by Brittany, Bebe, and Patty. And of course the camera crew. Everyone squished into our little cedar-paneled den and jumped up and down as if they had won the Super Bowl.

Aunt Addie was the only one who looked disappointed. "Mary cut up my beautiful wedding dress for nothing," she said dejectedly.

Mom patted her on the back. "It's all right, Aunt Adelaide. If you get married again I'm sure Mary can find a way to put it back together." Marva snorted and Corinne covered her mouth.

Scarlett unzipped the bag and pulled out the somewhat wrinkled, but very fancy designer wedding dress. The asymmetrical neckline fringed with silk rosette flowers, ruched bodice with crystal beads, yards of layered organza, and dramatic back with the trail of silk petals, was as beautiful as I remembered it. The other ladies in the room sighed.

"It's even more beautiful than on TV," Mom said.

I was just about to knock on the bedroom door in case Charlotte hadn't heard the commotion when the door opened and Charlotte stepped through.

My breath caught in my chest as my eyes traveled over her. Charlotte swayed from side to side, showing off a full, gauzy, white tulle skirt draped over a satin underlay which must have been part of Aunt Addie's original dress. But anything resembling that dress stopped there. A V-neck satin bodice gently cupped Charlotte's figure, overlaid with transparent tulle trimmed with the most delicate-looking lace I had ever seen. The waist was tied with a wide satin bow, making the dress sophisticated and classically simple at the same time.

I don't know how she did it, but Mary had created a stunning dress that rivaled the designer dress. Looking at Charlotte's face, I knew she loved it as well.

I stepped away from her so that the rest of the room could see.

One by one the ladies in the room grew silent as they examined the dress Charlotte wore. One of the cameramen whistled from the corner.

"Turn around, Charlotte," said Jessica. Excitement was written all over her face.

Charlotte turned around and showed us the back of the dress. It was high in back, with a lace trellis climbing up the sides. A small pearl button at the top was the perfect touch for the romantic silhouette.

"How did you do that?" Mom asked Mary, who appeared in the doorway wearing a huge smile.

"I used Addie's dress, some of the girls' prom dress lace, organza and boning, leftover christening lace from Marva's daughter's baptism, a satin bow from Dorothy Weideman's Easter dress, and the button in back was from Corinne's favorite Christmas sweater."

"Who knew anyone could create something so beautiful from all of *that*?" said Brittany.

"Well, all the Adler cousins who stayed at my house last night helped," said Mary.

"It is nice," said Scarlett. "But look, your real wedding dress has arrived." She made a sweeping gesture with her hand at the voluminous dress she and June held. I couldn't help but think that if it took two people to hold, surely it would overwhelm one small woman. But I kept my mouth shut.

Charlotte looked at each of the ladies. She walked over to a full-length mirror near the back door and tilted her head. While the designer dress was magnificent and incredibly complex in detail, the new dress was simple and delicate.

Scarlett marched up to her, dragging June along with her, and thrust the dress out in front of Charlotte, blocking Mary's creation in the mirror.

"Come on, Charlotte. Show everyone how beautiful this looks on you."

Charlotte pushed the Bellasposa dress aside and stared in the mirror, looking at herself from every angle. Her lips curled the same way they did when as children we'd played Here Comes the Bride in the freshly washed sheets.

"Hmm. No. I don't think so," she said, still staring at herself.

"What?" Scarlett's face was turning, well . . . scarlet. The cameras were rolling now.

"Thank you both so much for tracking down the dress for me. But this . . ." She dreamily looked down at the skirt and then back at herself in the mirror. "This is what I want to wear for my wedding!"

The other ladies in the room clapped. Even June nodded her approval, earning a scowl from Scarlett.

"Of course it's a little different," said Aunt Addie to anyone who would listen. "But just as beautiful as the original."

A rosy haze cascaded through the huge picture window as the sun began to set. I stood at the top of the lobby stairs waiting for my cue as Ian played Pachelbel's Canon in D on the piano. Below me, Bebe, Patty, and Jessica took their places opposite the groomsmen. Henry shifted nervously from his position next to the minister and fingered his bow tie. I should have given him a reassuring signal, but all I could see was Nick.

He stood beside Henry, his hands behind his back, and looked up at me with the intense, serious expression that I had grown accustomed to over the years. Our eyes met and held. Then he smiled, and his face transformed. I almost missed my cue. But Ian had been looking at us from behind the piano and he played a thunderous chord, making me jump. I guessed it was going to take Ian a little time to get used to Nick and me.

I descended the stairs, careful not to trip on my long, flowing, blue bridesmaid's dress. I felt almost as beautiful as the bride. My hair was pinned to the side and secured with an antique clasp that Charlotte had given me before the ceremony. If Nick's eyes were honest, I looked as good as I felt.

A crowd of over a hundred guests stood together in the lobby, as I took my place next to Jessica in front of the large stone fireplace. People I recognized from Atlanta stood with neighbors I had grown up with. Their faces looked both happy and relieved. *The Morning Show* camera crew videotaped unobtrusively from the top of the stairs and

Alain's bulky body darted back and forth in front of the steps, catching the wedding party from different angles with his camera.

Little sobs were already escaping Aunt Addie's throat and she blew her nose into a tissue so loudly that I saw Scarlett Francis inch away from her. Marva and Corinne patted Aunt Addie's shoulder sympathetically and dabbed their own eyes.

I shifted my gaze upward. Charlotte and Mom stood at the top of the stairs with their arms linked together. Mom stood proudly in her navy long-sleeve velvet dress that made her look young again, and Charlotte looked more enchanting than a fairy princess. I felt a warm rush of pride.

Henry stood straighter now. He and Charlotte beamed at each other like kids as the space between them grew smaller. When they finally stood together and turned toward the minister, Ian played the last note of the song and joined the groomsmen.

Later in the ceremony, the minister asked, "Who gives this woman to be married to this man?"

Mom, Ian, Aunt Addie, and I all joined in together. "We do."

We hugged Charlotte and Henry. Travis Hartwick led Aunt Addie to a nearby chair because she was blubbering so much she couldn't stand upright.

She wasn't alone. By the time the ceremony drew to a close, there were more than a few guests wiping away tears.

A massive cheer went up when Henry and Charlotte finally sealed their wedding vows with a kiss. When their lips met, Ian began to play Billy Idol's "White Wedding" vigorously on the piano. He was supposed to play a more traditional recessional song, and Aunt Addie shook her head and scowled. The cameras were rolling and Ian grinned for the audience as he received a thumbs-up from both Charlotte and Henry. They kissed each other a second time.

Henry escorted Charlotte through the jubilant crowd to the doorway. Mary Conrad met them and placed a red cape around Charlotte's shoulders and handed Henry a blanket. Then Grady threw open the doors to reveal a horse and sleigh.

"Where did you find that?" Charlotte said, clapping her hands to her cheeks.

Grady straightened his shoulders. "Just a little something I had up my sleeve," he said bashfully. Within minutes, the blissful couple was helped into the sleigh and whisked off to the mystery reception.

I stood by the fireplace and watched as the guests and the rest of the wedding party grabbed their coats. Wedding guests filed out the front door to follow the couple to their destination. The dim gray light of dusk was settling over the snow drifts and I moved toward the front door and watched as a parade of red lights made their way down Winding Road. I didn't want to leave the inn just yet. There was something I needed to do.

"I'll be right back," I said. Nick eyed me curiously as the rest of the wedding party moved past us.

The lobby was almost empty when I returned. Nick leaned against the stairway railing, waiting for me. He didn't look surprised at what I had in my hands.

"I know she has Alain and the camera crew, but I'm not sure I trust them to do this right." I slung the camera bag over my shoulder.

"I'm sorry about your dad's camera," he said.

I shrugged my shoulders. "Are we going to be late?"

"I know a shortcut," he said, kissing me thoroughly. "You look beautiful. The only thing that kept me from attacking you all day was the tongue-lashing Ian gave me after breakfast."

"You aren't going to let him keep us apart, are you?"

"No. But I told him I would give him until sunset to get used to it. After that, all is fair."

"It's sunset now."

"I know." He grinned.

"It's still light outside!" a voice bellowed from the front doorway.

"Barely," I called out.

"If you aren't at the reception in ten minutes I'm sending Aunt Addie to find you!" Ian stalked out the front door. I hoped he would get over this soon. We didn't need another family meltdown.

Nick helped me with my coat and together we walked toward the doorway.

"Wait," I said, pulling away as he reached for the door. Stepping to the side, my hands ran along the plaque my father had carved all those years ago. *Where There Is Love There Is Life.*

For the thousandth time I adjusted it. *I love you, Dad.*

Chapter 23

"My legs are freezing! How long is this ride going to last?" I screamed over Nick's shoulder from the back of the snowmobile.

"Why didn't you put on boots like everyone else?"

"Who wears boots to a wedding reception? Besides, you said we were taking a shortcut, but you never mentioned the snowmobile!"

Nick's hand reached around and he ran his gloves up and down my legs.

"We're almost there," he assured me over the sound of the motor. The wind tugged at my dress where I had hitched it up. My matching blue pumps were propped on the running board. A helmet kept my hair from flying all over the place, and I hoped my beautiful hairdo wasn't going to be flattened by the time we arrived at this mystery location.

I had a strange feeling I knew where we were going.

We raced over the back nine, past the golf shack, and through the copse of trees that separated our property from the Conrads' land. By the time we cleared the ridge, many of the guests had already arrived.

Nick drew up alongside the old barn and stopped the snowmobile. He turned his head. "Here we are."

I placed my hand on my heart and looked around.

Nestor and several other men stood by an industrial-size grill between the barn and the house. Smoke billowed into the nearby forest and a savory smell of something wonderful lingered in the air. A bonfire raged to our left and I could see Travis Hartwick passing beer around, looking for all the world like he belonged.

Nick jumped off the snowmobile and lifted me.

"I can walk," I protested.

He shook his head. "Not in those shoes." He carried me through the barn's double doors. When he finally put me down, he waited while my eyes drank in the scene before me.

Russell Conrad's workshop had never looked so magical. The barn was illuminated with hundreds of tiny white lights strung from the beams above our heads. They reminded me of stars in the sky. Glowing lanterns were suspended from the rafters and cast a warm haze over the room. The light flickered across the wood planks on the walls, making the old barn feel alive. Dozens of our tables from the inn were draped with white tablecloths and small panels of burlap. They were adorned with our beautiful flower arrangements of deep pink and white roses, surrounded by shimmering candles.

"Are those—"

"Uh-huh, Cozy Candles from Marva. She was so excited. But I think I'm signed up to host a candle party, now," Nick said.

Good for her. It was breathtaking.

The memory of the beautiful Lakeland Hills Country Club in Atlanta couldn't even compare. There was something so unique about the rustic room and the twinkling lights, so incredibly appropriate, that all I could do was shake my head and look up at Nick in wonder.

"Do you like it?" he said with hope in his eyes.

I threw my arms around him. "Oh, Nick, it's incredible."

He exhaled and pulled me off my feet. "Well, don't look too close. I am sure there are still birds nesting in the rafters."

When he put me down I couldn't help taking another look. "How did you do this?"

"We had a lot of help. Some of the men from the Elks Lodge came by and cleaned up the dust and grime. George Bloodworth lent us a forklift to string the lights. Jerry Landry rallied a few trucks to cart the tables and chairs here. I guess you could say it was a town effort."

George Bloodworth and Jerry Landry stood on the opposite end of the barn talking with Scarlett Francis and I tried to make sense of what Nick had just said. I thought he hated those men for what they'd put his dad through.

Nick saw my dismay. "Maybe they figured they owed me, I don't know."

I thought of all the things he had overcome to make this happen. He had been so angry at George Bloodworth and Jerry Landry for how they treated his father. And now, not only had they worked together but they had done it here, in the one place that brought back so many bittersweet memories for Nick.

"Thank you." I lifted my hand and cupped his cheek. He leaned into it, closed his eyes, and kissed my palm.

"I did it for you, Annie," he said, lifting his lids.

"I love you," I said.

"I know."

Then I pulled my hand away and slapped him on the shoulder. "You love me too!"

"I know," he said meaningfully, with hooded eyes.

This was going to be a long night if he kept looking at me like that. The sun had set, after all.

In a corner of the room I could hear the first notes of a song. A keyboard, drum set, and guitars were set up in front of a makeshift dance floor. Somehow Ian's bandmates had made it through the snow-covered roads all the way from Detroit.

"It's New Year's Eve, everyone," Ian shouted into the microphone. "This first song goes out to my little sister, Mrs. Henry Lowell. Let's party!" He launched into an updated version of Barry Manilow's "Copacabana." He changed some of the words and I was pretty sure I heard a reference to a roof caving in.

I turned around to see Charlotte glowering, her hands on her hips. I pulled out my camera and handed my bag to Nick. This was the kind of picture I wanted. Charlotte saw me and stuck out her tongue just as my shutter clicked.

"You're the one who wanted to be treated like me," I said.

"*Excusez-moi*, mademoiselle. Leave the photography to a professional like me, *s'il vous plaît*," Alain said loudly as he stomped toward me, shaking a finger.

Charlotte put her arm around my shoulders and turned to him. "Oh, Annie knows what she is doing, Alan. Believe me. You know she won the Fiske photography scholarship to NYU a few years back."

"Well, I didn't stay at—" I started.

"You won the—Wait a moment—*you*?" Alain had suddenly lost his French accent. "I was passed over for that . . . How could that be?"

His face turned purple under the lantern light as he stumbled over the words.

Charlotte just nodded and smiled sweetly. Her grip on my shoulder told me she would allow no explanations from me. So I laughed and pointed my camera toward Alain.

"Smile."

As the evening unfolded it became clear that Charlotte's wedding was the event of the decade, whether you were from Truhart or Atlanta. Nestor cooked a meal that made even Scarlett Francis rave. Aunt Addie basked in the attention from the younger generation, who demanded more stories about the good ol' days. The wedding cake had been replaced with a cupcake tower, thanks to dozens of donations from the ladies in town. And Ian enjoyed the attention of the video cameras and the ladies in the crowd. At one point, he pulled the microphone stand sideways and crooned for a group of women that included Brittany, of all people. She bounced up and down and gazed at Ian with the adoring eyes of a teenybopper fan. Of course he pretended not to notice her, but I saw the way he checked her out when she wasn't looking.

"If he even thinks about dating her, I'll disown him," I muttered.

Nick had been nuzzling my neck telling me all the ways he loved me as we pretended to dance on the crowded floor. "Why?" he asked.

"Because she reminds me of a spoiled debutante."

"Well, that's kind of strange," he said, "since she thinks you're great."

I turned my head into Nick's shoulder so he couldn't see me redden. Well, maybe it was time I knocked that chip off my shoulder.

Nearby someone was talking over the music about the designer dress Charlotte hadn't worn. "I hear she is going to auction it off on eBay and donate the money to the inn. After she puts the story on *The Morning Show* it should fetch double what she paid for it."

Nick drew back and raised his eyebrows. That would help out a lot. Mom had promised to wait a few more weeks to make a decision about the inn, so maybe we had a reprieve from a sale. I crossed my fingers in front of me and Nick kissed them and laughed.

"So, I have been thinking," he said slowly as Ian sang a sappy song. "That small division in my firm that renovates old buildings needs a lead architect. I really liked what they did with that old office building in Detroit and I'm thinking of putting my name in for the job. It's in Ann Arbor."

My heart skipped a beat. "Really?"

He nodded. "Have you ever thought of taking some more photography classes? Maybe finish that degree? Ann Arbor is the perfect place for that."

"Funny, I was thinking about that just today." Maybe it was time for me to give photography a try again.

Nick kissed me.

"Get a room, you two!" I turned to see Charlotte cupping her hands over her mouth.

"Oh my God, I think Ian and I have created a monster," I said in between kisses.

When the song finished, the lights flickered.

"It's almost midnight," someone yelled.

Nick left me to help Ian and Grady usher everyone out. I grabbed my camera and stood on a chair near the doors, taking pictures of the crowd as they wandered outside. Several men, including George Bloodworth and Travis Hartwick, handed out large sky lanterns and explained what to do with them. I don't know who arranged it, but I was glad they did. When midnight hit it was going to be one beautiful sea of flying lanterns.

Charlotte and Henry stood together in the center of the crowd holding a large white lantern. Grady handed my mother a red lantern and said something that made her smile. Aunt Addie, Marva, Corinne, and Mary stood together, laughing at their clumsy attempts to light their paper wicks. Ian intervened and held up a lighter for them, earning a peck on the cheek from Aunt Addie.

I found myself captivated by the scene. Everywhere I looked people held lanterns. Their faces were illuminated by the soft light and they turned to each other, laughing and waiting for the signal.

Kevin and Bebe started counting down to midnight and the crowd joined in.

I saw Ian elbow his way toward Charlotte and Henry, clearing a path for Mom and Aunt Addie to follow. They stood together and lifted their lanterns high.

Wait, a part of me screamed. In a few seconds it would be a new year. Everything was changing. Where would we be next year? Would we still be in Truhart? Images of childhood flashed in my mind.

Quick. I lifted my camera and took a picture.

"Nine, eight, seven," the crowd was chanting.

"Annie," called Nick over the noise. He stood by the doorway to the barn, holding a lantern that lit up his face. He held out his free hand.

I lowered my camera and joined him.

Truhart Twister

with special thanks to my friend Deborah Andris Caputo

Ingredients

- 2 oz. Valentine White Blossom vodka
- 1 oz. McClary Bros. Michigan Cherry drinking vinegar
- ½ oz. freshly squeezed lemon juice
- ½ oz. simple syrup (equal parts sugar and water boiled down)
- 2 oz. dry sparkling wine or dry Prosecco (or club soda, if you must . . .)
- 3 Bada Bing Cherries (you will never have any other kind again!)

Preparation

Combine the first four ingredients with ice in a cocktail shaker (do not add the sparkling wine or club soda yet). Shake. Strain into a cocktail glass. Top off with the sparkling wine or club soda. Skewer the three cherries and place in the glass. Enjoy with friends!

Cynthia Tennent was the original book thief, stealing romance novels from underneath her mother's bed when she was just twelve. As an adult, she grew serious and studied international relations, education, and other weighty matters while living all over the world. In search of happy endings, she rediscovered love stories and wrote her own when her daughters were napping. She lives in Michigan with her husband, three daughters, and her collie dog, Jack. This is her first novel.

You can visit her at www.cynthiatennent.com

Made in the USA
Middletown, DE
21 November 2016